THINGS ARE MEANING LESS

<u>THINGS</u> <u>ARE</u> <u>MEANING</u> <u>LESS</u>
COMICS BY AL BURIAN
DRAWN 1997-1998
PUBLISHED 2003 BY
MICROCOSM PUBLISHING
PO BOX 14332
PORTLAND, OR 97293
THANKS JOE BIEL.
THANKS DAVE LANEY FOR
COVER DESIGN AND GENERAL
ENCOURAGEMENT.

things
are
meaning
less

"DRINK BLACK COFFEE / DRINK BLACK COFFEE/
DRINK BLACK COFFEE / AND STARE AT THE WALL."

— BLACK FLAG

1.

THE NARRAGANSET POWER PLANT IN PROVIDENCE, RI IS NOTABLE FOR ITS THREE LOOMING TOWERS. I HAVE A GOOD VIEW OF THEM FROM MY WINDOW. THE COOL THING ABOUT THEM IS THAT THEY EACH HAVE A SET OF FLASHING LIGHTS, BUT THE LIGHTS BLINK AT DIFFERENT INTERVALS SO THAT THEY ARE CONSTANTLY SHIFTING THE PATTERN IN WHICH THEY BLINK.

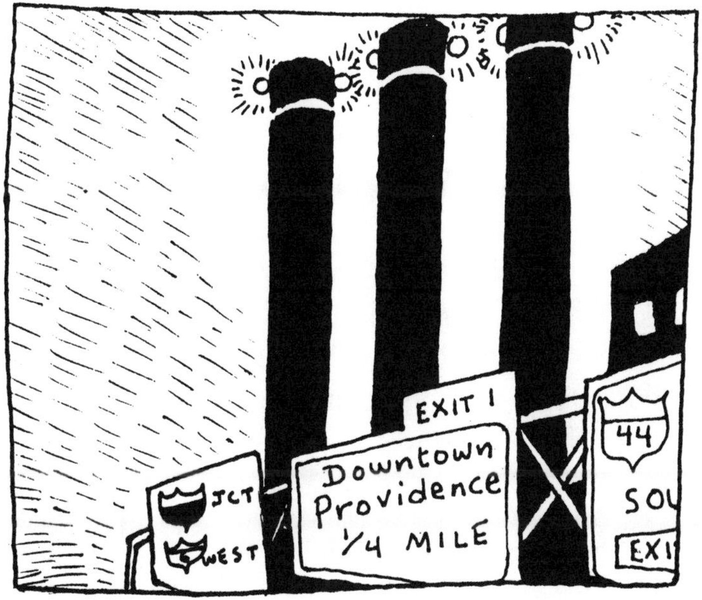
JCT
WEST
EXIT 1
Downtown
Providence
1/4 MILE
44
SOU
EXI

I USED TO SPEND AN EMBARRASING AMOUNT OF TIME WATCHING THE PATTERNS OF THESE BLINKING LIGHTS, TRYING TO CALCULATE THE SEQUENCE -- TWO-ONE, ONE-TWO-THREE, AND SO ON. BUT I COULD NEVER FIGURE IT OUT. WITH THREE SETS OF LIGHTS, IT'S JUST TOO COMPLICATED.

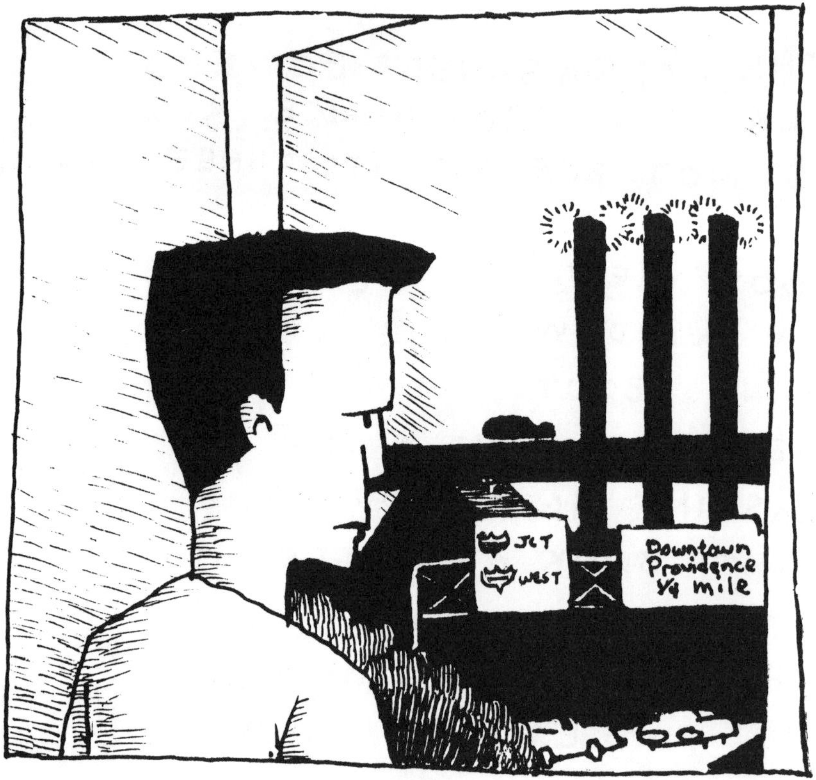
JCT
WEST
Downtown
Providence
1/4 mile

I'VE NEVER BEEN GOOD AT MATH. I'M NOT A SCIENTIFIC PERSON, REALLY. DESPITE MY PROFESSED ATHEISM, I'M DEEPLY SUPERSTITIOUS AT HEART. SO IT'S ONLY NORMAL THAT MY NEXT STEP AFTER FAILING TO FIND LOGICAL PATTERNS WOULD BE TO ASCRIBE SYMBOLIC MEANINGS TO THE BLINKING OF THOSE LIGHTS. AND I CAME TO THINK OF THE THREE LIGHTS BLINKING IN UNISON AS THE FATES ALL ALIGNING IN MY FAVOR.

THREE FATES, JUST LIKE IN ANCIENT MYTHOLOGY: IT WAS A GOOD TIME FOR ME. I FELT LUCKY WHEN I MOVED TO PROVIDENCE, LIKE I HAD STUMBLED ON A SITUATION OF ALMOST SUPERNATURAL AWE-SOMENESS. WAS IT JUST COINCEDENCE THAT MY PEN-PAL SEAN WORKED ACROSS THE STREET FROM MY XEROX STORE JOB AT THE GAS STATION AND GAVE ME FREE CANDY BARS?

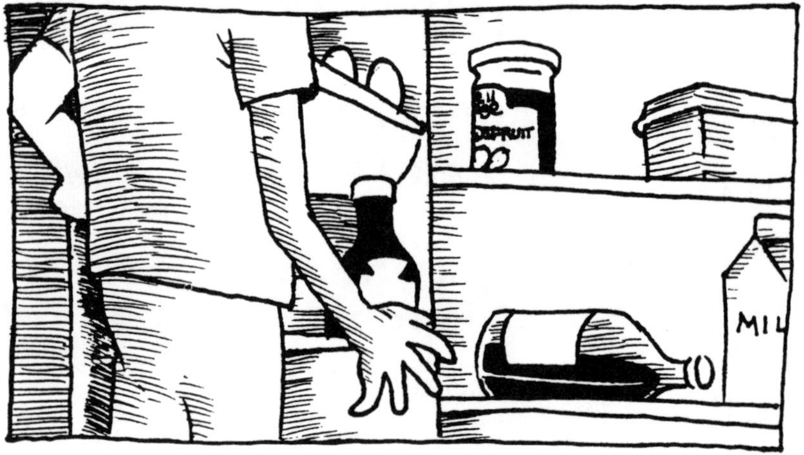

MIL

THINGS WERE JUST TOO
GOOD. MY DOWNSTAIRS
NEIGHBORS WERE HILARIOUS.
I WAS IN A GOOD BAND.
THE WINTRY RHODE
ISLAND AIR JUST SEEMED
TO MAKE PEOPLE ROSY-
CHEEKED AND VIGOROUSLY
HAPPY.

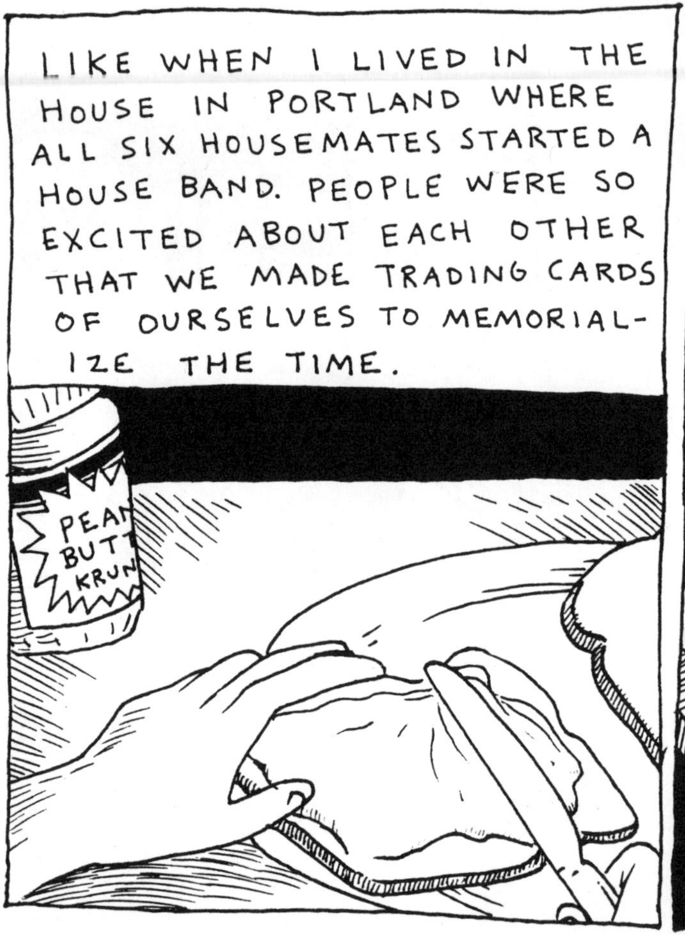
LIKE WHEN I LIVED IN THE HOUSE IN PORTLAND WHERE ALL SIX HOUSEMATES STARTED A HOUSE BAND. PEOPLE WERE SO EXCITED ABOUT EACH OTHER THAT WE MADE TRADING CARDS OF OURSELVES TO MEMORIALIZE THE TIME.
PEAN
BUTT
KRUN

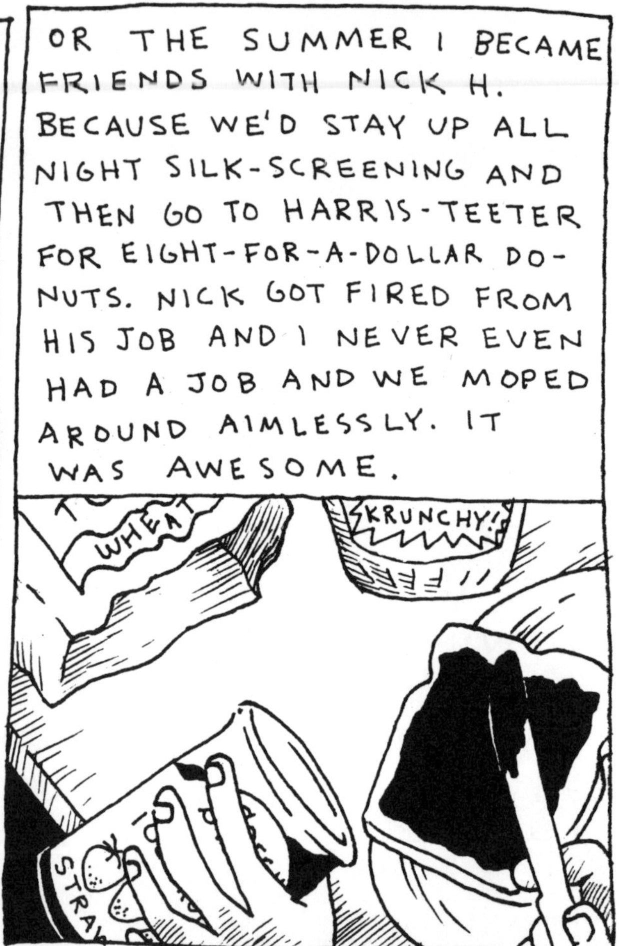
OR THE SUMMER I BECAME FRIENDS WITH NICK H. BECAUSE WE'D STAY UP ALL NIGHT SILK-SCREENING AND THEN GO TO HARRIS-TEETER FOR EIGHT-FOR-A-DOLLAR DONUTS. NICK GOT FIRED FROM HIS JOB AND I NEVER EVEN HAD A JOB AND WE MOPED AROUND AIMLESSLY. IT WAS AWESOME.
WHEAT
KRUNCHY!
STRA

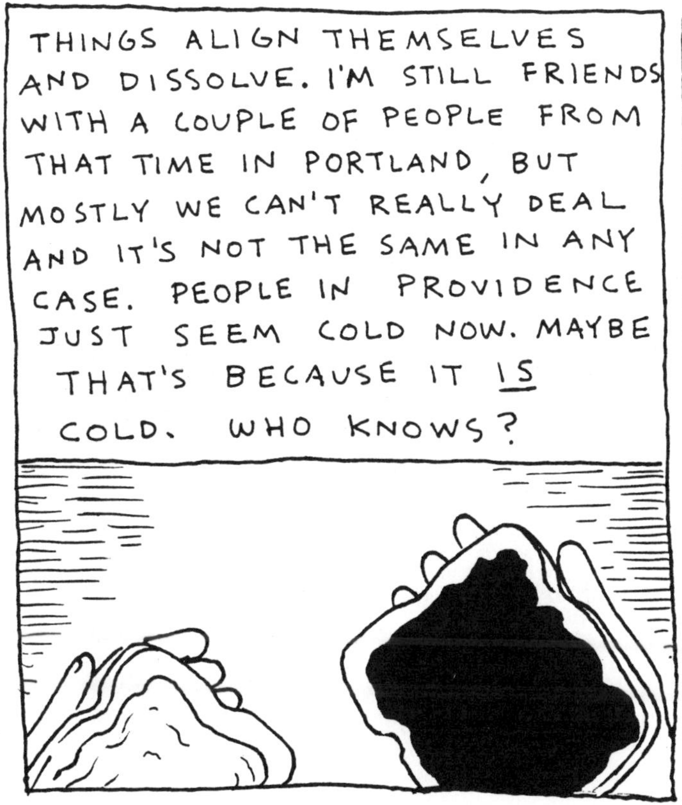
THINGS ALIGN THEMSELVES AND DISSOLVE. I'M STILL FRIENDS WITH A COUPLE OF PEOPLE FROM THAT TIME IN PORTLAND, BUT MOSTLY WE CAN'T REALLY DEAL AND IT'S NOT THE SAME IN ANY CASE. PEOPLE IN PROVIDENCE JUST SEEM COLD NOW. MAYBE THAT'S BECAUSE IT IS COLD. WHO KNOWS?

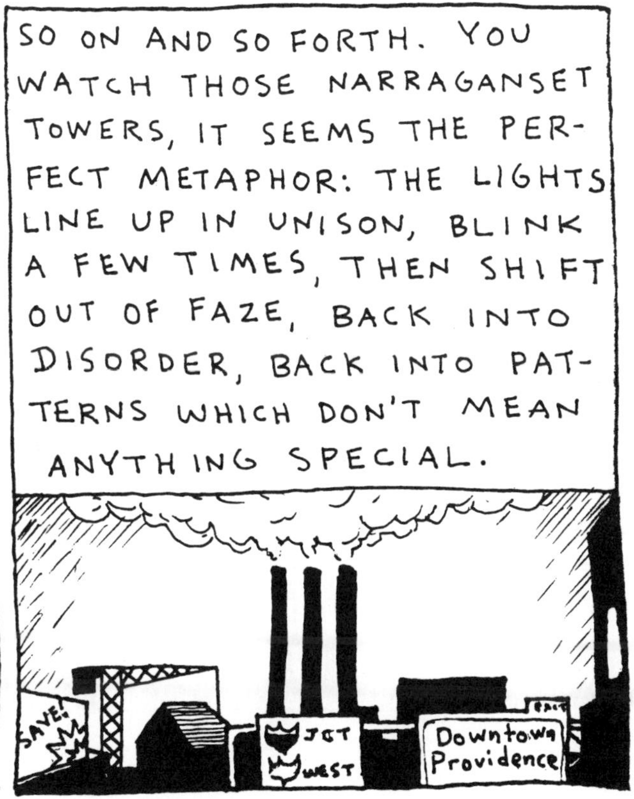
SO ON AND SO FORTH. YOU WATCH THOSE NARRAGANSET TOWERS, IT SEEMS THE PERFECT METAPHOR: THE LIGHTS LINE UP IN UNISON, BLINK A FEW TIMES, THEN SHIFT OUT OF FAZE, BACK INTO DISORDER, BACK INTO PATTERNS WHICH DON'T MEAN ANYTHING SPECIAL.
SAVE!
JCT
WEST
Downtown
Providence

LIFE EBBS AND FLOWS. IT SEEMS TO BE A PATTERN THAT PEOPLE AND SITUATIONS ALIGN AND THINGS SEEM SO PERFECT AND MAGICAL FOR A WHILE YOU CAN'T BELIEVE IT. THESE SORTS OF THINGS HAPPEN ALL THE TIME.

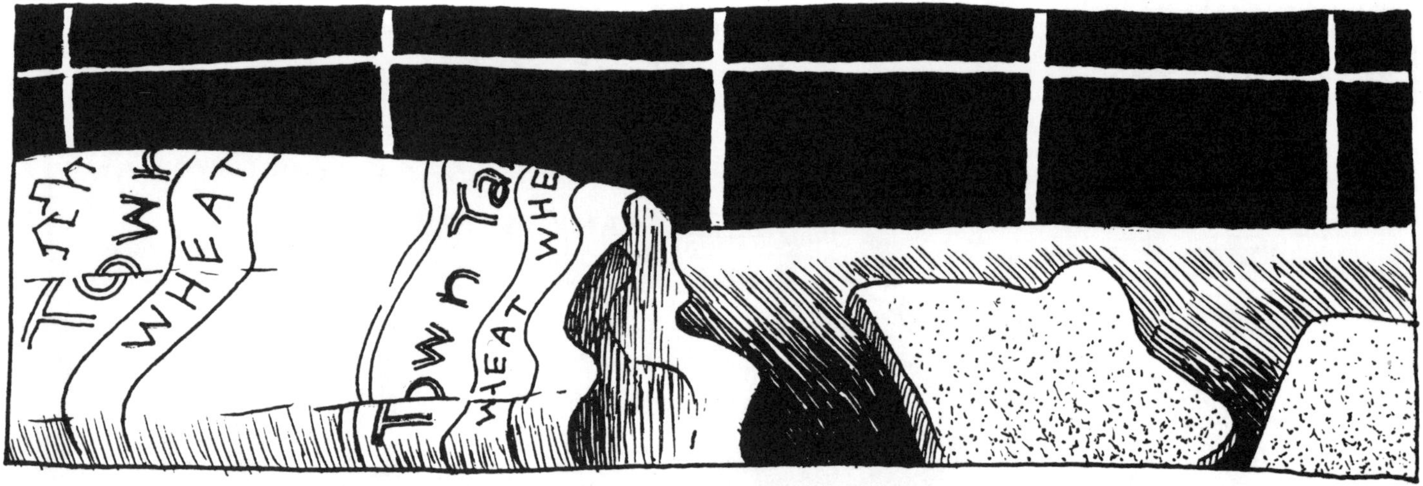
WHEAT
WHEAT

AND I WONDER: DOES THIS CYCLE JUST GO ON FOREVER? RIGHT NOW I'M IN THE VALLEY, WAITING FOR THE NEXT PEAK, THE NEXT ALIGNMENT OF CIRCUMSTANCES AND PEOPLE WHICH WILL CONVINCE ME THAT LIFE IS AWESOME AND MAGIC. BUT JUST BECAUSE THEY HAVE TENDED TO COME WITH ALARMING REGULARITY, DOES THAT MEAN ANOTHER ONE WILL COME?

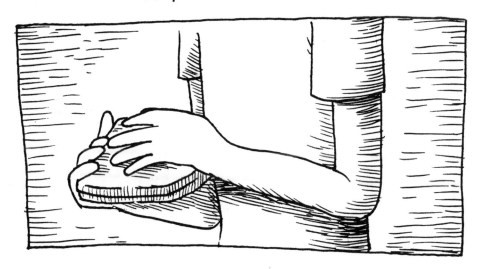

AND BESIDES, YOU
CAN'T JUST KEEP
MOVING AND SHIFTING
AND RE-ALIGNING
FOREVER. YOU HAVE
TO GROW UP SOME
TIME.

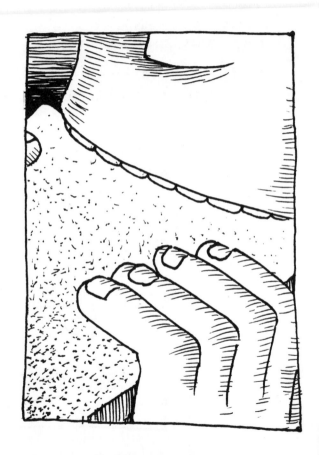

BEING AN ADULT SEEMS ALL ABOUT STASIS TO ME. BEING GROWN UP SEEMS TO MEAN SETTLING ON SOMETHING. AND THE AWESOME THINGS CAN'T BE SETTLED ON, THEY ARE FLEETING AND SLIP AWAY. SO DOES BEING A GROWN UP MEAN SETTLING FOR LIFE IN THE VALLEY OF LAMENESS? OR DOES MATURITY MEAN THAT YOU FIND A WAY TO SUSTAIN THAT TRANSITORY BEAUTY?

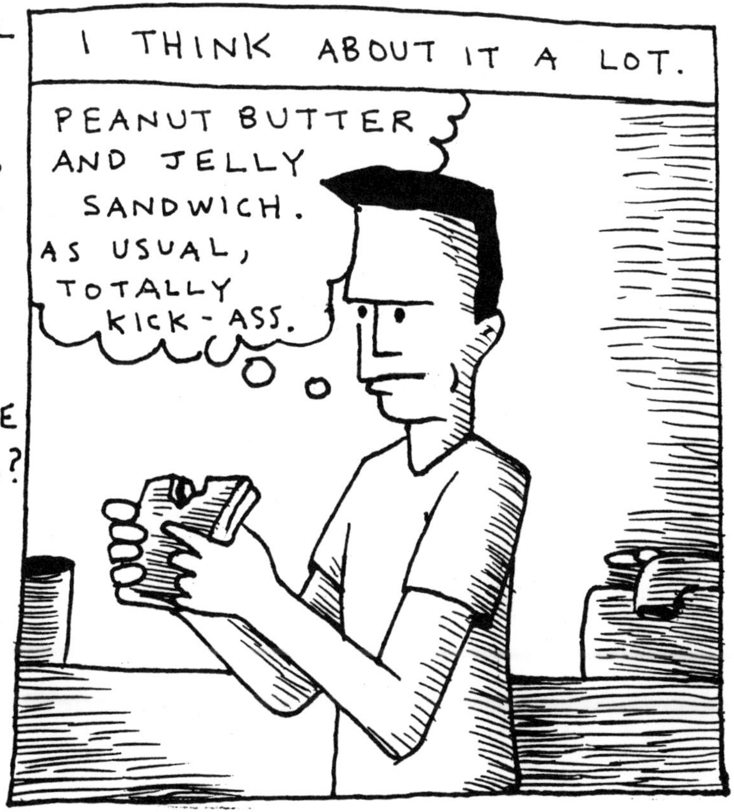
I THINK ABOUT IT A LOT.
PEANUT BUTTER AND JELLY SANDWICH. AS USUAL, TOTALLY KICK-ASS.

2.

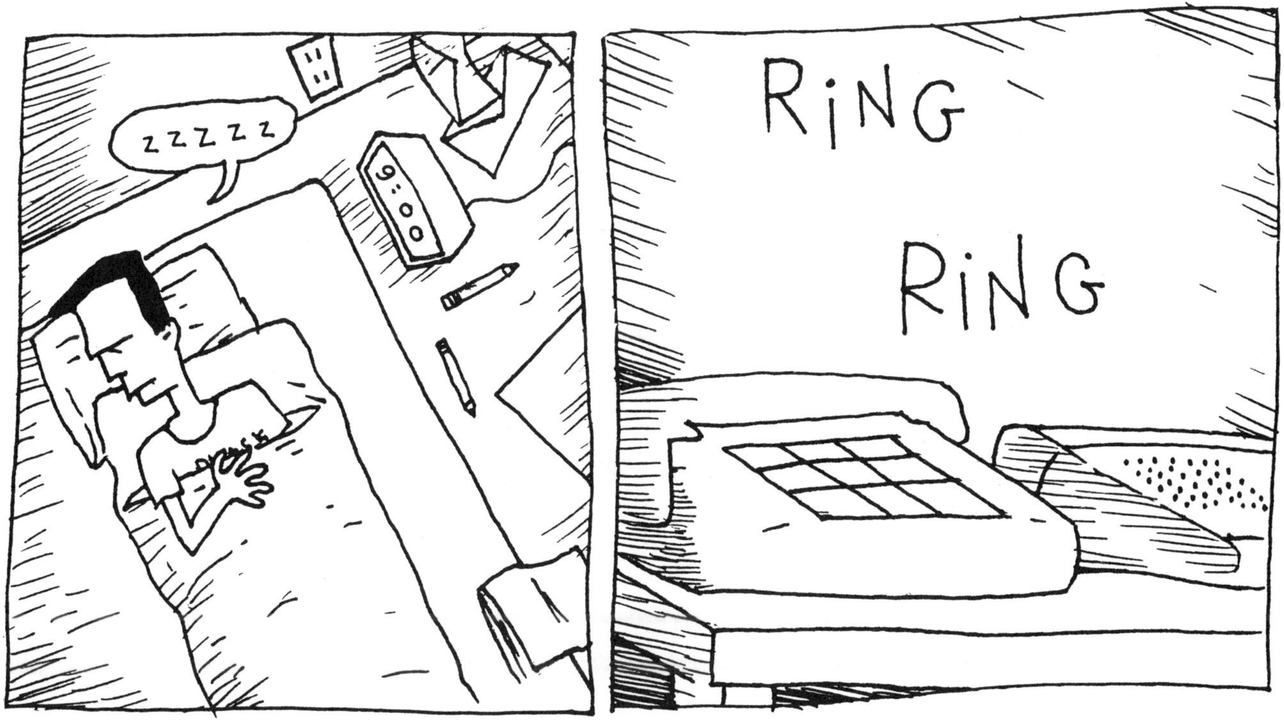
ZZZZZ
9:00
RiNG
RiNG

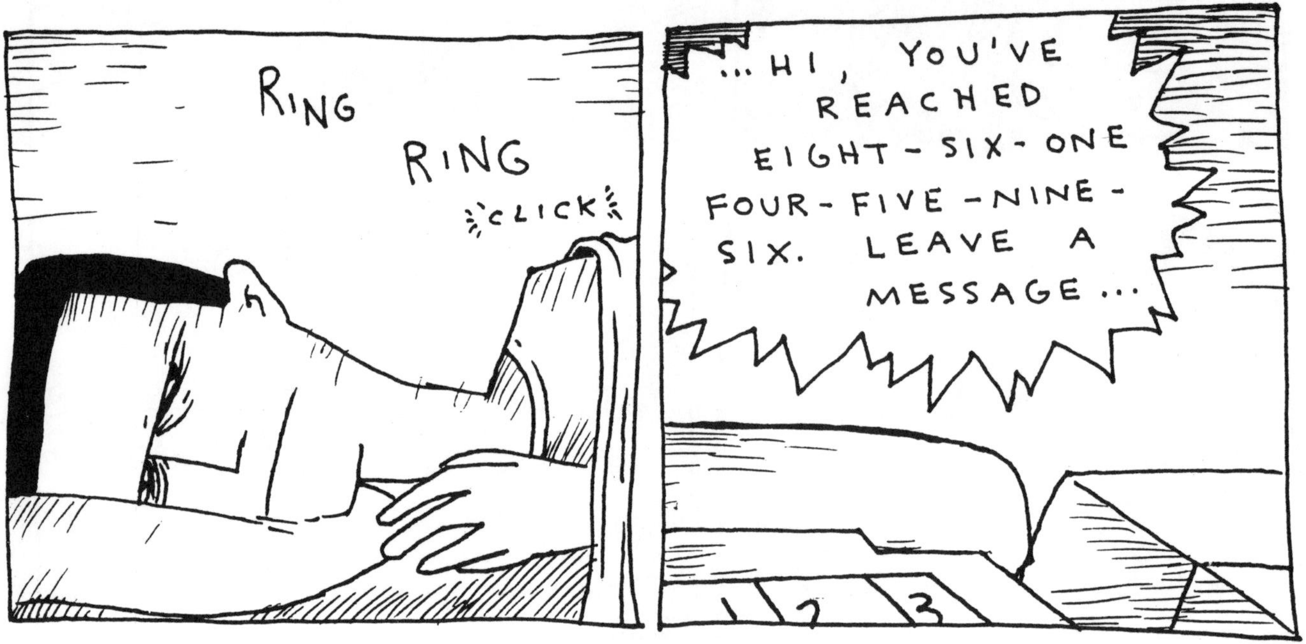
RING
RING
CLICK
...HI, YOU'VE REACHED EIGHT-SIX-ONE FOUR-FIVE-NINE-SIX. LEAVE A MESSAGE...
1
2
3

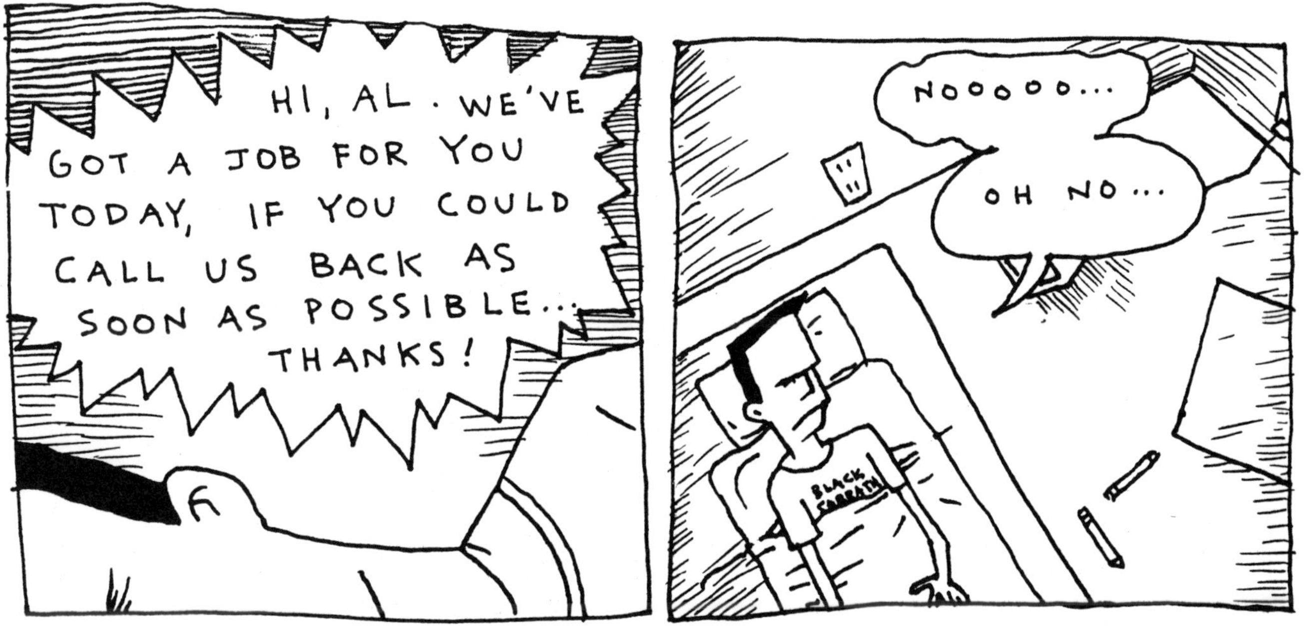
HI, AL. WE'VE GOT A JOB FOR YOU TODAY, IF YOU COULD CALL US BACK AS SOON AS POSSIBLE... THANKS!
NOOOOO...
OH NO...
BLACK SABBATH

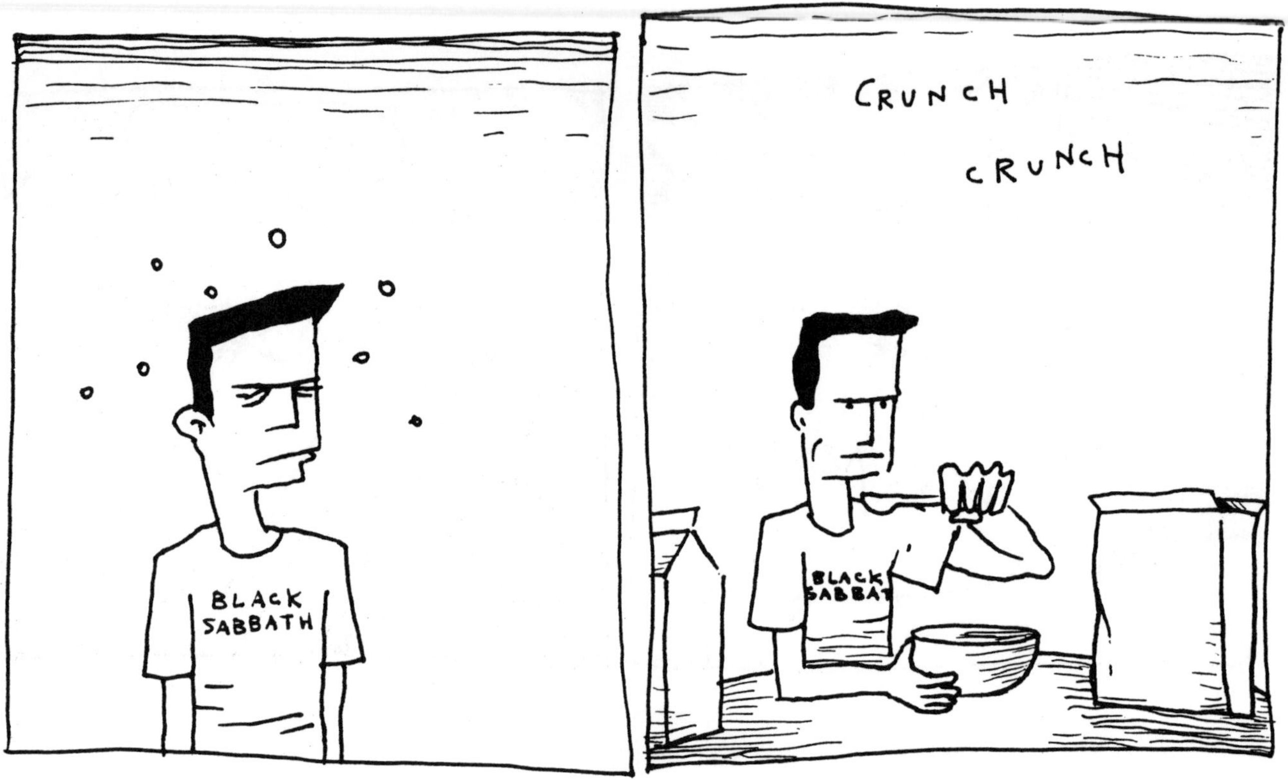
BLACK SABBATH
CRUNCH
CRUNCH
BLACK SABBATH

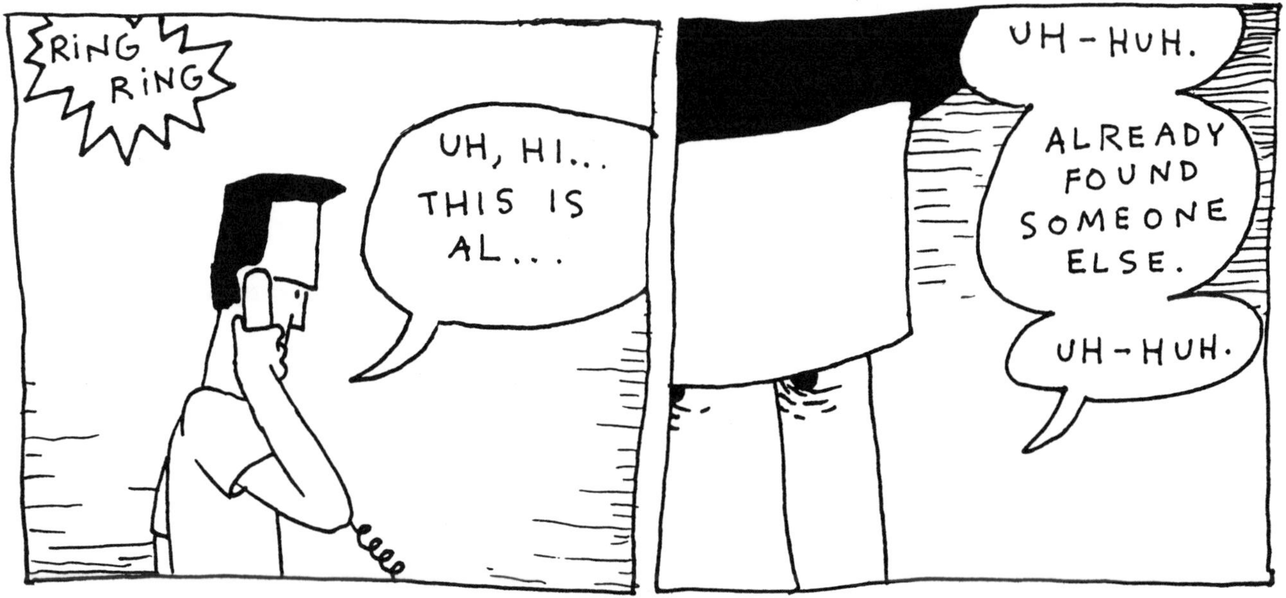
RING RING
UH, HI... THIS IS AL...
UH-HUH.
ALREADY FOUND SOMEONE ELSE.
UH-HUH.

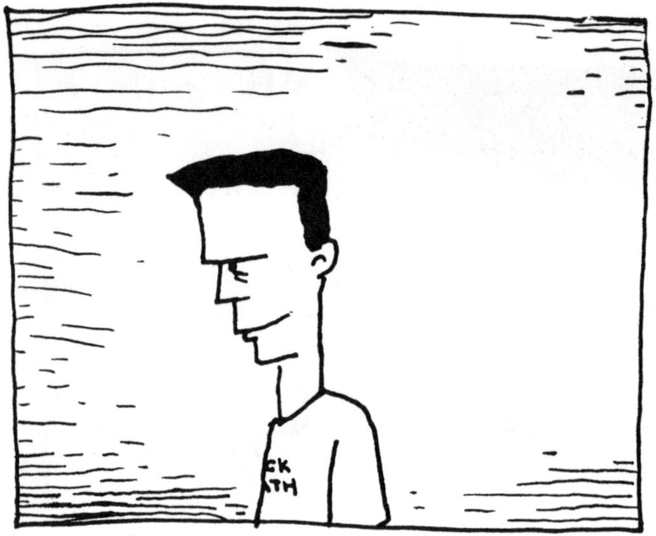
CK
ATH

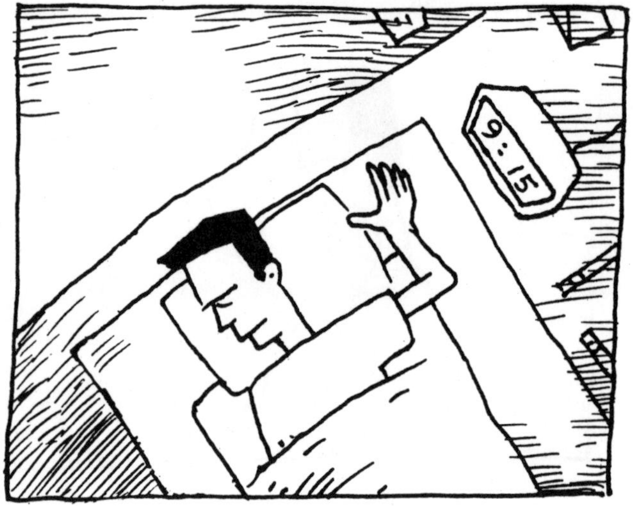
9:15

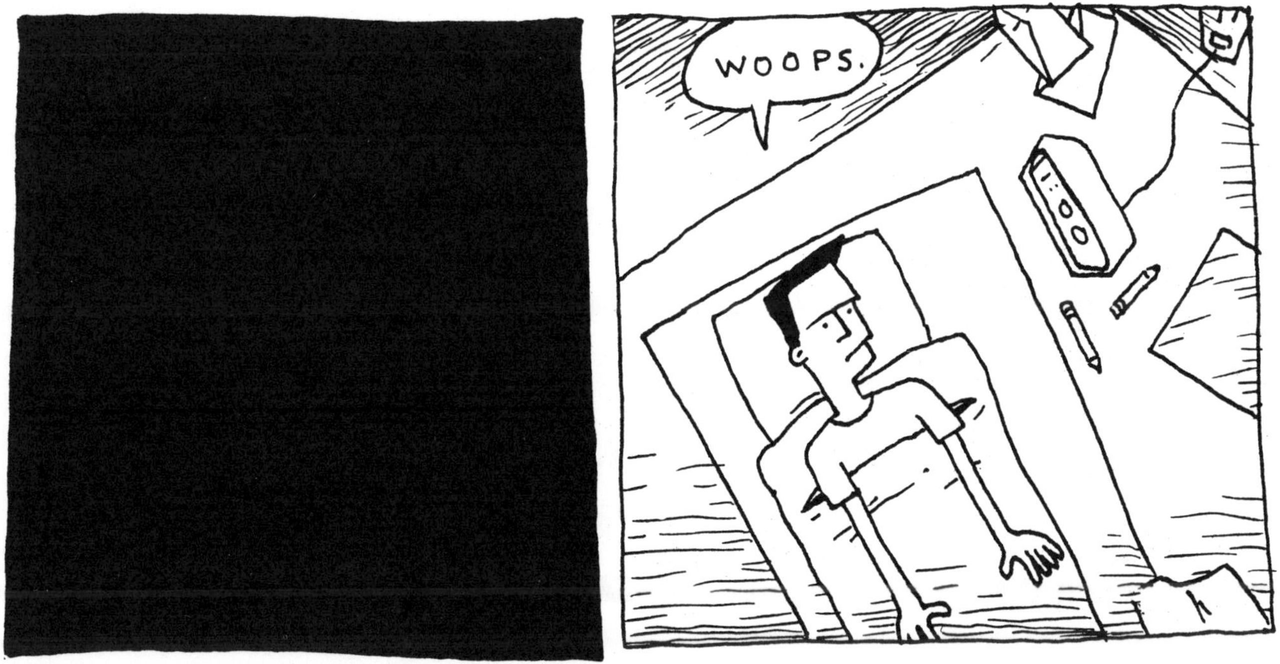
WOOPS.

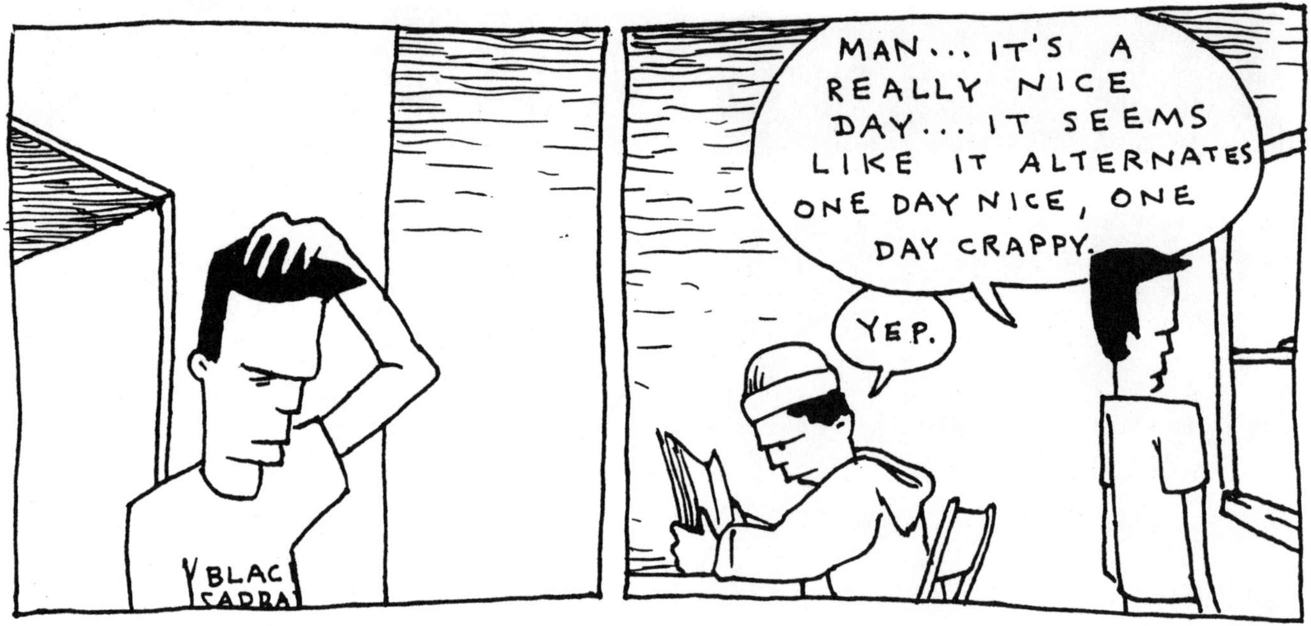
MAN... IT'S A REALLY NICE DAY... IT SEEMS LIKE IT ALTERNATES ONE DAY NICE, ONE DAY CRAPPY.
YEP.

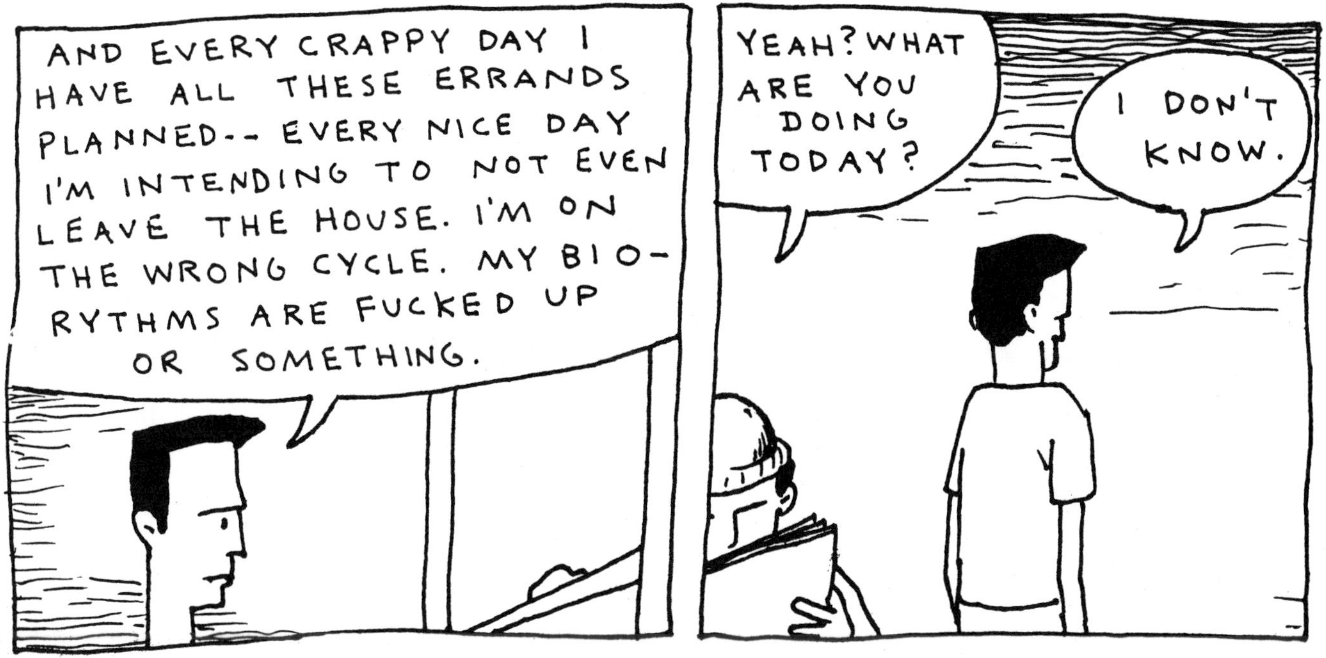
AND EVERY CRAPPY DAY I HAVE ALL THESE ERRANDS PLANNED-- EVERY NICE DAY I'M INTENDING TO NOT EVEN LEAVE THE HOUSE. I'M ON THE WRONG CYCLE. MY BIO-RYTHMS ARE FUCKED UP OR SOMETHING.
YEAH? WHAT ARE YOU DOING TODAY?
I DON'T KNOW.

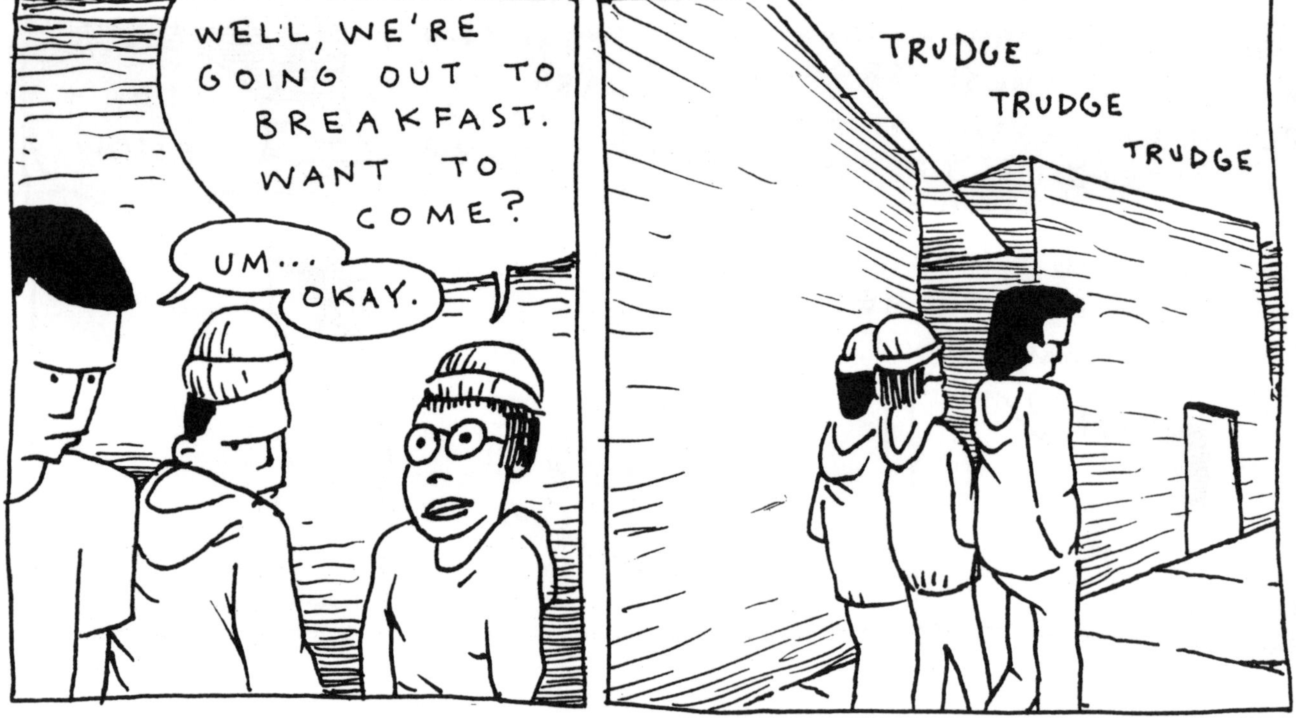
WELL, WE'RE GOING OUT TO BREAKFAST. WANT TO COME?
UM... OKAY.
TRUDGE
TRUDGE
TRUDGE

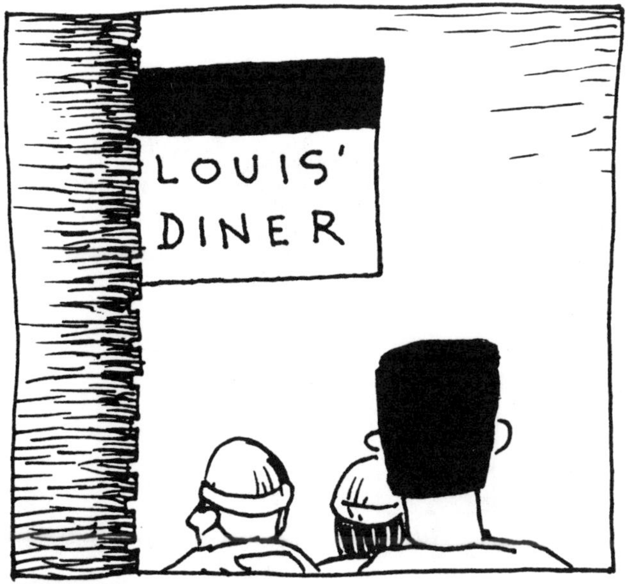
LOUIS'
DINER

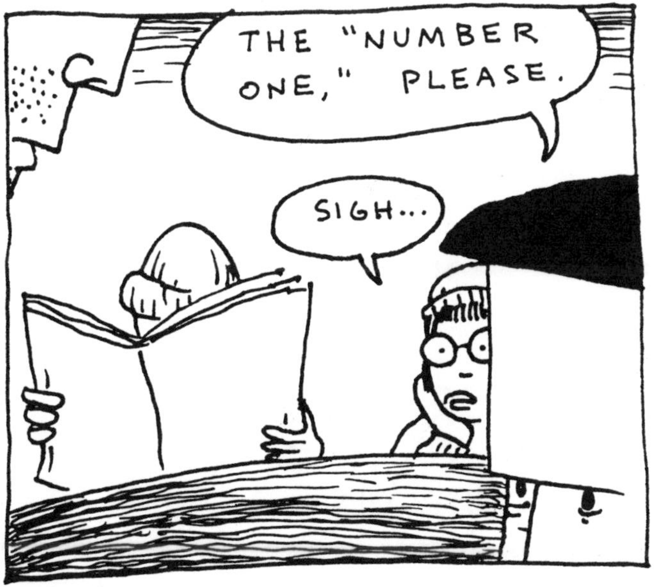
THE "NUMBER ONE," PLEASE.
SIGH...

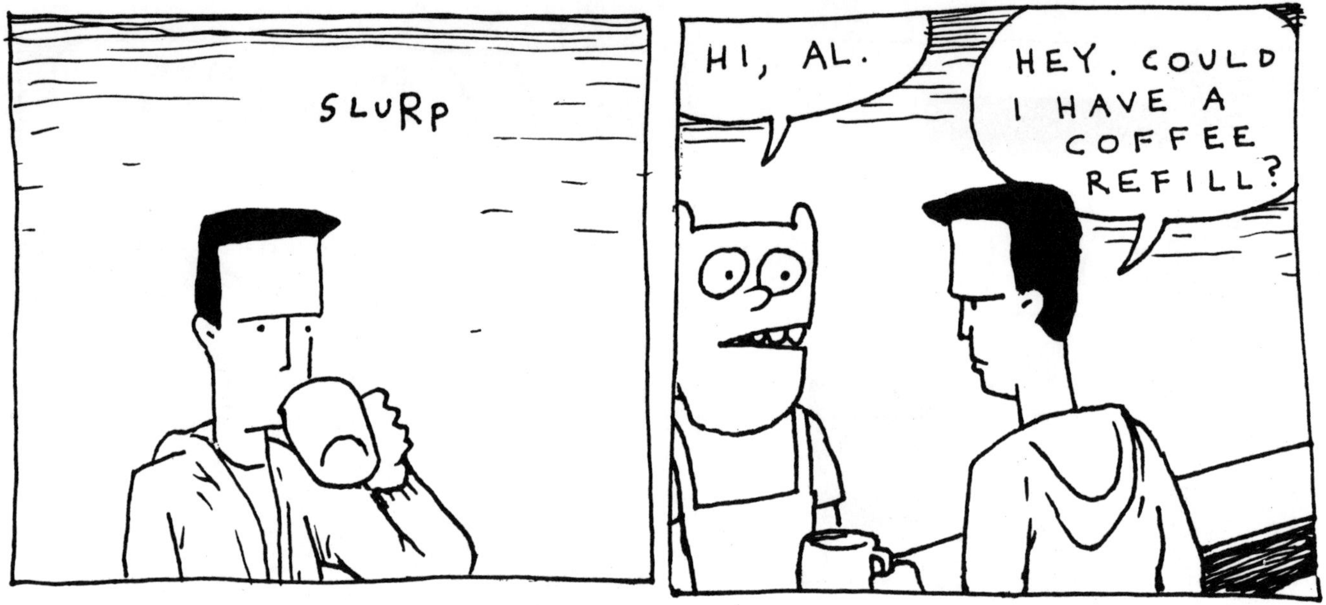
SLURP
HI, AL.
HEY. COULD I HAVE A COFFEE REFILL?

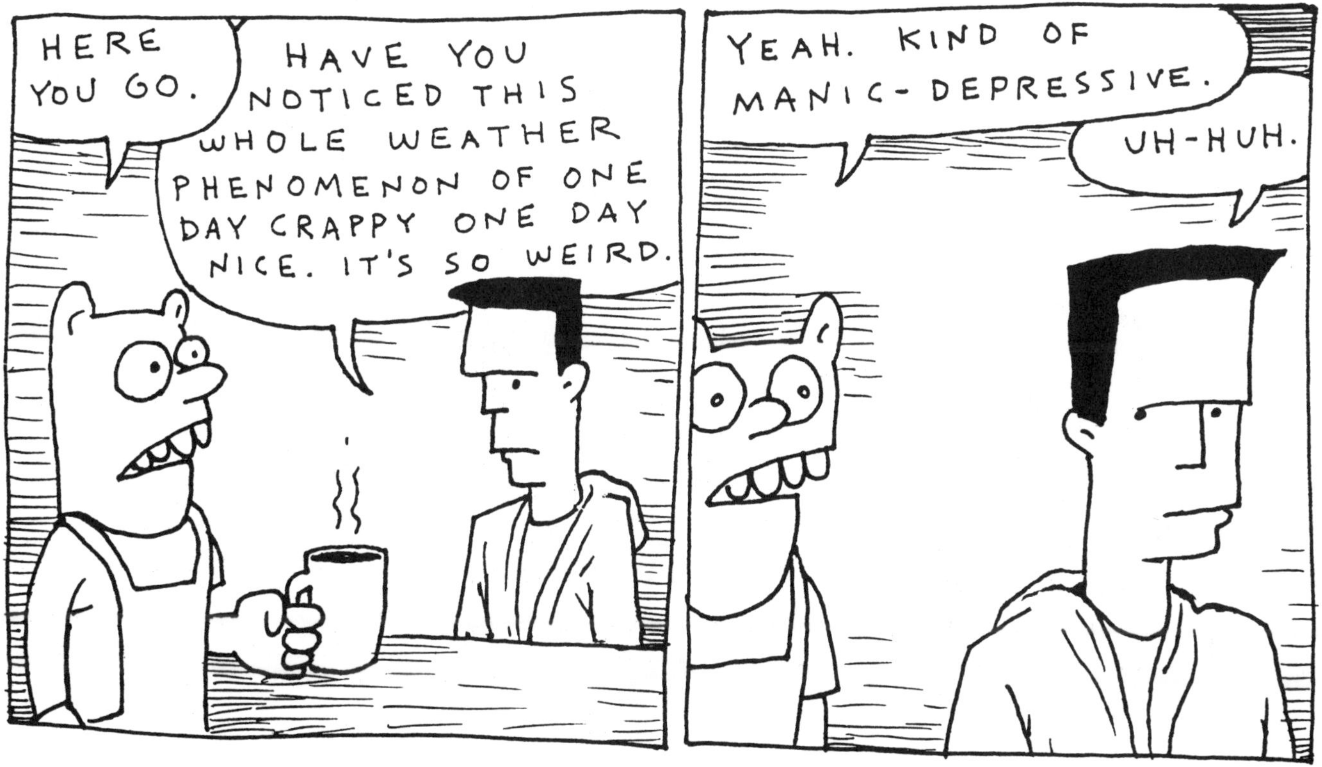
HERE YOU GO.
HAVE YOU NOTICED THIS WHOLE WEATHER PHENOMENON OF ONE DAY CRAPPY ONE DAY NICE. IT'S SO WEIRD.
YEAH. KIND OF MANIC-DEPRESSIVE.
UH-HUH.

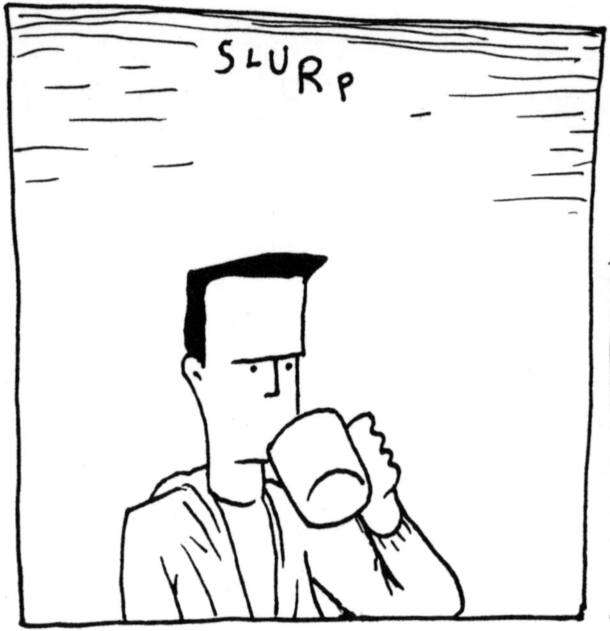
SLURP

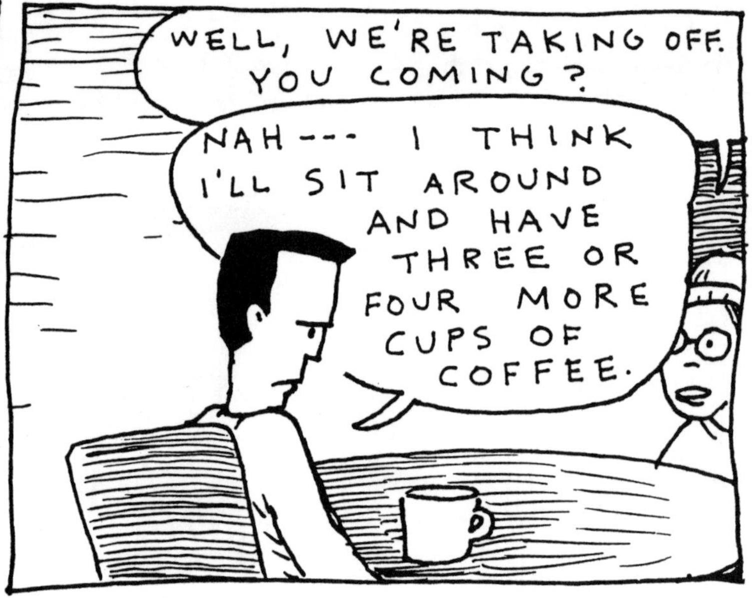
WELL, WE'RE TAKING OFF. YOU COMING?
NAH--- I THINK I'LL SIT AROUND AND HAVE THREE OR FOUR MORE CUPS OF COFFEE.

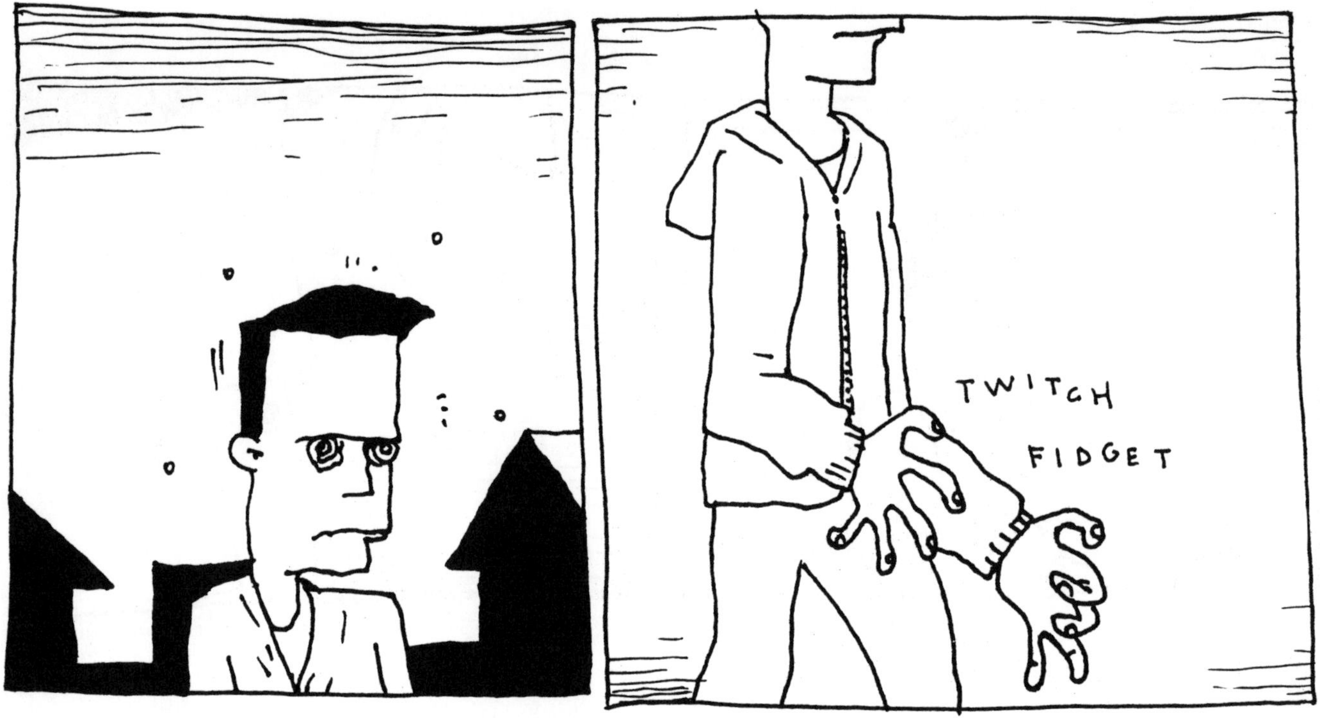
TWITCH
FIDGET

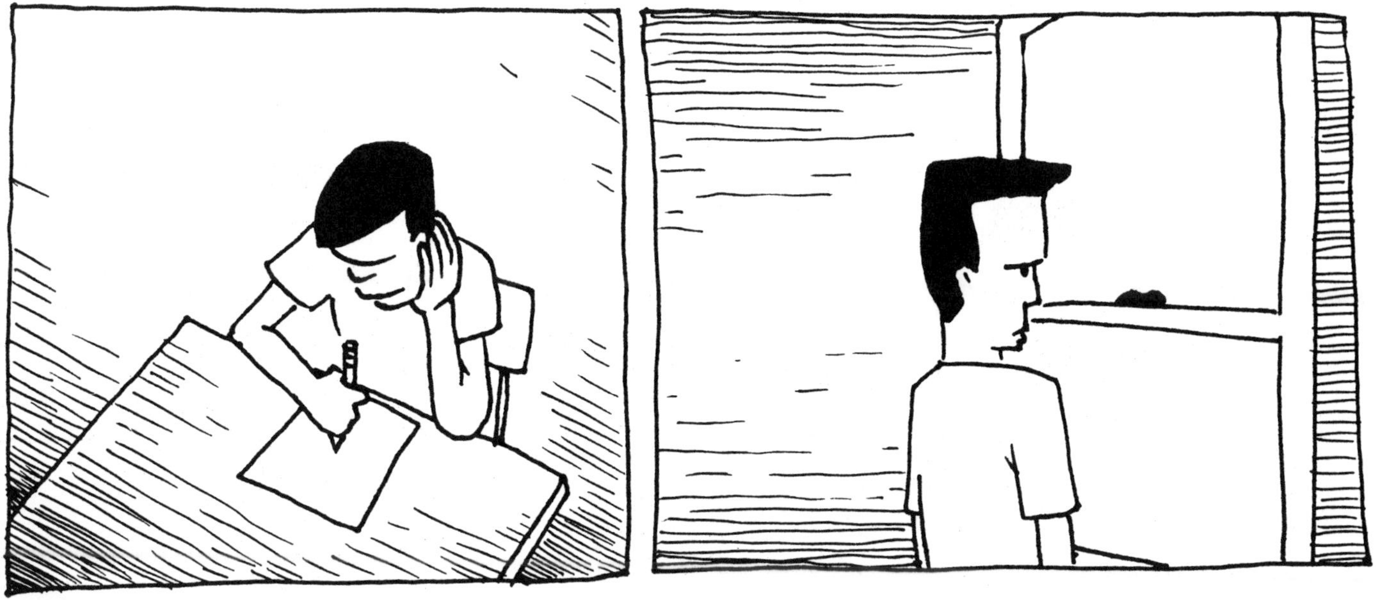

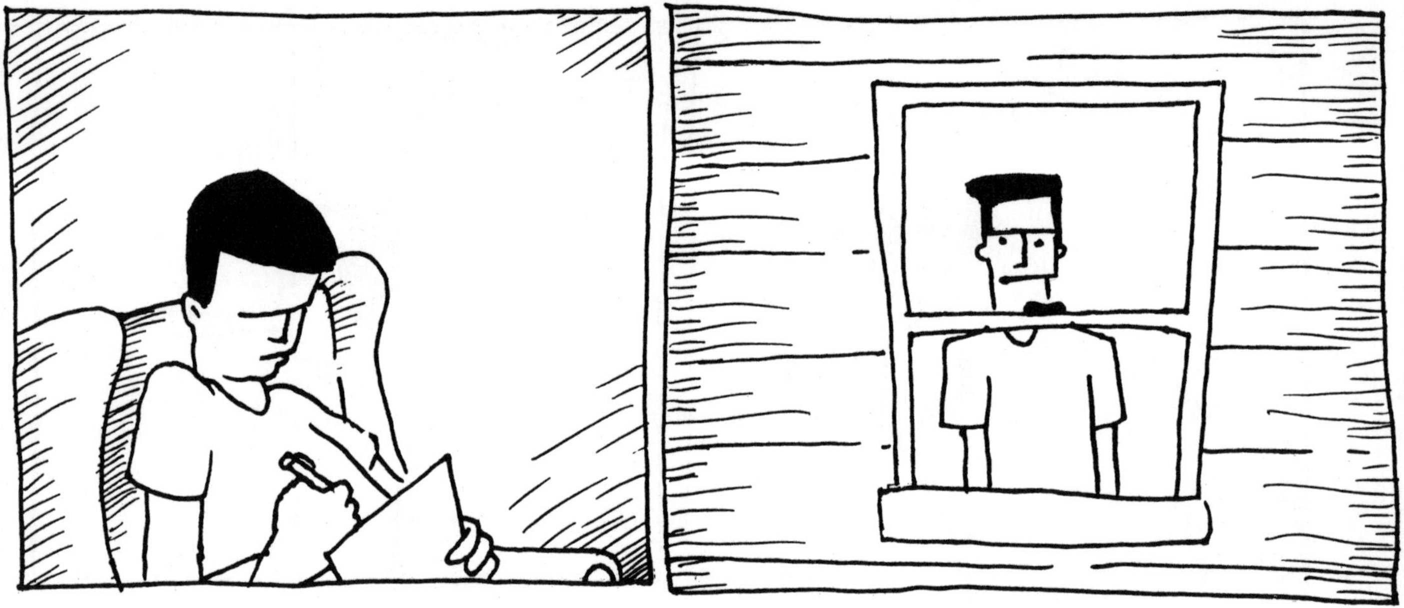

3.

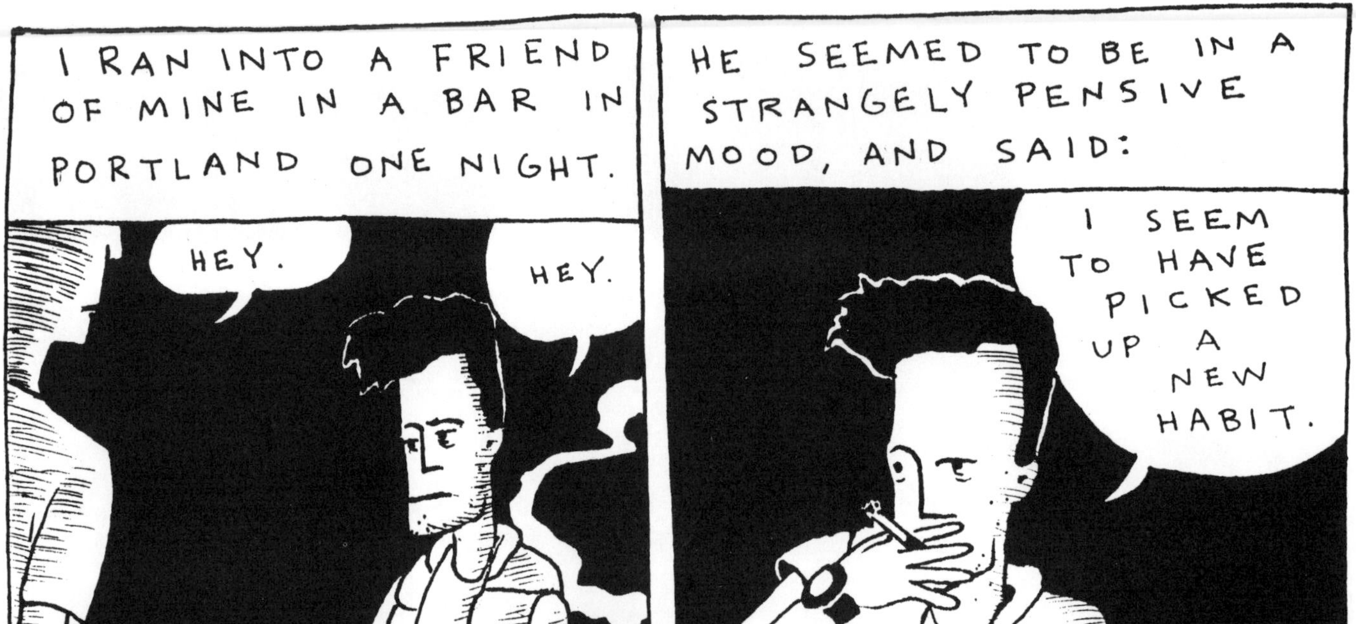
I RAN INTO A FRIEND OF MINE IN A BAR IN PORTLAND ONE NIGHT.
HEY.
HEY.
HE SEEMED TO BE IN A STRANGELY PENSIVE MOOD, AND SAID:
I SEEM TO HAVE PICKED UP A NEW HABIT.

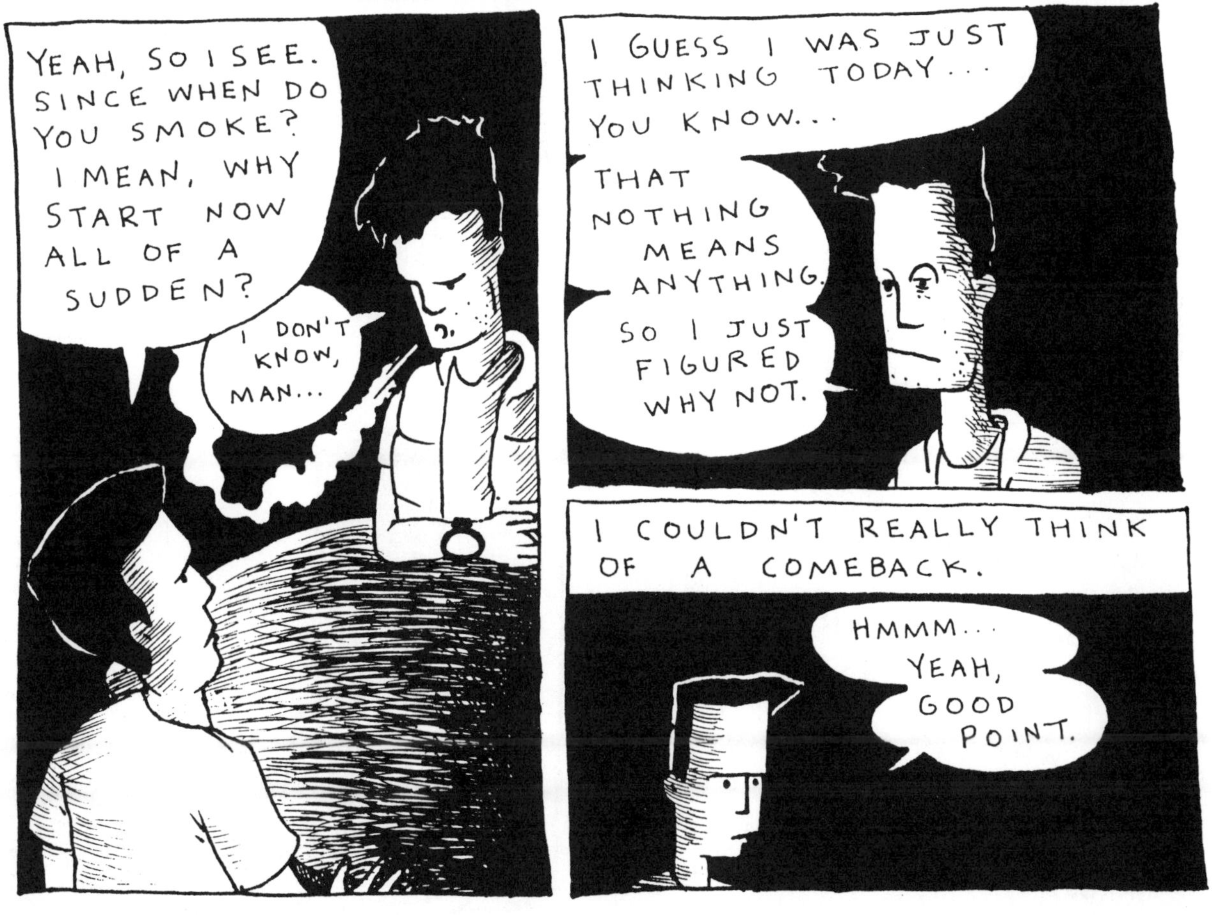
YEAH, SO I SEE. SINCE WHEN DO YOU SMOKE? I MEAN, WHY START NOW ALL OF A SUDDEN?
I DON'T KNOW, MAN...
I GUESS I WAS JUST THINKING TODAY... YOU KNOW...
THAT NOTHING MEANS ANYTHING.
SO I JUST FIGURED WHY NOT.
I COULDN'T REALLY THINK OF A COMEBACK.
HMMM... YEAH, GOOD POINT.

IT NEVER SURPRISES ME THAT TEENAGERS TAKE UP SMOKING. BEING A TEEN IS ALL ABOUT SUBVERTING ADULT AUTHORITY (I.E, IMPOSED MORALITY) AT ANY OPPORTUNITY. KIDS HAVE NO SENSE OF RIGHT AND WRONG, JUST WHAT THEY CAN AND CAN'T GET AWAY WITH. BUT ADULTS ARE SUPPOSED TO HAVE AN INTERNALIZED SET OF MORALS - LYING IS BAD, STEALING IS BAD, LEAVING THE SCENE OF A CAR ACCIDENT IS BAD. BUT WHAT IS OBJECTIVELY WRONG? HOW MUCH OF THAT HAVE WE JUST HAD BROW-BEATEN INTO US?

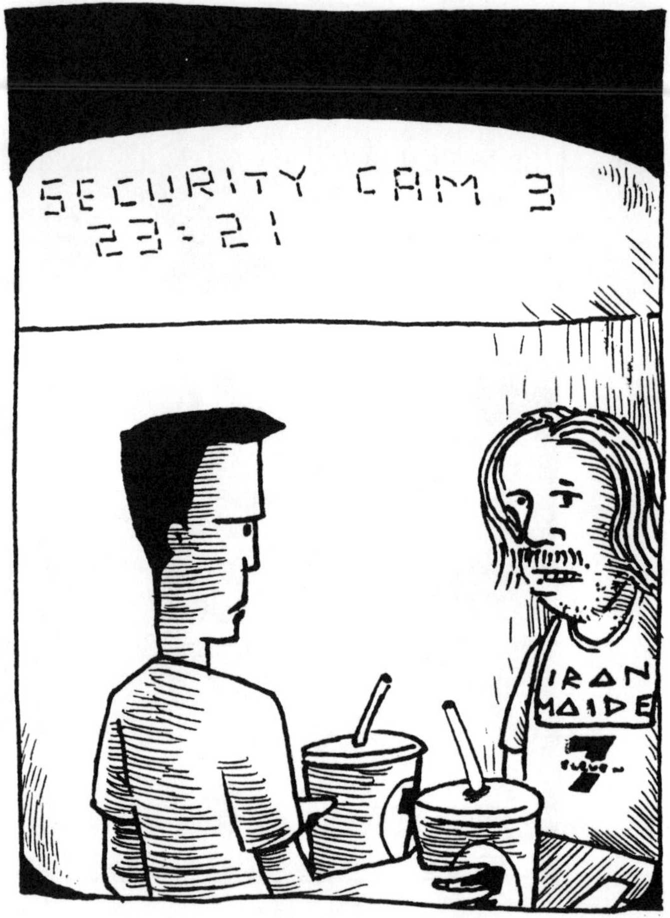
SECURITY CAM 3
23:21
IRON MAIDEN

IT'S EASY TO THINK ABOUT ANY ABSTRACT MORAL CODE OR SET OF "RIGHT" AND "WRONG" AND COME TO THE CONCLUSION THAT IT'S ARBITRARY, THAT NOTHING MEANS ANYTHING, THAT EVERYTHING IS JUST CHAOS AND FUCKED UPNESS. BUT YOU CAN'T REALLY LIVE LIKE THAT. RIGHT?

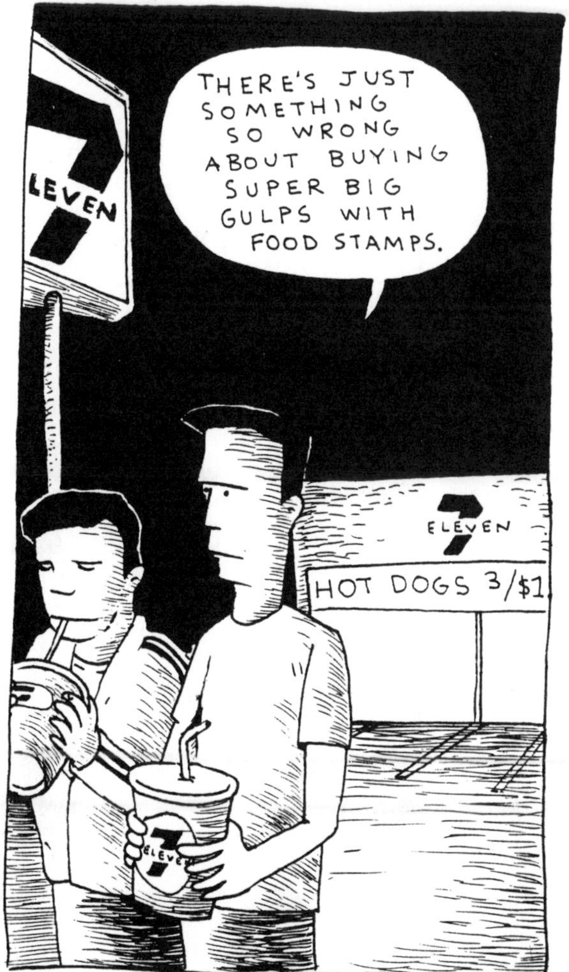

LEVEN
THERE'S JUST SOMETHING SO WRONG ABOUT BUYING SUPER BIG GULPS WITH FOOD STAMPS.
ELEVEN
HOT DOGS 3/$1

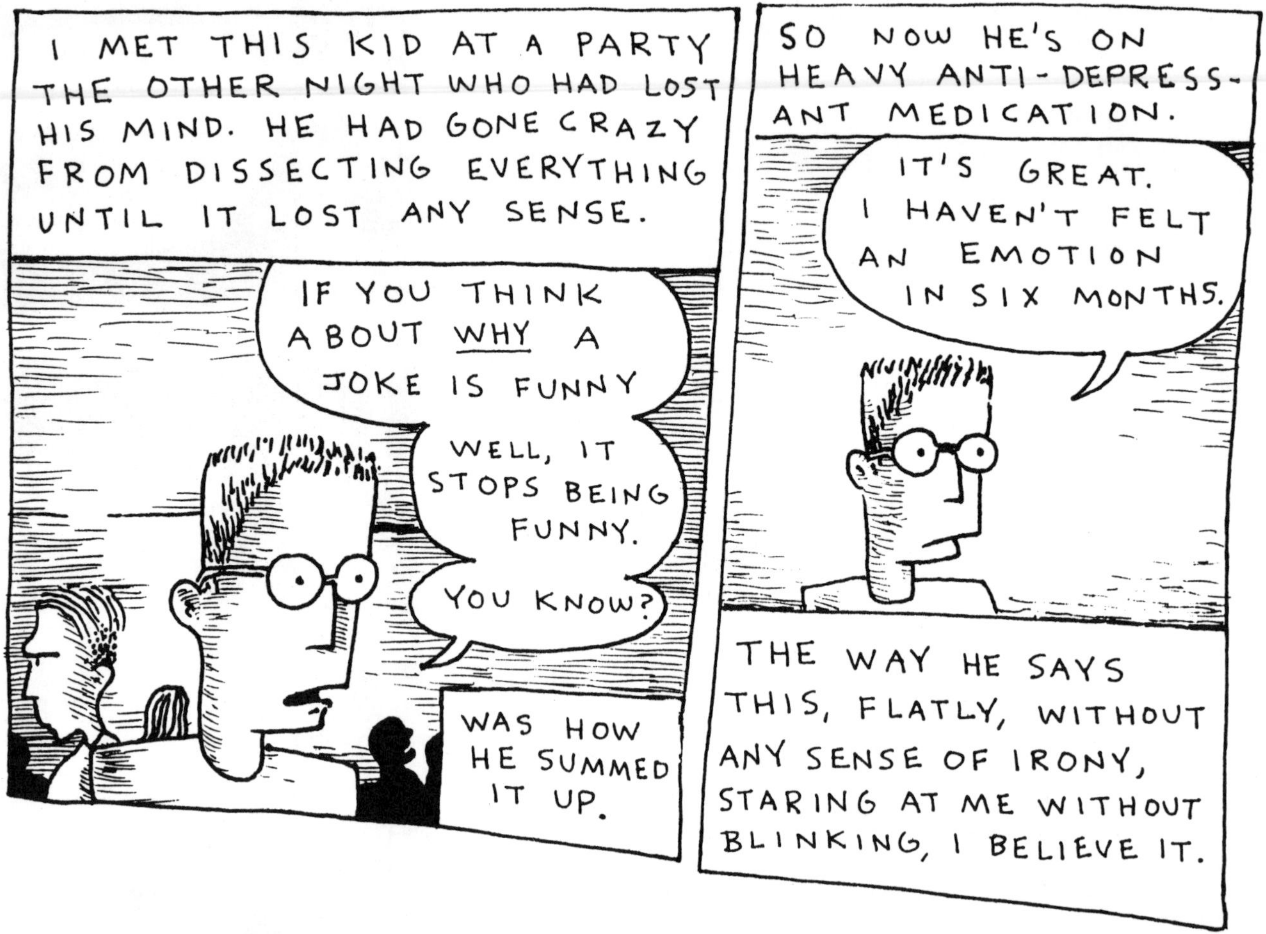
I MET THIS KID AT A PARTY THE OTHER NIGHT WHO HAD LOST HIS MIND. HE HAD GONE CRAZY FROM DISSECTING EVERYTHING UNTIL IT LOST ANY SENSE.
IF YOU THINK ABOUT WHY A JOKE IS FUNNY
WELL, IT STOPS BEING FUNNY.
YOU KNOW?
WAS HOW HE SUMMED IT UP.
SO NOW HE'S ON HEAVY ANTI-DEPRESSANT MEDICATION.
IT'S GREAT. I HAVEN'T FELT AN EMOTION IN SIX MONTHS.
THE WAY HE SAYS THIS, FLATLY, WITHOUT ANY SENSE OF IRONY, STARING AT ME WITHOUT BLINKING, I BELIEVE IT.

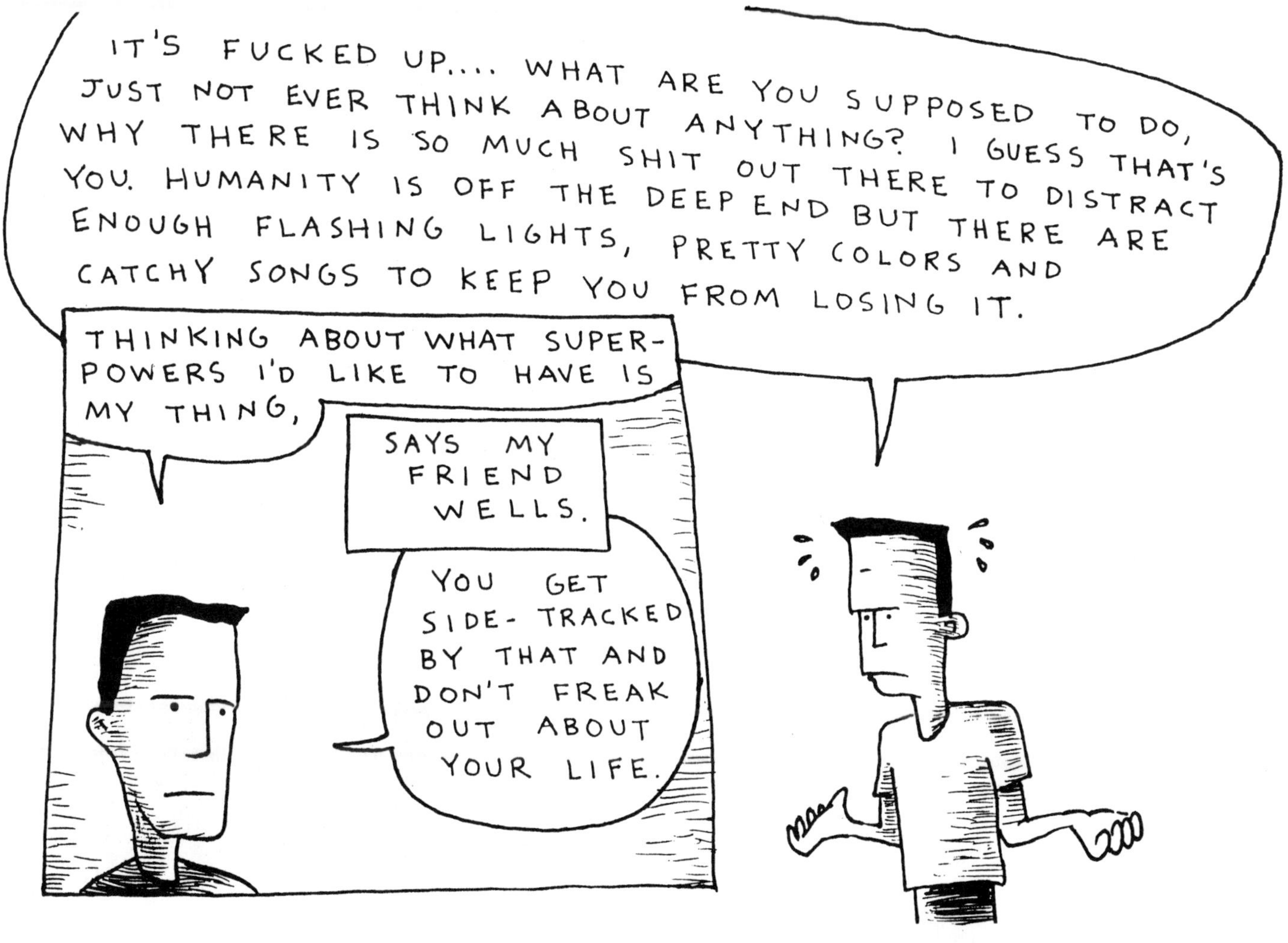
IT'S FUCKED UP.... WHAT ARE YOU SUPPOSED TO DO, JUST NOT EVER THINK ABOUT ANYTHING? I GUESS THAT'S WHY THERE IS SO MUCH SHIT OUT THERE TO DISTRACT YOU. HUMANITY IS OFF THE DEEP END BUT THERE ARE ENOUGH FLASHING LIGHTS, PRETTY COLORS AND CATCHY SONGS TO KEEP YOU FROM LOSING IT.
THINKING ABOUT WHAT SUPER-POWERS I'D LIKE TO HAVE IS MY THING,
SAYS MY FRIEND WELLS.
YOU GET SIDE-TRACKED BY THAT AND DON'T FREAK OUT ABOUT YOUR LIFE.

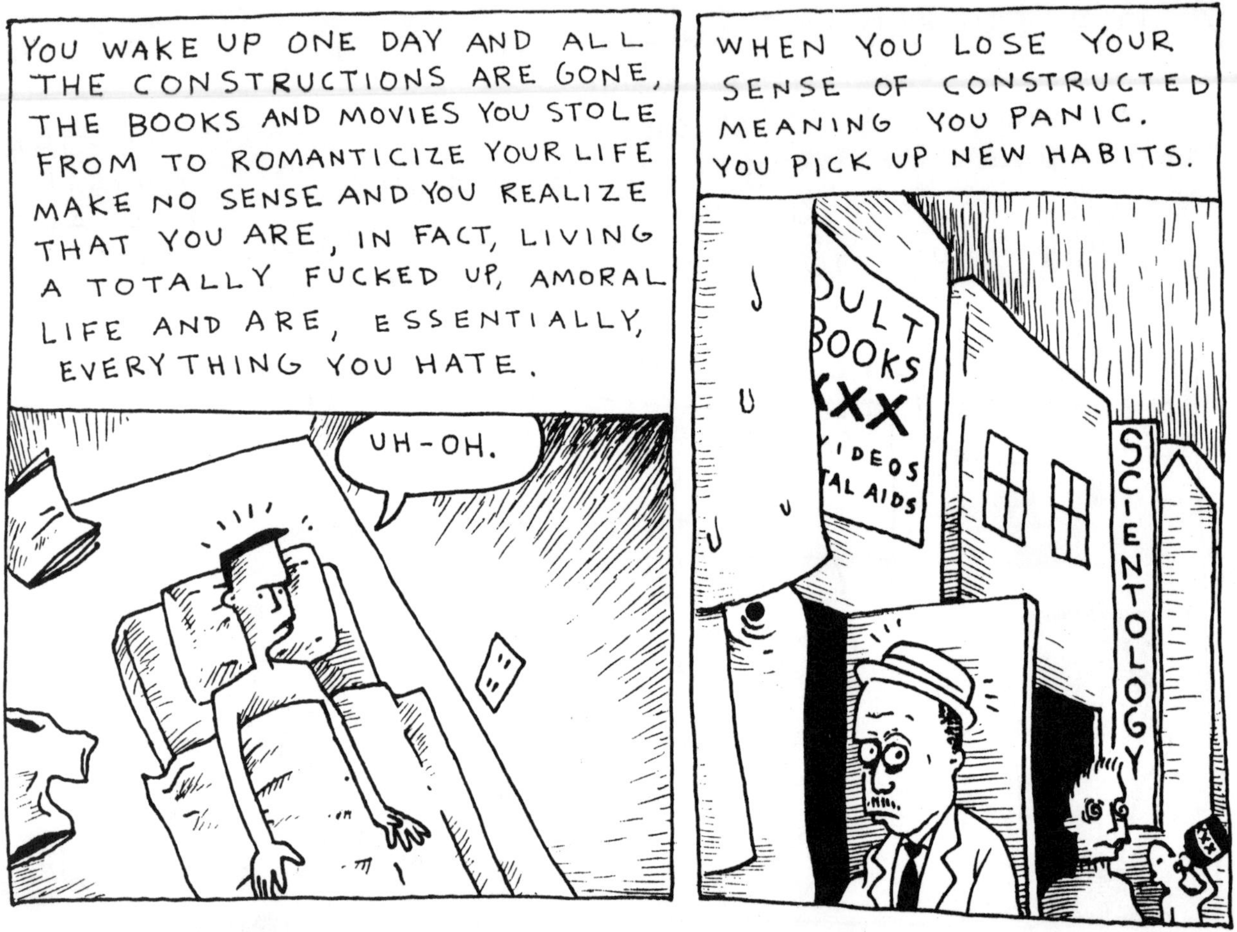
YOU WAKE UP ONE DAY AND ALL THE CONSTRUCTIONS ARE GONE, THE BOOKS AND MOVIES YOU STOLE FROM TO ROMANTICIZE YOUR LIFE MAKE NO SENSE AND YOU REALIZE THAT YOU ARE, IN FACT, LIVING A TOTALLY FUCKED UP, AMORAL LIFE AND ARE, ESSENTIALLY, EVERYTHING YOU HATE.
UH-OH.
WHEN YOU LOSE YOUR SENSE OF CONSTRUCTED MEANING YOU PANIC. YOU PICK UP NEW HABITS.
BOOKS
XXX
SCIENTOLOGY

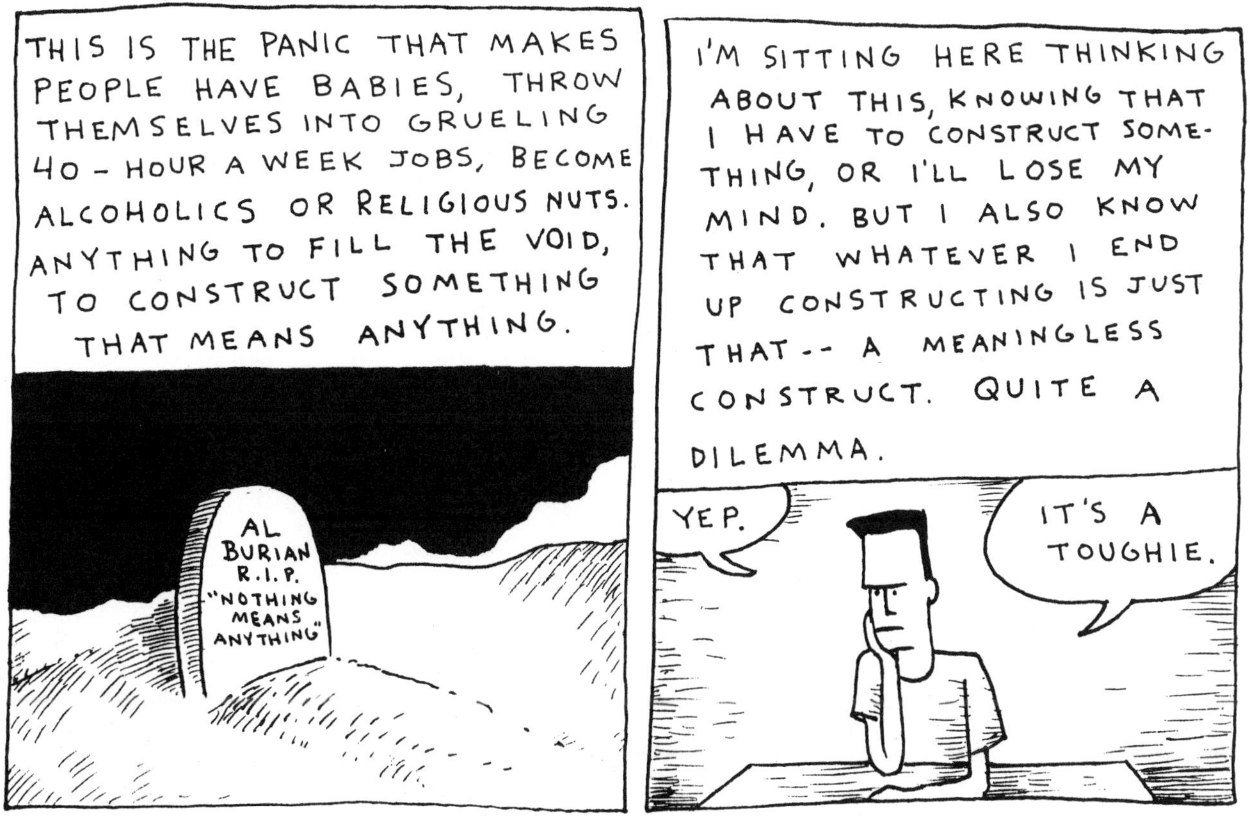
THIS IS THE PANIC THAT MAKES PEOPLE HAVE BABIES, THROW THEMSELVES INTO GRUELING 40-HOUR A WEEK JOBS, BECOME ALCOHOLICS OR RELIGIOUS NUTS. ANYTHING TO FILL THE VOID, TO CONSTRUCT SOMETHING THAT MEANS ANYTHING.
AL BURIAN R.I.P. "NOTHING MEANS ANYTHING"
I'M SITTING HERE THINKING ABOUT THIS, KNOWING THAT I HAVE TO CONSTRUCT SOMETHING, OR I'LL LOSE MY MIND. BUT I ALSO KNOW THAT WHATEVER I END UP CONSTRUCTING IS JUST THAT -- A MEANINGLESS CONSTRUCT. QUITE A DILEMMA.
YEP.
IT'S A TOUGHIE.

4.

TALKING ABOUT THE WEATHER IS GENERALLY CONSIDERED FAIRLY PASSÉ, THE SORT OF THING YOU REEL OFF AS CONVERSATIONAL FILLER BECAUSE IT IS SO NON-IDEOLOGICAL AND EASY — PRETTY MUCH EVERYONE THINKS THAT RAIN SUCKS AND SUNNY DAYS ARE NICE. I THINK THIS CONDESCENDING VIEW OF THE WEATHER CONVERSATION IS KIND OF MISLEADING, THOUGH. CONVERSATION IS PRETTY MUCH JUST PEOPLE'S ATTEMPT TO FIND COMMONALITY AND THUS CONNECTEDNESS, AND YOU HAVE CERTAIN CONVERSATIONAL CORRIDORS YOU CAN AND CAN'T PASS DOWN WITH EVERYONE — POLITICS, MUSICAL TASTE, OR EVEN JUST WHETHER YOU HAVE THE FREEDOM TO SAY "TERRIBLE" WHEN SOMEONE ASKS, "HOW'S IT GOING?"

WEATHER, THOUGH: EVERYONE'S GOT SOMETHING
TO SAY ABOUT IT, AND YOU DON'T FIND MANY RADICAL
THINKERS IN THE WORLD OF CLIMATE PREFERENCE. EVEN
IF YOU DO, DO YOU REALLY FEEL STRONGLY ENOUGH ABOUT
BAROMETRIC PRESSURE OR WHETHER WE'RE DUE FOR ANOTHER
COLD FRONT THAT YOU'D BE WILLING TO GET IN A FIST
FIGHT OR EVEN RAISE YOUR VOICE IN DEFENSE OF YOUR
CONVICTIONS? WHEN RODNEY KING ASKED WHY WE CAN'T
ALL GET ALONG, THE OBVIOUS ANSWER IS, BECAUSE THE
CONVERSATION ISN'T ABOUT THE WEATHER.
    I ENJOY A GOOD WEATHER CONVERSATION. I SPEND
A LOT OF TIME PONDERING THE EFFECT OF THE SEASONS
ON PEOPLE. WHEN YOU'RE REALLY BUMMED OUT, IT'S EASY TO
CONVINCE YOURSELF THAT YOU HAVE THE MOST GRANDIOSE
OF MOTIVATIONS, THAT IT'S THE VAST INJUSTICES OF
THE WORLD AND THE BARBARISM OF HOW MAN TREATS
MAN WHICH HAS GOT YOU DOWN. NOBODY WANTS TO
THINK IT'S JUST A FEW CONSECUTIVE DAYS OF RAIN.
WE LIKE TO THINK WE HAVE MORE CONTROL OF
OUR BRAIN THAN THAT.

OF COURSE, INEVITABLY THE
SUN COMES OUT, REVEALING THE SHALLOW NATURE OF
OUR EMOTIONAL LIVES AS WE PUT ON SHORTS AND
HOOTERS T-SHIRTS AND GET READY TO GO TO THE
BEACH. "HEY, WHAT ABOUT THE VAST INJUSTICES OF
THE WORLD?" SOMEONE WHO YOU CORNERED A FEW
DAYS AGO WHEN THE WEATHER WAS BAD AND GAVE AN
EARFULL TO, ASKS. "MAN, HOW ABOUT THIS SUN," YOU
SAY. "THINK THERE'S ANOTHER COLD FRONT COMING IN,
OR WHAT?"

IT'S RAINING TODAY AND I'M BIKING AROUND,
HALF-ASSEDLY LOOKING FOR A JOB. WHENEVER I FEEL
LIKE GOING TO THE RECORD STORE OR READING SOME
MAGAZINES, I JUST GO AND ASK IF THEY'RE HIRING.
THEY'RE INEVITABLY NOT, AND THEN OF COURSE SINCE
I'M THERE ANYWAY I MIGHT AS WELL SPEND FORTY
FIVE MINUTES SEEING IF THEY HAVE ANYTHING NEW

WHICH I MIGHT BE INTERESTED IN BUYING WHEN
I GET THAT JOB. I'M ESPECIALLY HALF-ASSED
TODAY, BECAUSE THE RAIN MAKES ME SLUGGISH
AND MOODY AND MAKES ME FEEL FAR AWAY,
DISCONNECTED FROM MY SURROUNDINGS AND PREOCCUPIED
WITH OTHER PLACES AND OTHER TIMES. THE RAIN
REMINDS ME OF PORTLAND, MAKES MY EYES GLAZE
OVER AND MY THOUGHTS TURN TO FAR AWAY THINGS, AS
I CAREEN GLAZED-EYED DOWN THE STREET, SCARCELY
AWARE OF THE AUTOMOBILES NARROWLY MISSING ME
AND COMMENTING ON MY NOSTALGIA-CHARGED BIKING
STYLE WITH HONKS AND THE ALWAYS PERTINENT
MIDDLE FINGER.
    IT'S FUNNY HOW WE EVEN MISS THE THINGS WE
HATED, JUST BECAUSE THEY'RE GONE. IT RAINED FOR

SEVEN DAYS IN A ROW ONCE WHEN
I LIVED IN PORTLAND. I'M NOT
SAYING THERE WERE SEVEN CONSECU-
TIVE DAYS DURING WHICH AT SOME
POINT IT RAINED; I'M SAYING THAT
THERE WAS A ONE-HUNDRED AND SIXTY
EIGHT HOUR PERIOD DURING WHICH IT
WAS CONSTANTLY RAINING. THERE WOULD
BE THE OCCASIONAL TEN MINUTE
LULL, WHEREIN YOU HAD JUST ENOUGH
TIME TO HAUL ASS DOWN THE STREET
TO THE SPACE ROOM OR SOME OTHER
NEARBY DEN OF ILL REPUTE, BEFORE
THE WATER WOULD BARREL DOWN
AGAIN AND YOU'D BE CONSIGNED TO
A COUPLE DAYS HANGING OUT AT
THE SPACE ROOM, LOADED AND
DEPRESSED. SLEEP, DESPERATION
DRINKING, AND SLOTH—— ONLY THOSE
WHO HAVE SPENT SOME TIME IN THE
NORTHWESTERN UNITED STATES CAN
UNDERSTAND THE OMINOUS UNDER-
TONES IN THE OLYMPIA BREWING
COMPANY'S SLOGAN, "IT'S THE WATER."

BY DAY FIVE, PARALYZED AND UNABLE TO
THINK OF A REASON TO GET UP, I FOUND
THE ONLY WAY I COULD TALK MYSELF
INTO NON-HORIZONTAL EXISTENCE WAS BY
CALLING UP AN AIRLINE, BUYING A PLANE
TICKET TO NEW YORK, AND THEN GETTING AS
DRUNK AS POSSIBLE UNTIL IT WAS TIME
TO GO.

THE MORNING OF DAY EIGHT, I WOKE UP WITH
AN INCREDIBLY BAD HEADACHE. THE SUN WAS
GLARINGLY BRIGHT IN MY FACE. SEVERAL PEOPLE
I HAD BEEN FRIENDS WITH DAYS EARLIER WERE
NO LONGER SPEAKING TO ME. "AH, THE SUN,"
I MUMBLED DREAMILY, GOT UP, AND CAUGHT A BUS
TO THE AIRPORT.

5.

HONEY
ROASTED
PEANUTS?

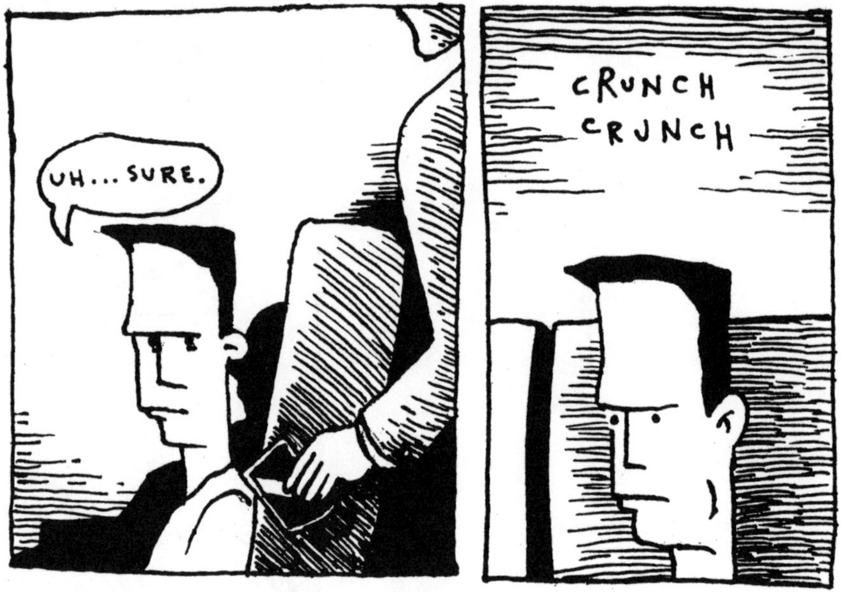
UH... SURE.
CRUNCH
CRUNCH

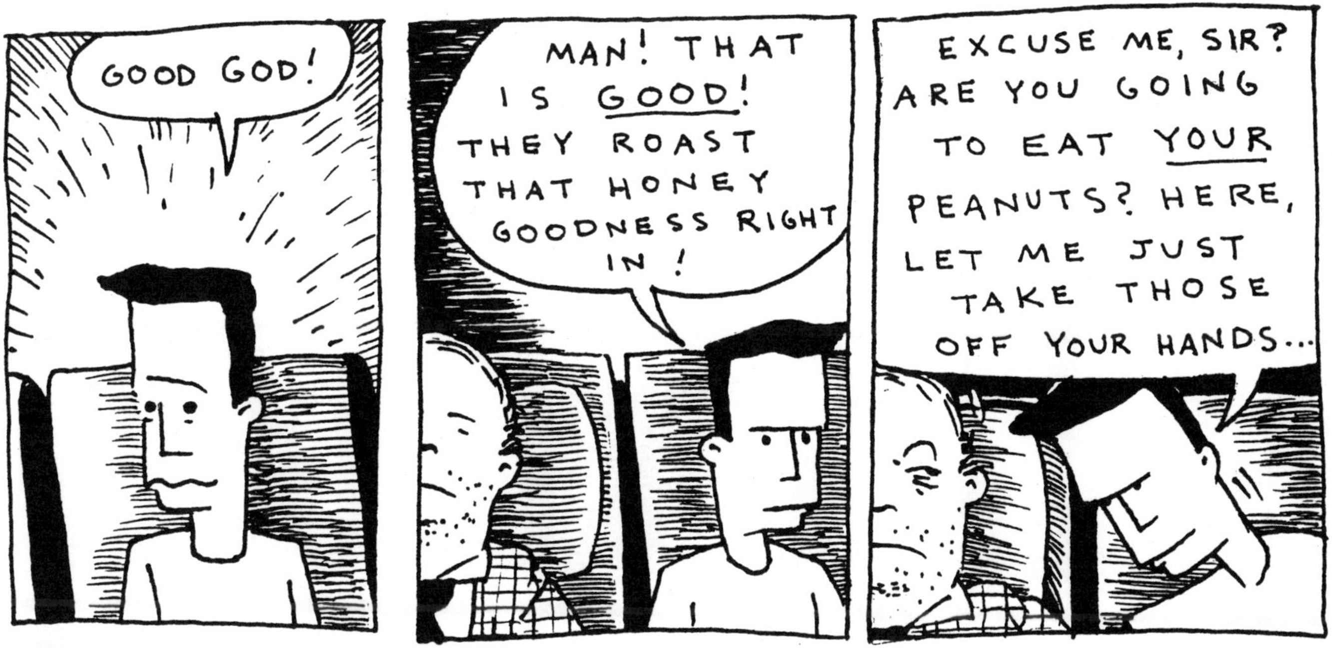
GOOD GOD!
MAN! THAT IS GOOD! THEY ROAST THAT HONEY GOODNESS RIGHT IN!
EXCUSE ME, SIR? ARE YOU GOING TO EAT YOUR PEANUTS? HERE, LET ME JUST TAKE THOSE OFF YOUR HANDS...

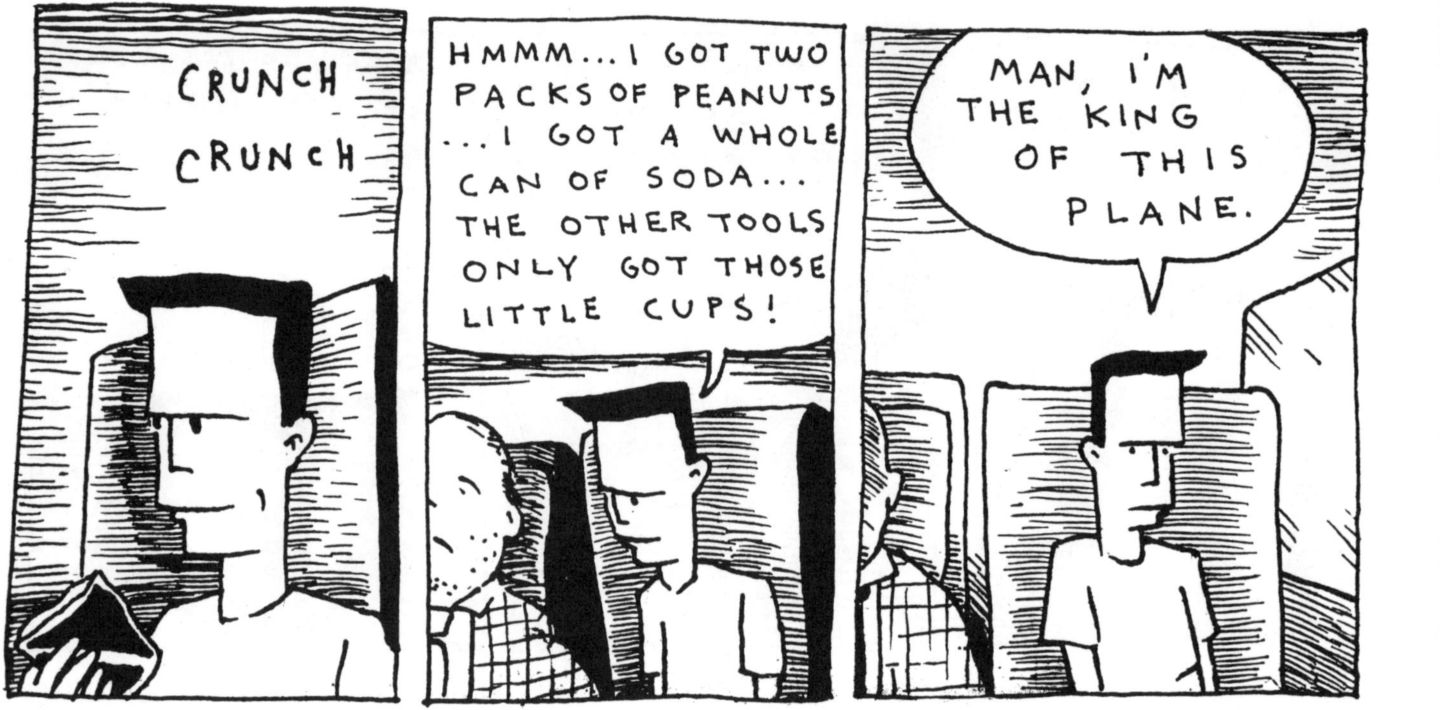
CRUNCH
CRUNCH
HMMM...I GOT TWO PACKS OF PEANUTS ...I GOT A WHOLE CAN OF SODA... THE OTHER TOOLS ONLY GOT THOSE LITTLE CUPS!
MAN, I'M THE KING OF THIS PLANE.

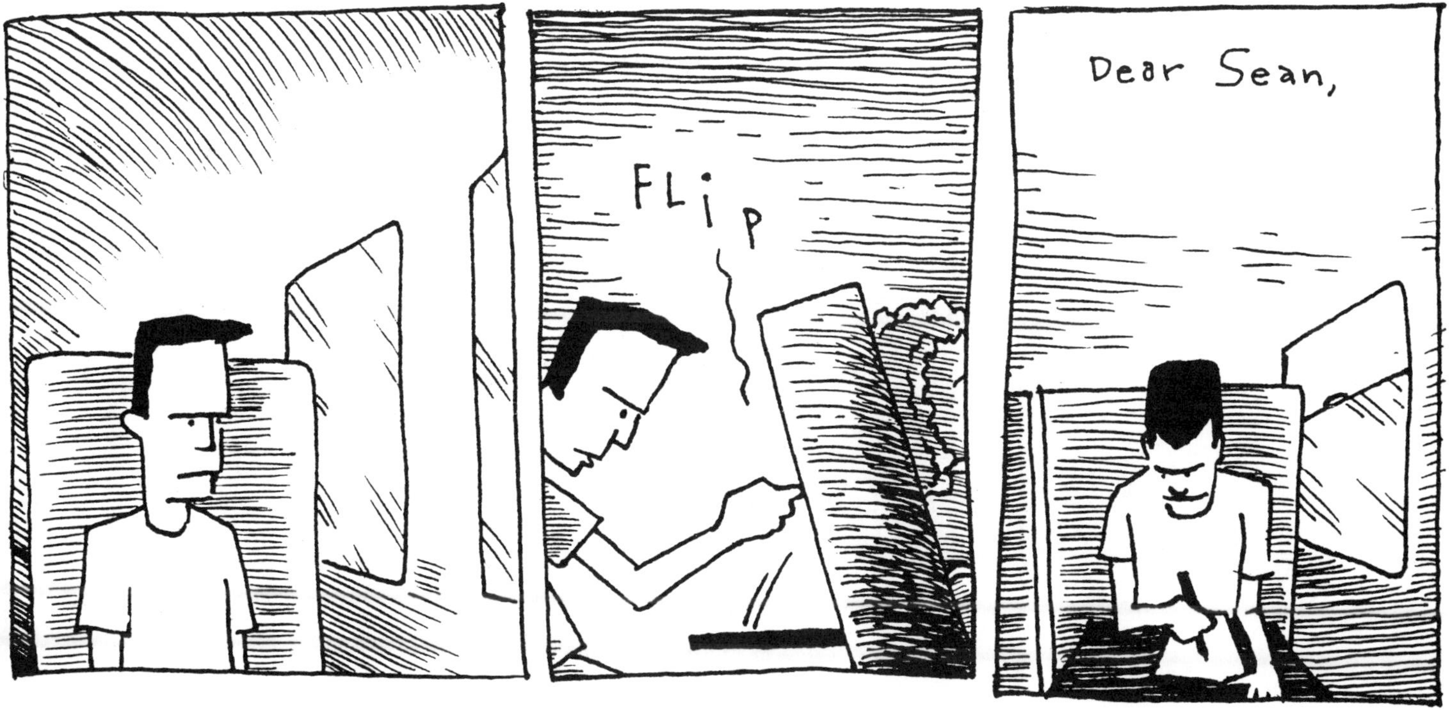
FLip
Dear Sean,

As I write this I'm at some ungodly altitude being zipped across America. I got my ticket for a few days so that I'd have some time to screw around.. I need a break from my fucked up life in Portland. Jeez, Portland: walking around with this girl the other night

passing by all the houses and hearing the dull thud of bands practicing

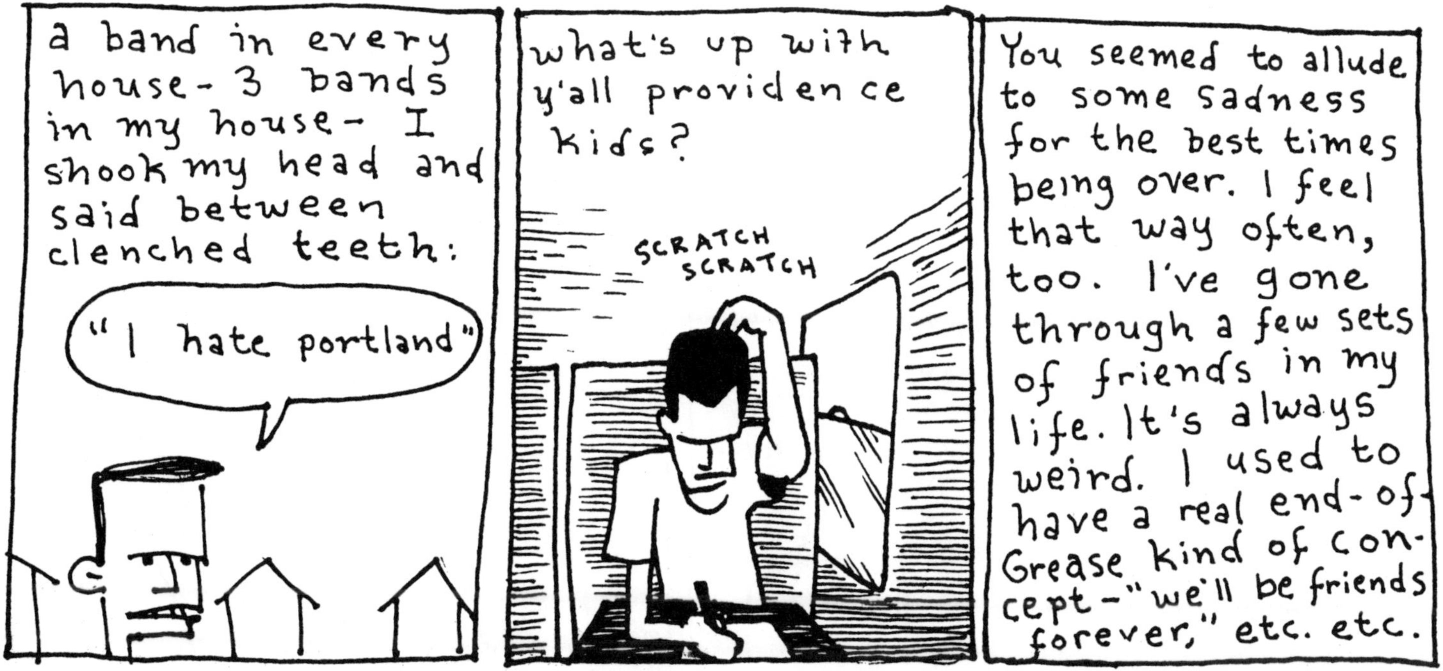
a band in every house - 3 bands in my house - I shook my head and said between clenched teeth:
"I hate portland"
what's up with y'all providence kids?
SCRATCH SCRATCH
You seemed to allude to some sadness for the best times being over. I feel that way often, too. I've gone through a few sets of friends in my life. It's always weird. I used to have a real end-of-Grease kind of con-cept - "we'll be friends forever," etc. etc.

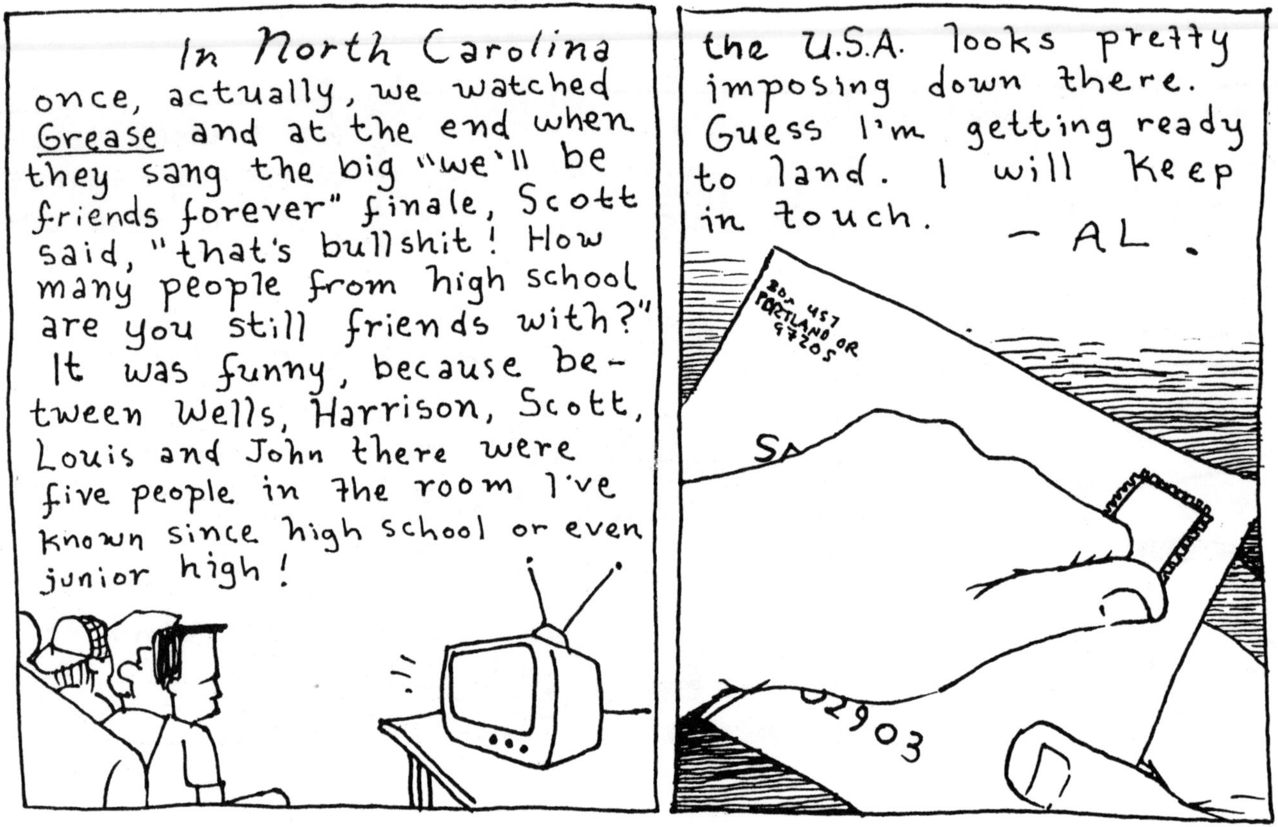
In North Carolina once, actually, we watched Grease and at the end when they sang the big "we'll be friends forever" finale, Scott said, "that's bullshit! How many people from high school are you still friends with?" It was funny, because between Wells, Harrison, Scott, Louis and John there were five people in the room I've known since high school or even junior high!
the U.S.A. looks pretty imposing down there. Guess I'm getting ready to land. I will keep in touch. - AL.
PORTLAND OR
97205
02903

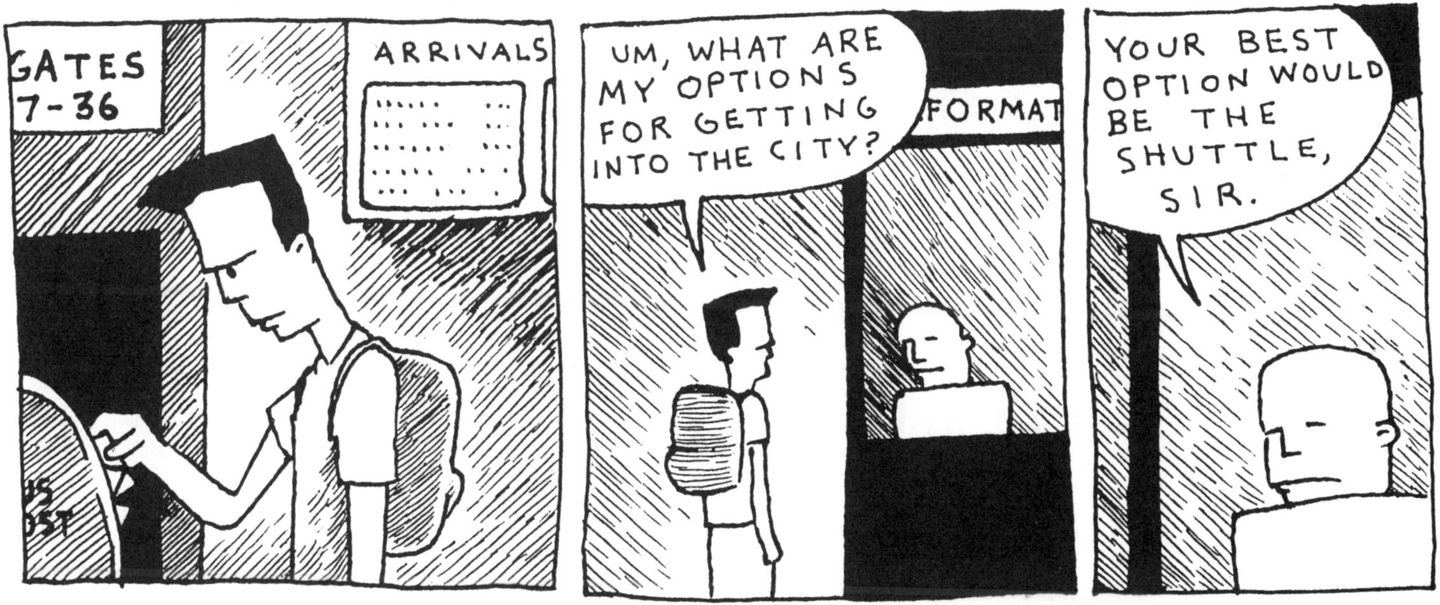
GATES
7-36
ARRIVALS
UM, WHAT ARE MY OPTIONS FOR GETTING INTO THE CITY?
FORMAT
YOUR BEST OPTION WOULD BE THE SHUTTLE, SIR.

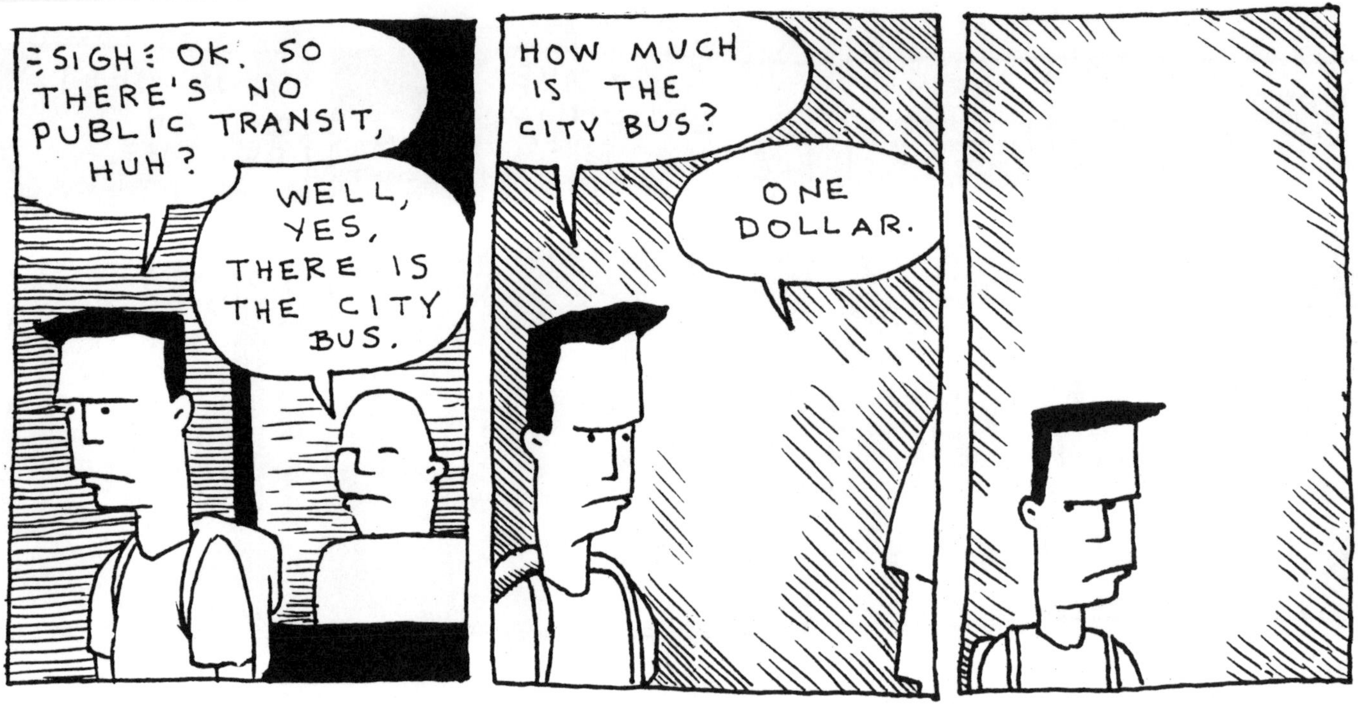

≡SIGH≡ OK. SO THERE'S NO PUBLIC TRANSIT, HUH?
WELL, YES, THERE IS THE CITY BUS.
HOW MUCH IS THE CITY BUS?
ONE DOLLAR.

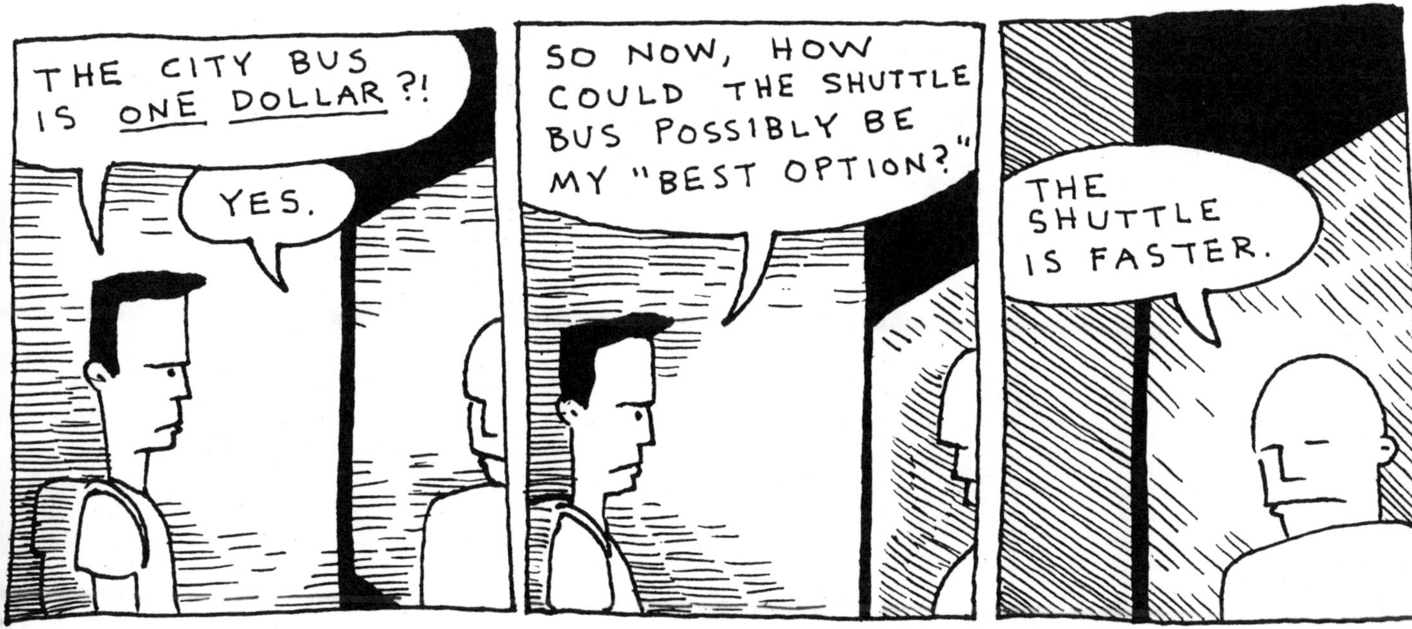
THE CITY BUS IS ONE DOLLAR?!
YES.
SO NOW, HOW COULD THE SHUTTLE BUS POSSIBLY BE MY "BEST OPTION?"
THE SHUTTLE IS FASTER.

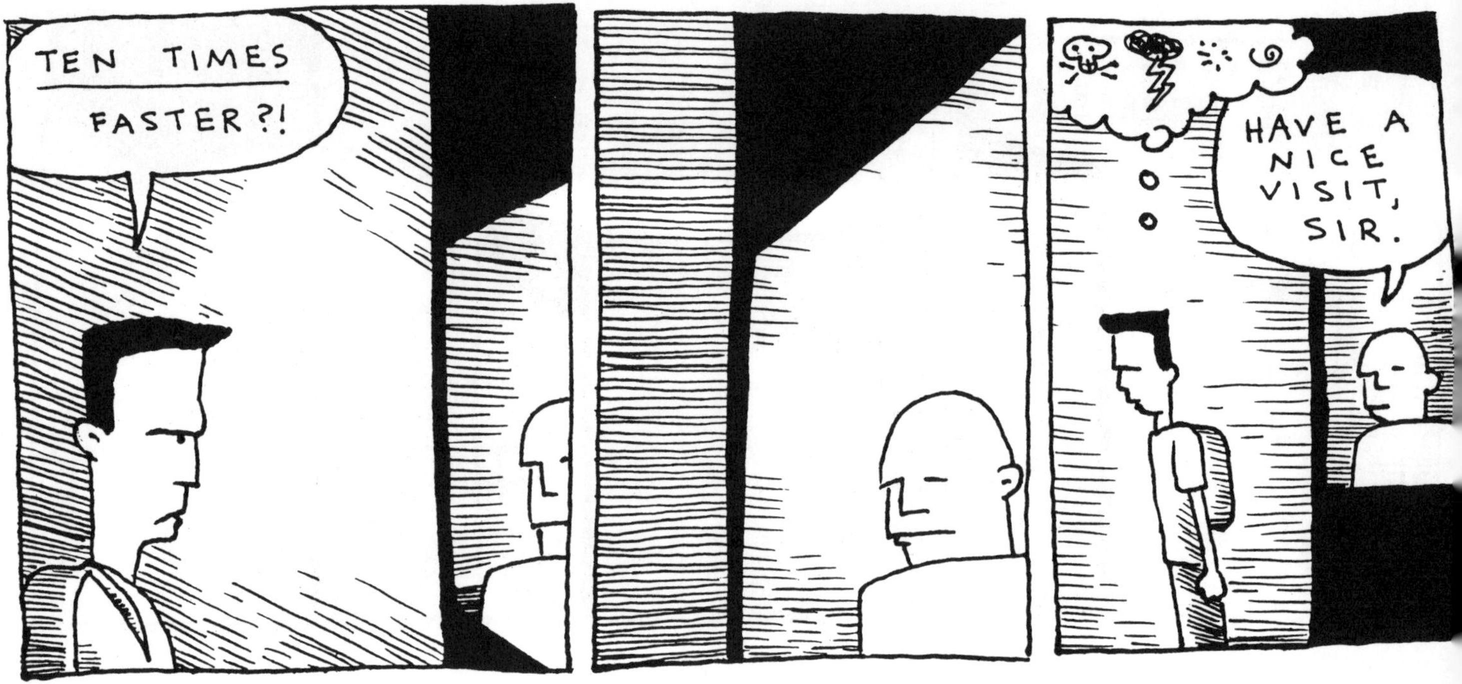
TEN TIMES FASTER?!
HAVE A NICE VISIT, SIR.

6.

NEW YORK! NEW YORK!
SO MUCH CITY THEY HAD
TO NAME IT TWICE. GOD,
I HATE IT WHEN PEOPLE
SAY DUMB SHIT LIKE THAT.

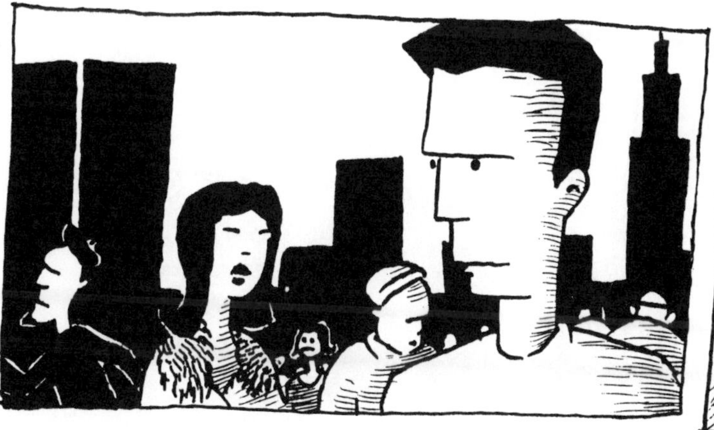

HANGING OUT WITH JIMMY FOUNTAIN. STICK A FORK INTO MY HAND IN A REST-AURANT TO PROVE A POINT.

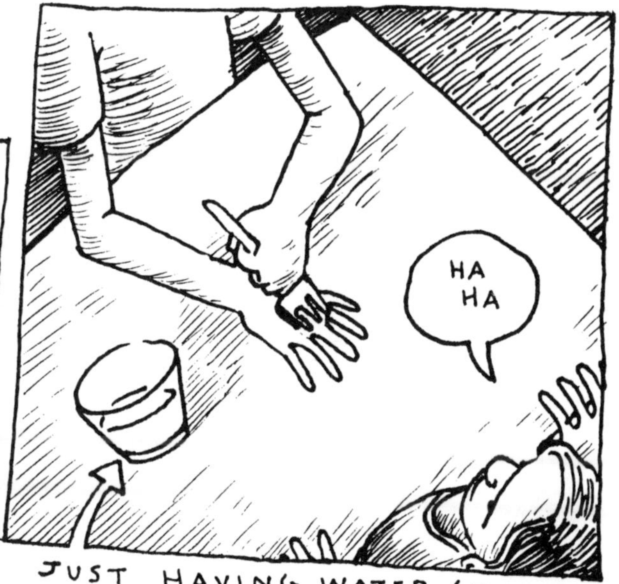
HA HA

JUST HAVING WATER (TYPICAL!)

EXISTENTIAL DESPAIR ABOUNDS.

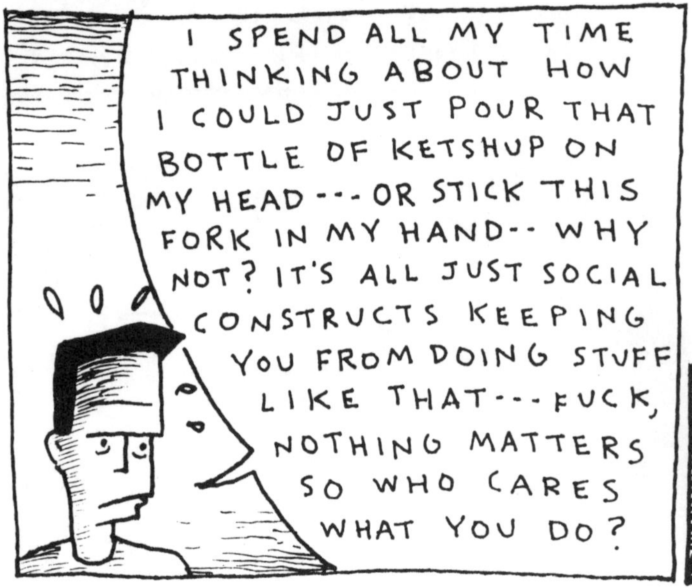
I SPEND ALL MY TIME THINKING ABOUT HOW I COULD JUST POUR THAT BOTTLE OF KETSHUP ON MY HEAD---OR STICK THIS FORK IN MY HAND-- WHY NOT? IT'S ALL JUST SOCIAL CONSTRUCTS KEEPING YOU FROM DOING STUFF LIKE THAT---FUCK, NOTHING MATTERS SO WHO CARES WHAT YOU DO?

BEEN HERE TWO DAYS. ALREADY HAVE A ROUTINE: A COFFEE SHOP I GO TO EVERY DAY. TWO DAYS AND THE REFILLS ARE ALREADY FREE (IN ANY OTHER TOWN, THAT'S THE EQUIVALENT ACCOMPLISHMENT OF BEING ELECTED MAYOR.)

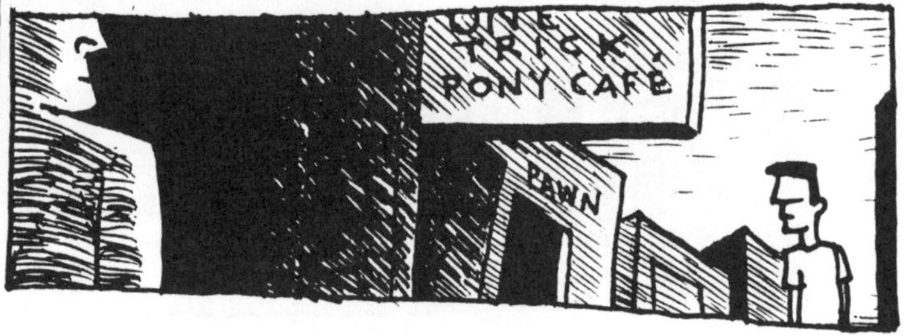
TRICK
PONY CAFÉ
PAWN

NOT A BAD ROUTINE. BUT AS EDDIE MURPHY SAID ABOUT THE HAUNTED HOUSE: "TOO BAD I CAN'T STAY."

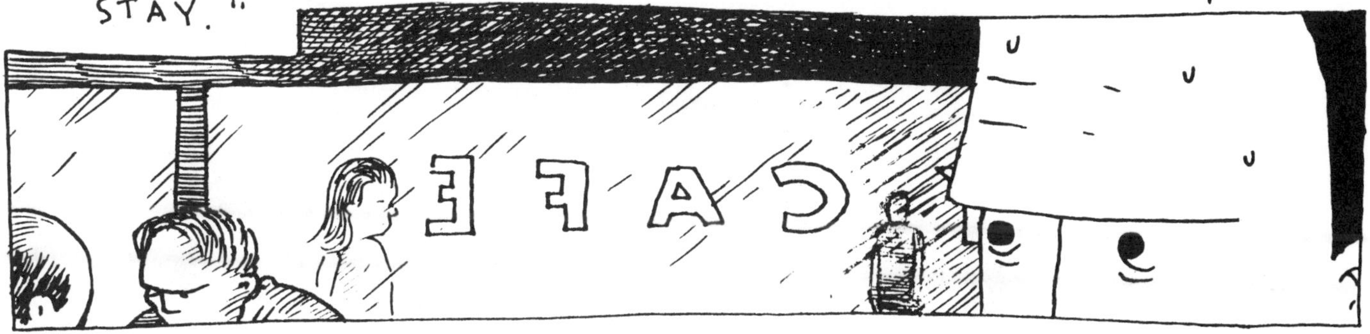
CAFE

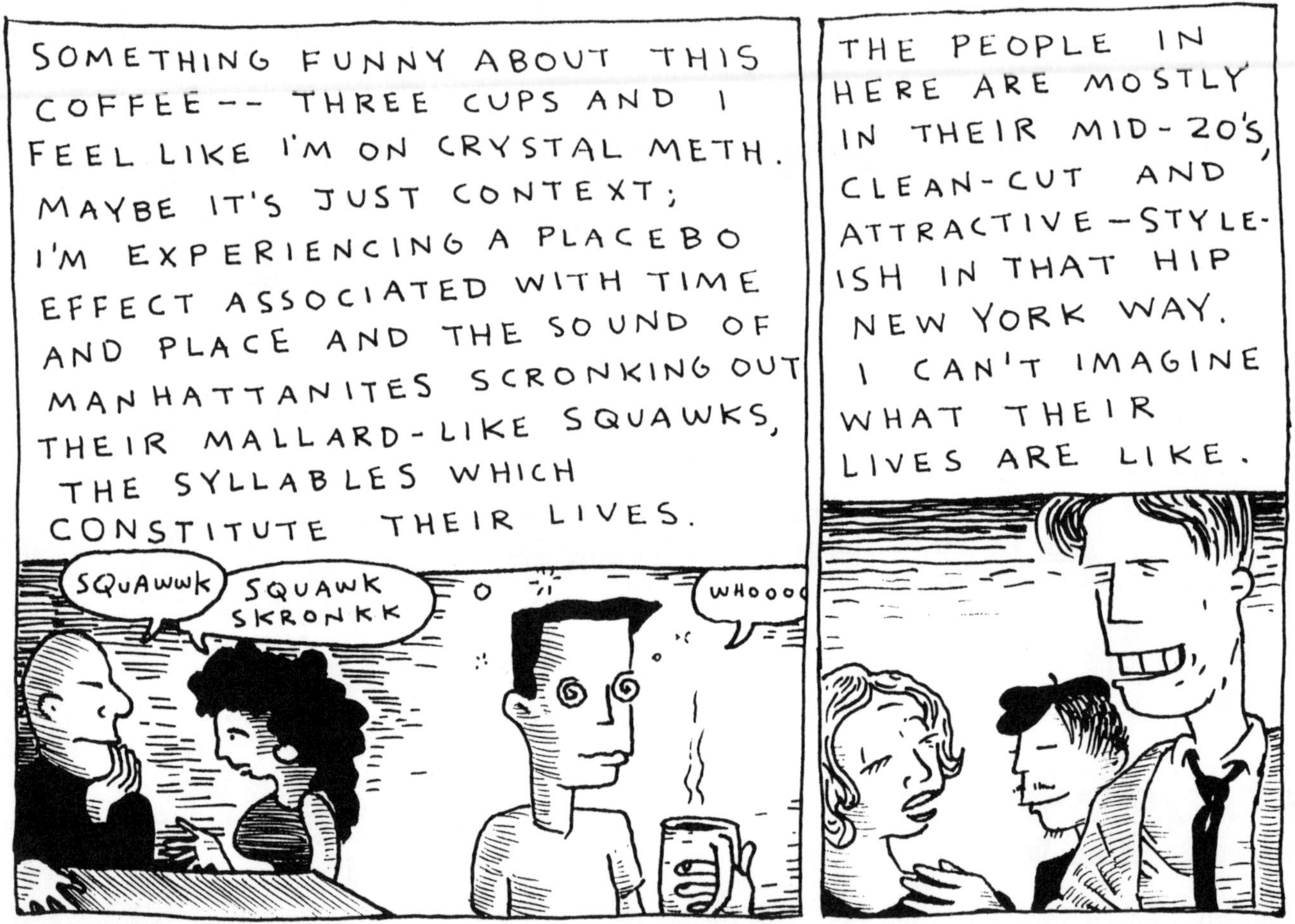
SOMETHING FUNNY ABOUT THIS COFFEE -- THREE CUPS AND I FEEL LIKE I'M ON CRYSTAL METH. MAYBE IT'S JUST CONTEXT; I'M EXPERIENCING A PLACEBO EFFECT ASSOCIATED WITH TIME AND PLACE AND THE SOUND OF MANHATTANITES SCRONKING OUT THEIR MALLARD-LIKE SQUAWKS, THE SYLLABLES WHICH CONSTITUTE THEIR LIVES.
SQUAWWK
SQUAWK SKRONKK
WHOOOO
THE PEOPLE IN HERE ARE MOSTLY IN THEIR MID-20'S, CLEAN-CUT AND ATTRACTIVE—STYLE-ISH IN THAT HIP NEW YORK WAY. I CAN'T IMAGINE WHAT THEIR LIVES ARE LIKE.

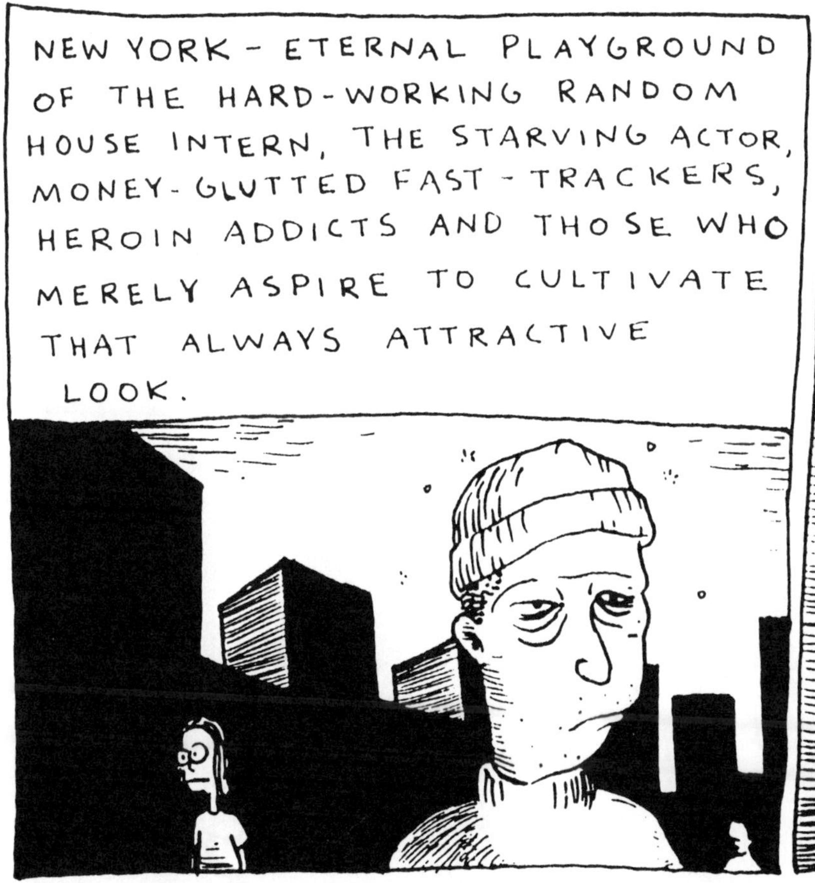
NEW YORK - ETERNAL PLAYGROUND OF THE HARD-WORKING RANDOM HOUSE INTERN, THE STARVING ACTOR, MONEY-GLUTTED FAST-TRACKERS, HEROIN ADDICTS AND THOSE WHO MERELY ASPIRE TO CULTIVATE THAT ALWAYS ATTRACTIVE LOOK.

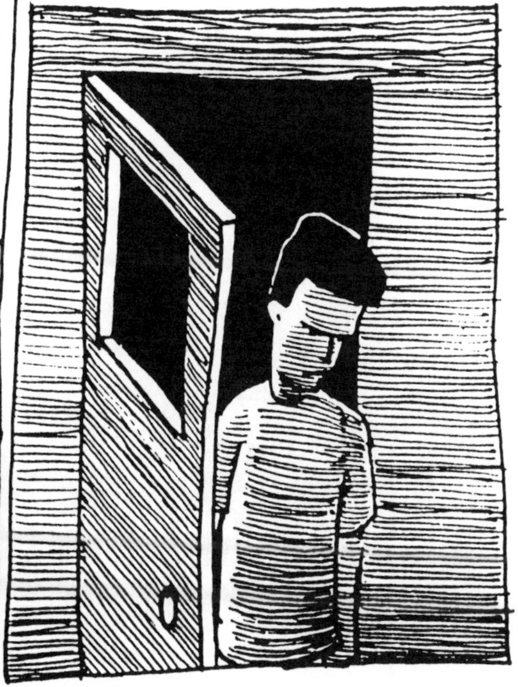
I CAN'T STAY. NEW YORK AND ME AGREE TO DISAGREE.

I'VE ALWAYS THOUGHT THAT WHEN YOU VISIT A PLACE YOU SHOULDN'T SAY YOU DON'T LIKE IT UNLESS YOU'VE HONESTLY THROWN YOURSELF INTO WHAT IS ESSENTIAL TO THAT PLACE. I TRY, BUT NEW YORK IS TOUGH, BECAUSE IT'S ESSENCE IS A GIANT INTESTINAL TRACT OF COMMERCE AND TRANSACTION - A CHURNING, WRITHING, CONSUMING AND DIGESTING, GORGE-EXCRETE-GORGE ECONOMY.

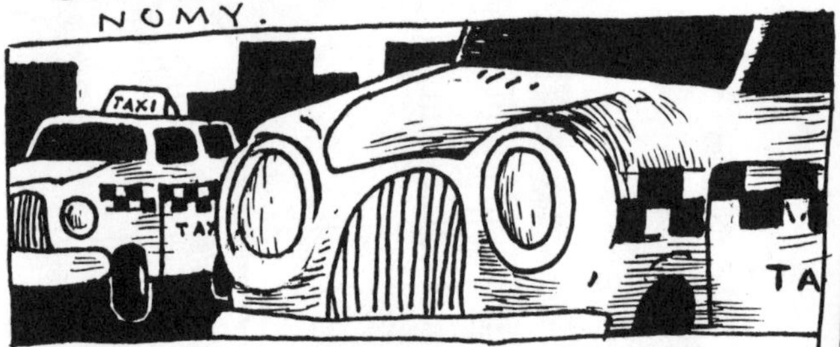

THE TAXI CAB IS CONSIDERED A STANDARD MODE OF TRANSPORT, FOR GOD'S SAKE.

SO THE TIME I'VE SPENT THERE IS ALWAYS SPENT WAITING TO "GET IT," SO THAT ALL THOSE NEW YORKER CARTOONS AND WOODY ALLEN MOVIES WILL MAKE SENSE AND I CAN DIE A COSMOPOLITAN, MUTTERING WITH CONVICTION ON MY DEATHBED,

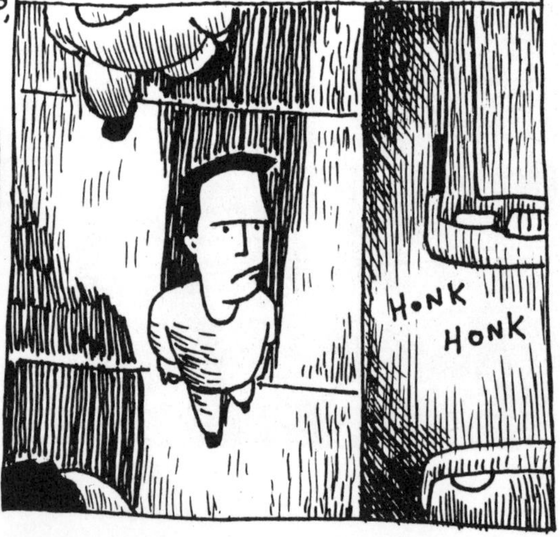
HONK
HONK

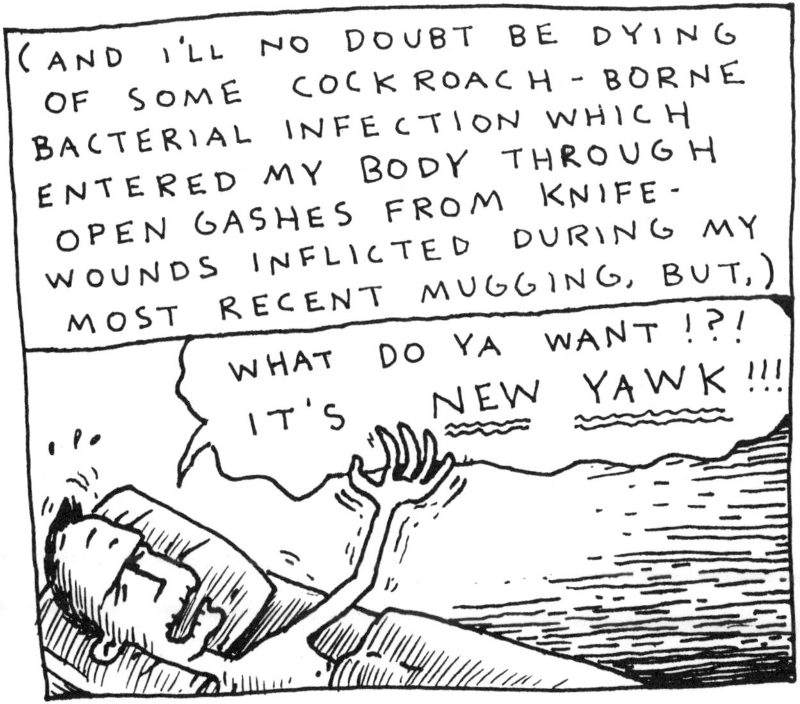
(AND I'LL NO DOUBT BE DYING OF SOME COCKROACH-BORNE BACTERIAL INFECTION WHICH ENTERED MY BODY THROUGH OPEN GASHES FROM KNIFE-WOUNDS INFLICTED DURING MY MOST RECENT MUGGING, BUT,)
WHAT DO YA WANT!?! IT'S NEW YAWK!!!

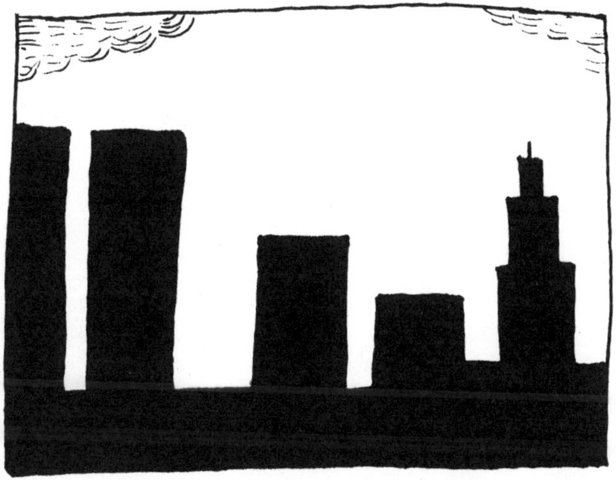

7.

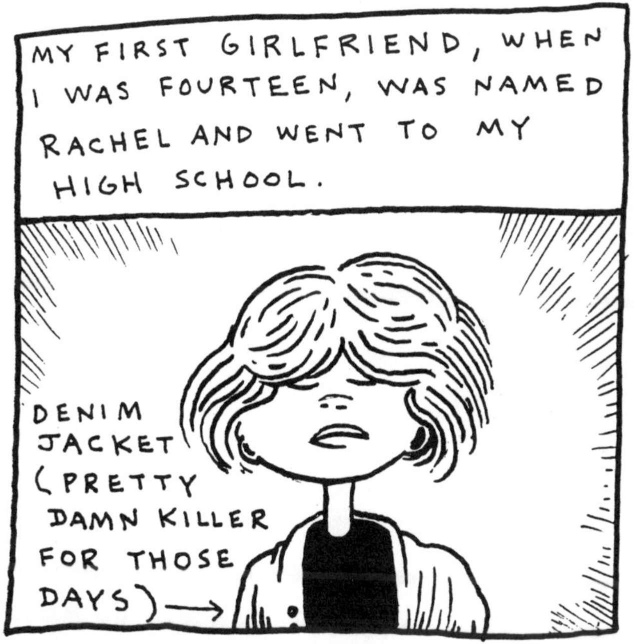
MY FIRST GIRLFRIEND, WHEN I WAS FOURTEEN, WAS NAMED RACHEL AND WENT TO MY HIGH SCHOOL.
DENIM JACKET (PRETTY DAMN KILLER FOR THOSE DAYS)

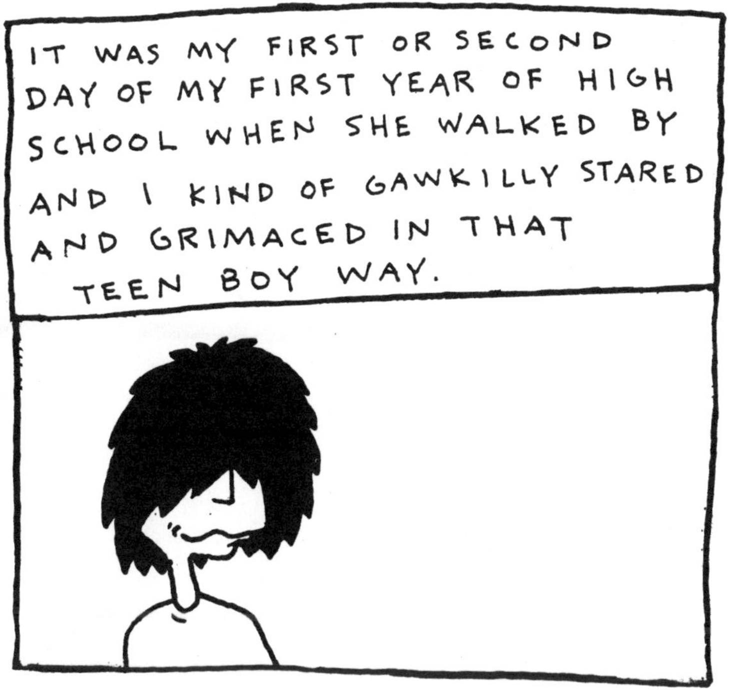
IT WAS MY FIRST OR SECOND DAY OF MY FIRST YEAR OF HIGH SCHOOL WHEN SHE WALKED BY AND I KIND OF GAWKILLY STARED AND GRIMACED IN THAT TEEN BOY WAY.

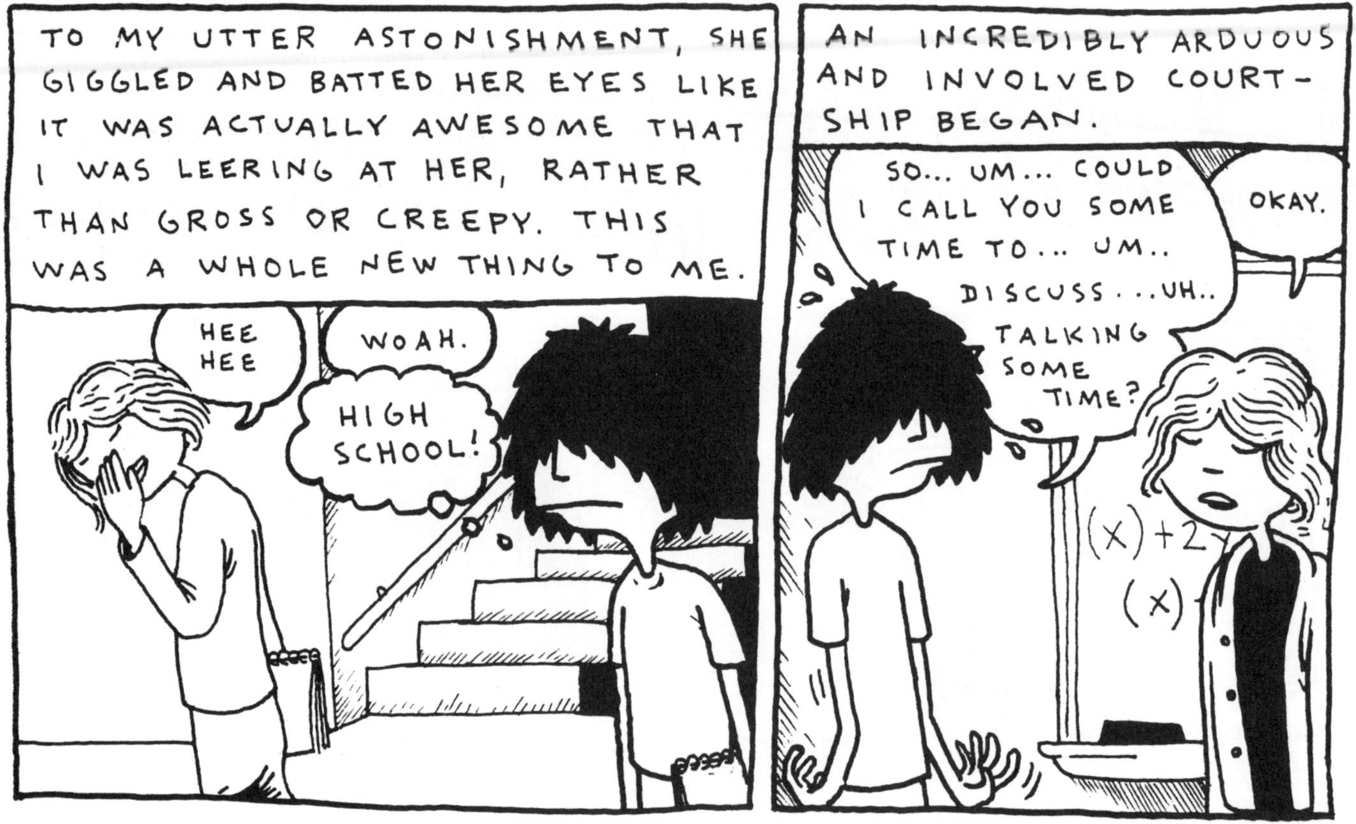
TO MY UTTER ASTONISHMENT, SHE GIGGLED AND BATTED HER EYES LIKE IT WAS ACTUALLY AWESOME THAT I WAS LEERING AT HER, RATHER THAN GROSS OR CREEPY. THIS WAS A WHOLE NEW THING TO ME.
HEE HEE
WOAH.
HIGH SCHOOL!
AN INCREDIBLY ARDUOUS AND INVOLVED COURT-SHIP BEGAN.
SO... UM... COULD I CALL YOU SOME TIME TO... UM.. DISCUSS...UH.. TALKING SOME TIME?
OKAY.

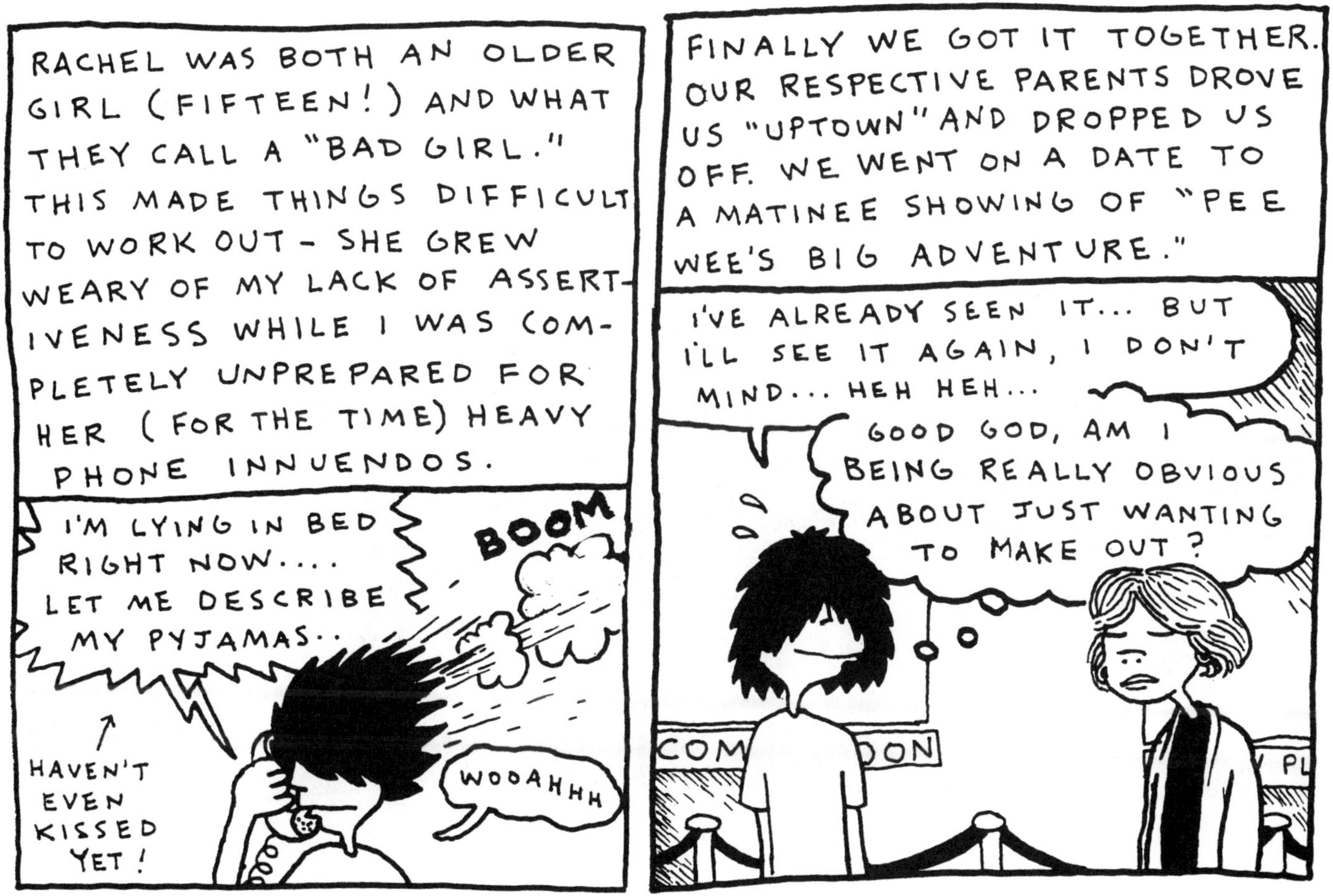
RACHEL WAS BOTH AN OLDER GIRL (FIFTEEN!) AND WHAT THEY CALL A "BAD GIRL." THIS MADE THINGS DIFFICULT TO WORK OUT - SHE GREW WEARY OF MY LACK OF ASSERTIVENESS WHILE I WAS COMPLETELY UNPREPARED FOR HER (FOR THE TIME) HEAVY PHONE INNUENDOS.
I'M LYING IN BED RIGHT NOW.... LET ME DESCRIBE MY PYJAMAS..
BOOM
WOOAHHH
HAVEN'T EVEN KISSED YET!
FINALLY WE GOT IT TOGETHER. OUR RESPECTIVE PARENTS DROVE US "UPTOWN" AND DROPPED US OFF. WE WENT ON A DATE TO A MATINEE SHOWING OF "PEE WEE'S BIG ADVENTURE."
I'VE ALREADY SEEN IT... BUT I'LL SEE IT AGAIN, I DON'T MIND... HEH HEH...
GOOD GOD, AM I BEING REALLY OBVIOUS ABOUT JUST WANTING TO MAKE OUT?
COM
OON
PL

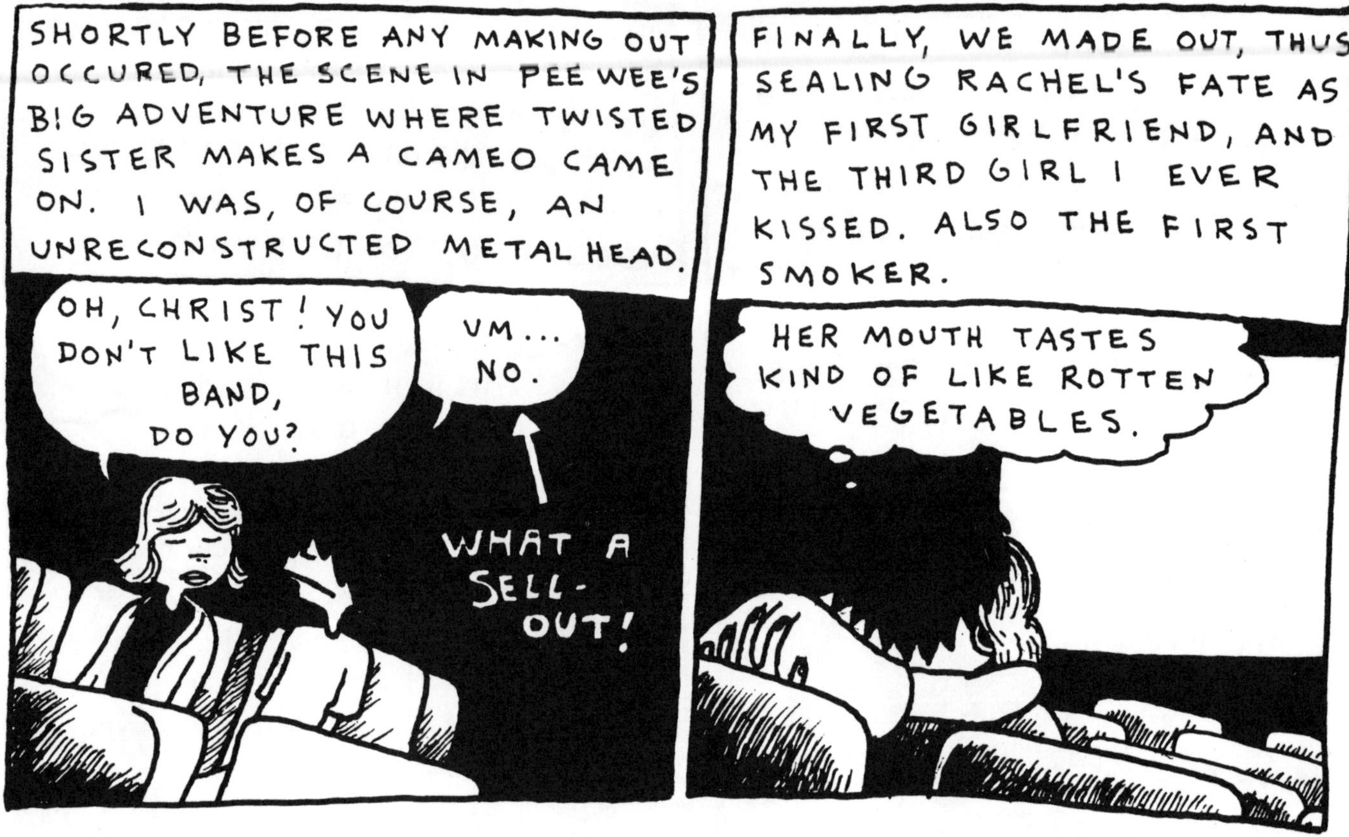
SHORTLY BEFORE ANY MAKING OUT OCCURED, THE SCENE IN PEE WEE'S BIG ADVENTURE WHERE TWISTED SISTER MAKES A CAMEO CAME ON. I WAS, OF COURSE, AN UNRECONSTRUCTED METAL HEAD.
OH, CHRIST! YOU DON'T LIKE THIS BAND, DO YOU?
UM... NO.
WHAT A SELL-OUT!
FINALLY, WE MADE OUT, THUS SEALING RACHEL'S FATE AS MY FIRST GIRLFRIEND, AND THE THIRD GIRL I EVER KISSED. ALSO THE FIRST SMOKER.
HER MOUTH TASTES KIND OF LIKE ROTTEN VEGETABLES.

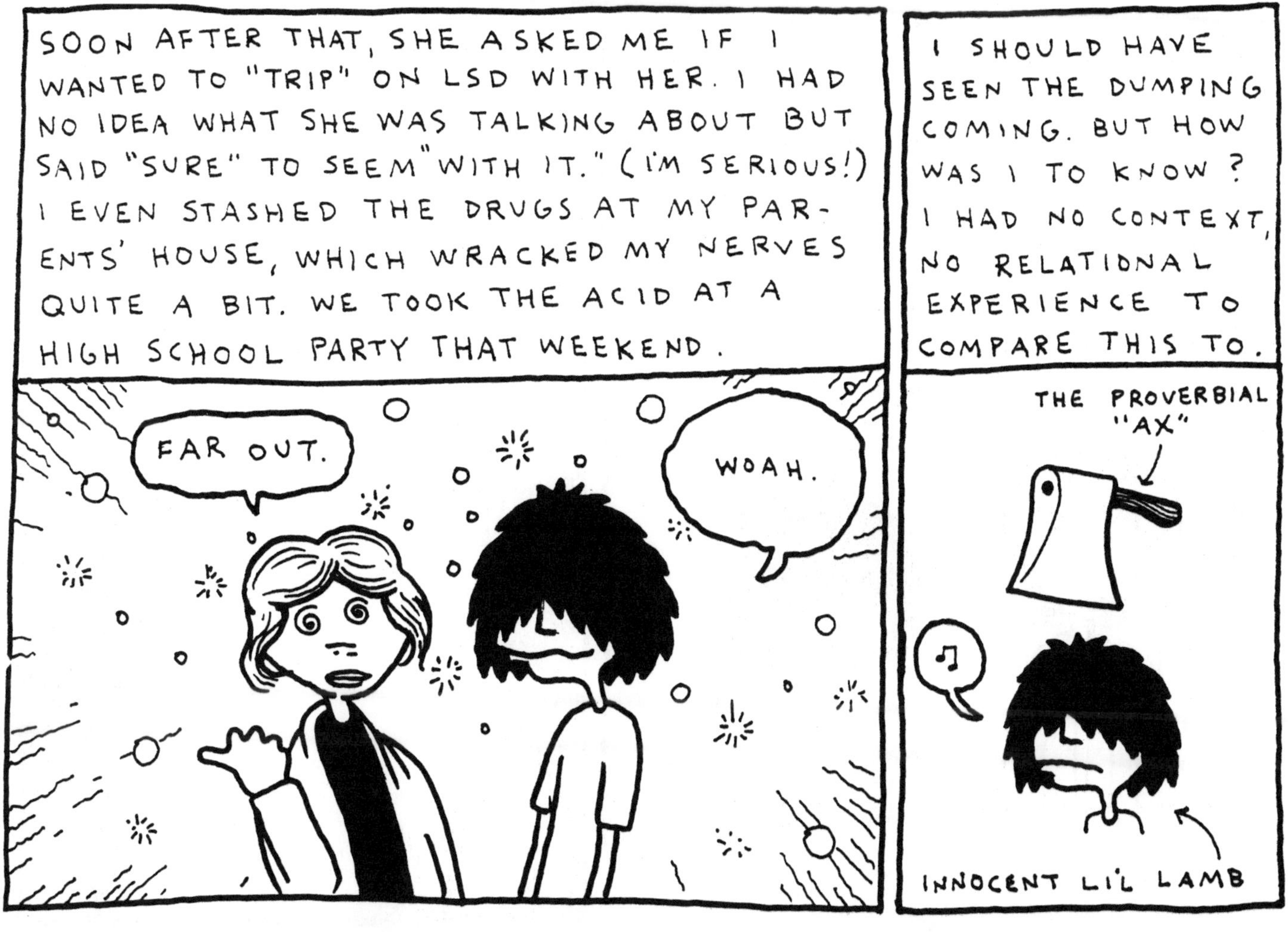
SOON AFTER THAT, SHE ASKED ME IF I WANTED TO "TRIP" ON LSD WITH HER. I HAD NO IDEA WHAT SHE WAS TALKING ABOUT BUT SAID "SURE" TO SEEM "WITH IT." (I'M SERIOUS!) I EVEN STASHED THE DRUGS AT MY PARENTS' HOUSE, WHICH WRACKED MY NERVES QUITE A BIT. WE TOOK THE ACID AT A HIGH SCHOOL PARTY THAT WEEKEND.
FAR OUT.
WOAH.
I SHOULD HAVE SEEN THE DUMPING COMING. BUT HOW WAS I TO KNOW? I HAD NO CONTEXT, NO RELATIONAL EXPERIENCE TO COMPARE THIS TO.
THE PROVERBIAL "AX"
INNOCENT LI'L LAMB

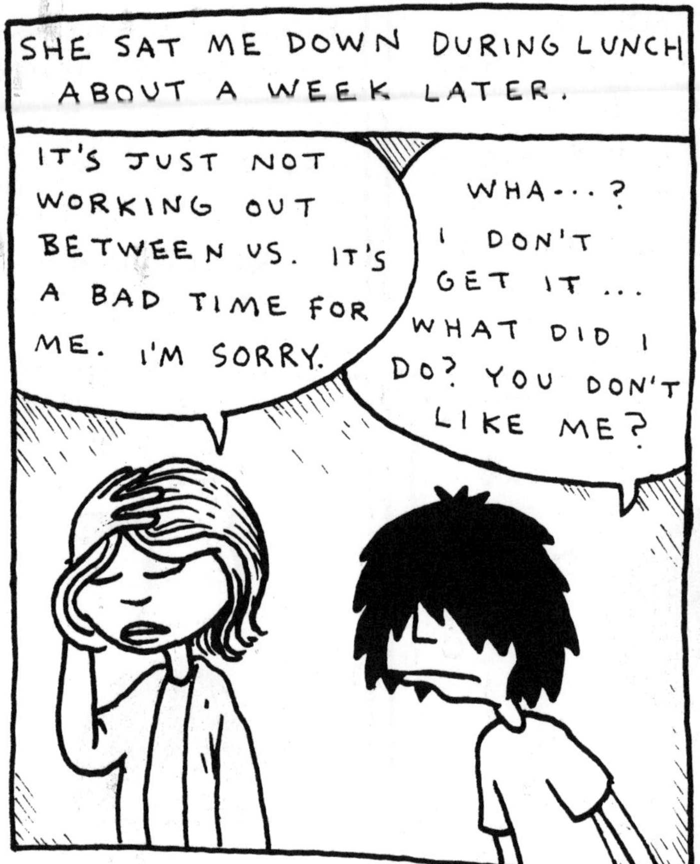
SHE SAT ME DOWN DURING LUNCH ABOUT A WEEK LATER.
IT'S JUST NOT WORKING OUT BETWEEN US. IT'S A BAD TIME FOR ME. I'M SORRY.
WHA...? I DON'T GET IT... WHAT DID I DO? YOU DON'T LIKE ME?

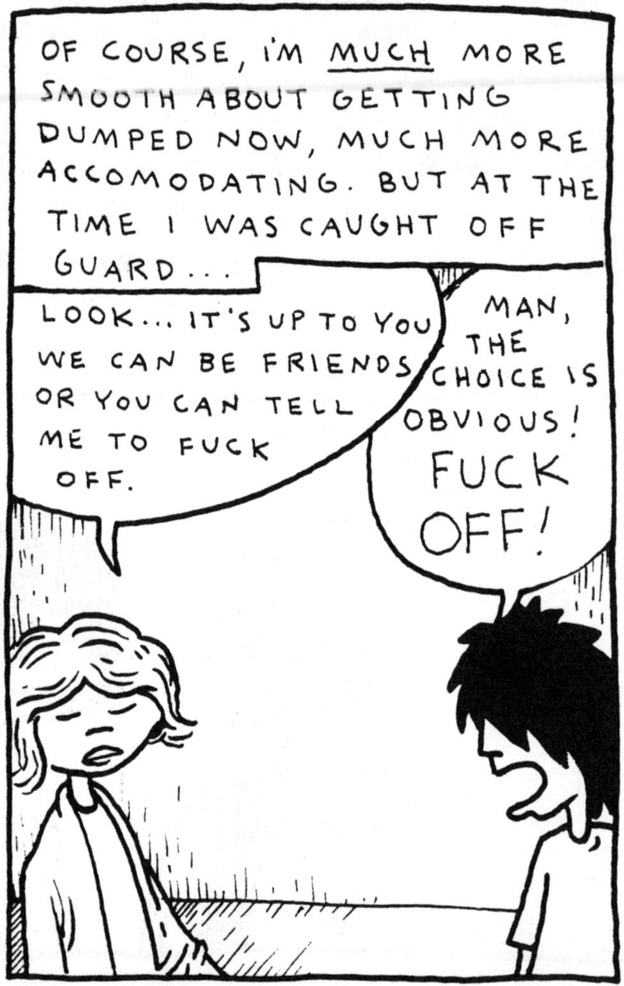
OF COURSE, I'M MUCH MORE SMOOTH ABOUT GETTING DUMPED NOW, MUCH MORE ACCOMODATING. BUT AT THE TIME I WAS CAUGHT OFF GUARD...
LOOK... IT'S UP TO YOU. WE CAN BE FRIENDS OR YOU CAN TELL ME TO FUCK OFF.
MAN, THE CHOICE IS OBVIOUS! FUCK OFF!

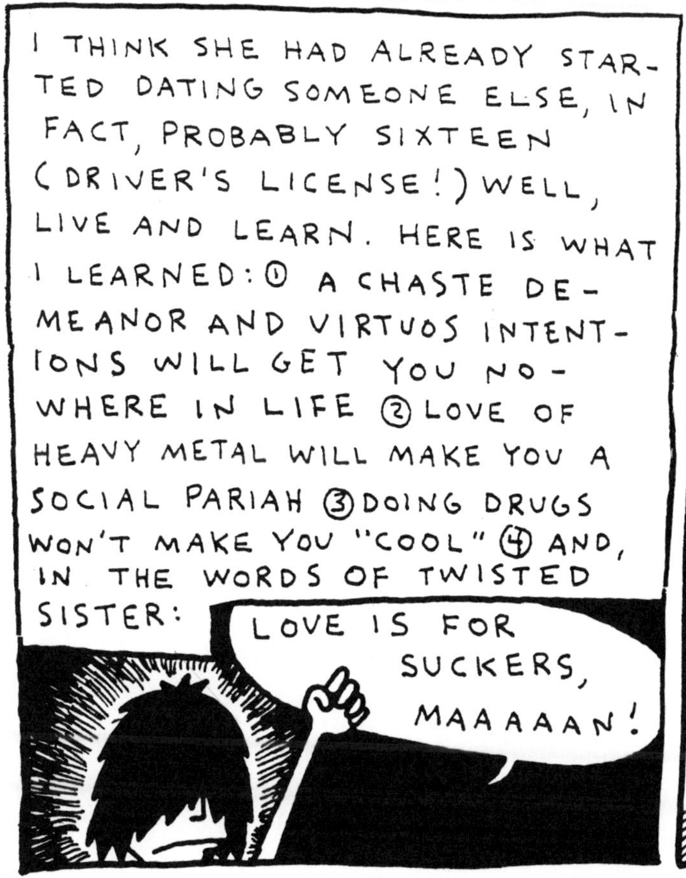
I THINK SHE HAD ALREADY STARTED DATING SOMEONE ELSE, IN FACT, PROBABLY SIXTEEN (DRIVER'S LICENSE!) WELL, LIVE AND LEARN. HERE IS WHAT I LEARNED: ① A CHASTE DEMEANOR AND VIRTUOS INTENTIONS WILL GET YOU NOWHERE IN LIFE ② LOVE OF HEAVY METAL WILL MAKE YOU A SOCIAL PARIAH ③ DOING DRUGS WON'T MAKE YOU "COOL" ④ AND, IN THE WORDS OF TWISTED SISTER:
LOVE IS FOR SUCKERS, MAAAAAN!

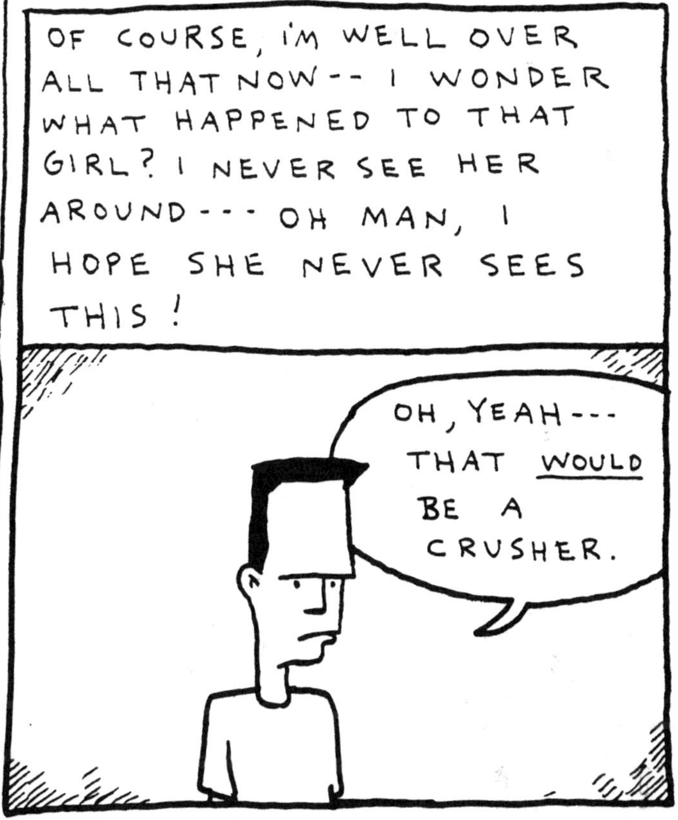
OF COURSE, I'M WELL OVER ALL THAT NOW-- I WONDER WHAT HAPPENED TO THAT GIRL? I NEVER SEE HER AROUND--- OH MAN, I HOPE SHE NEVER SEES THIS!
OH, YEAH--- THAT WOULD BE A CRUSHER.

8.

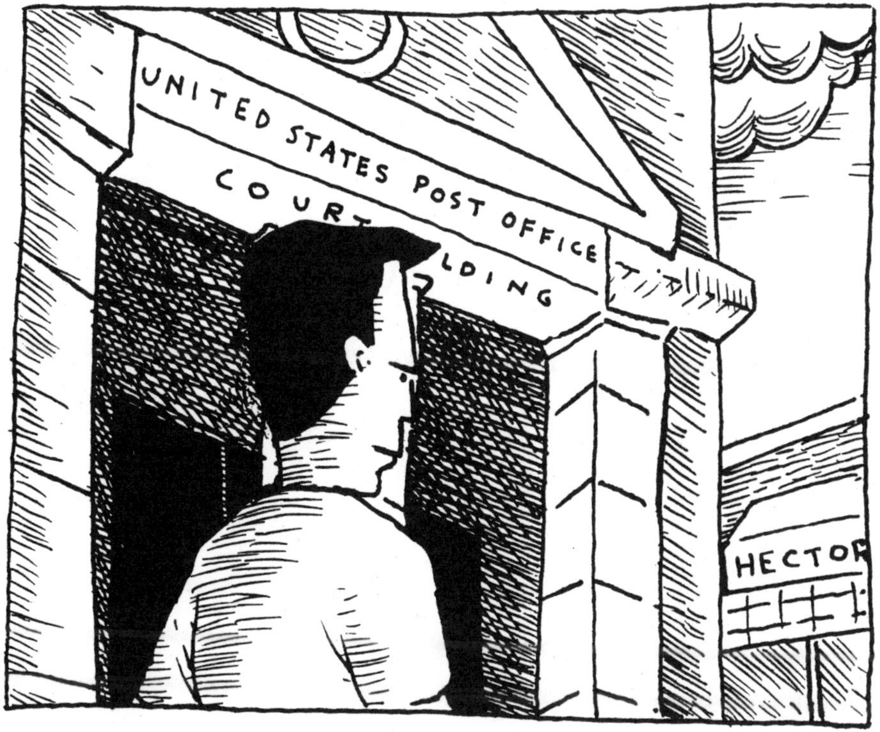
UNITED STATES POST OFFICE
COURT
LDING
HECTOR

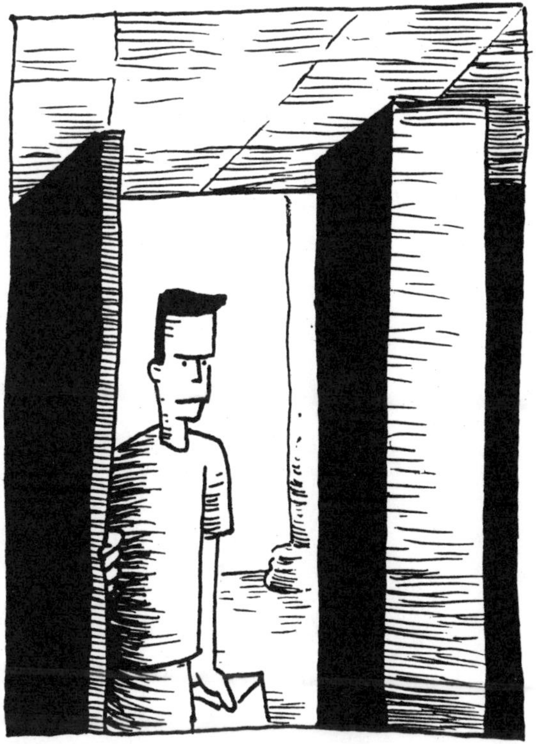

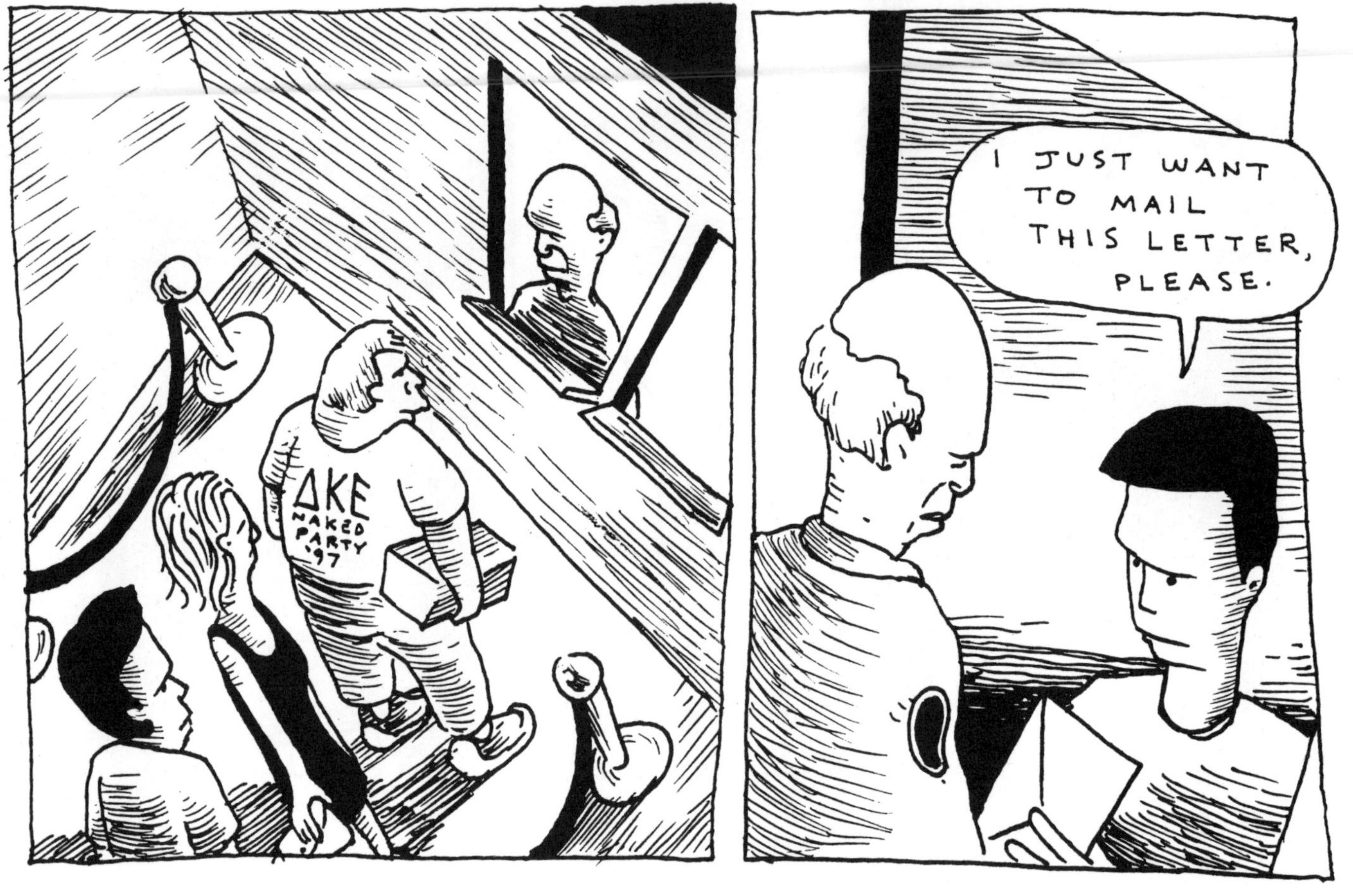
ΔKE
NAKED
PARTY
'97
I JUST WANT TO MAIL THIS LETTER, PLEASE.

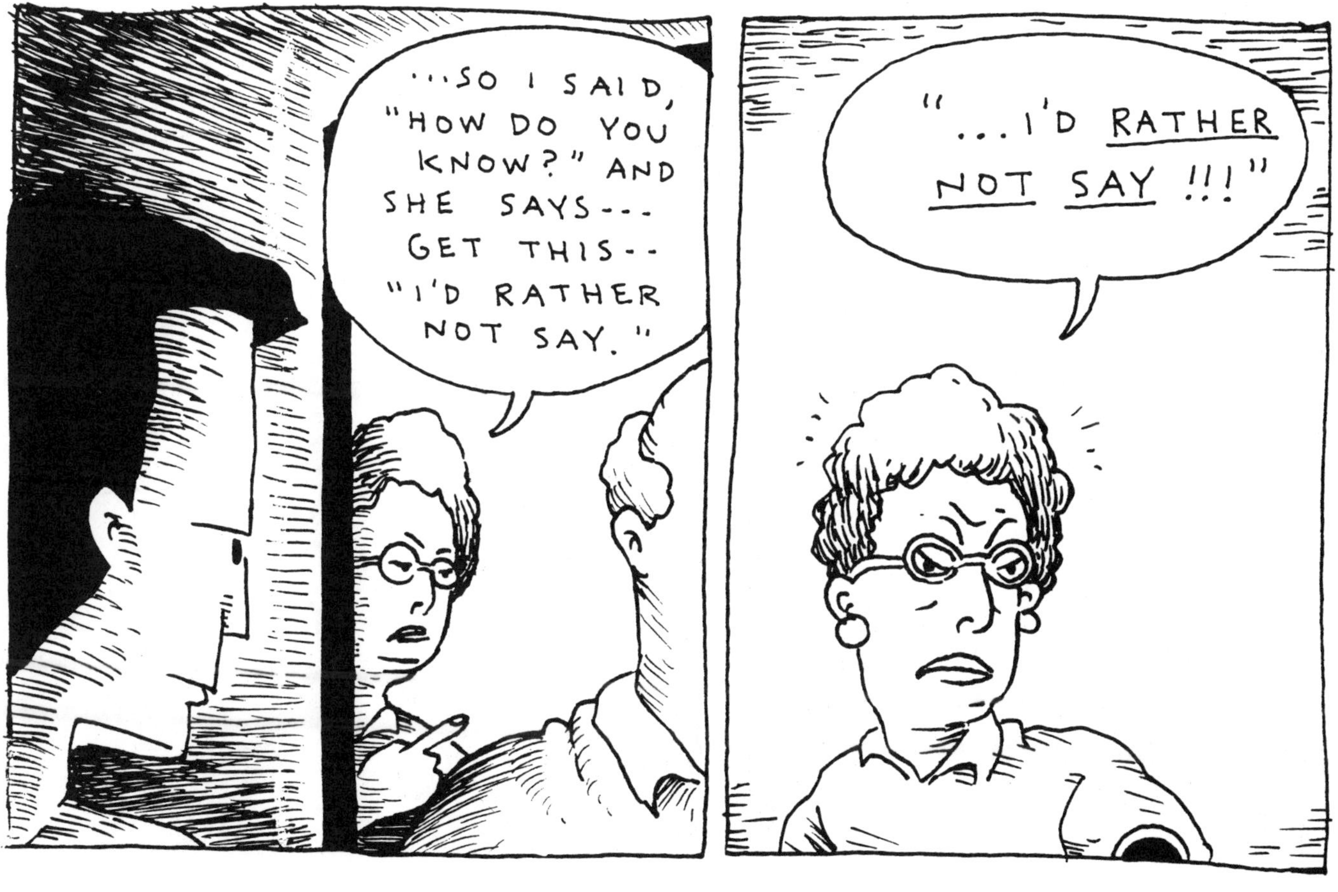
...SO I SAID, "HOW DO YOU KNOW?" AND SHE SAYS--- GET THIS-- "I'D RATHER NOT SAY."
"...I'D RATHER NOT SAY !!!"

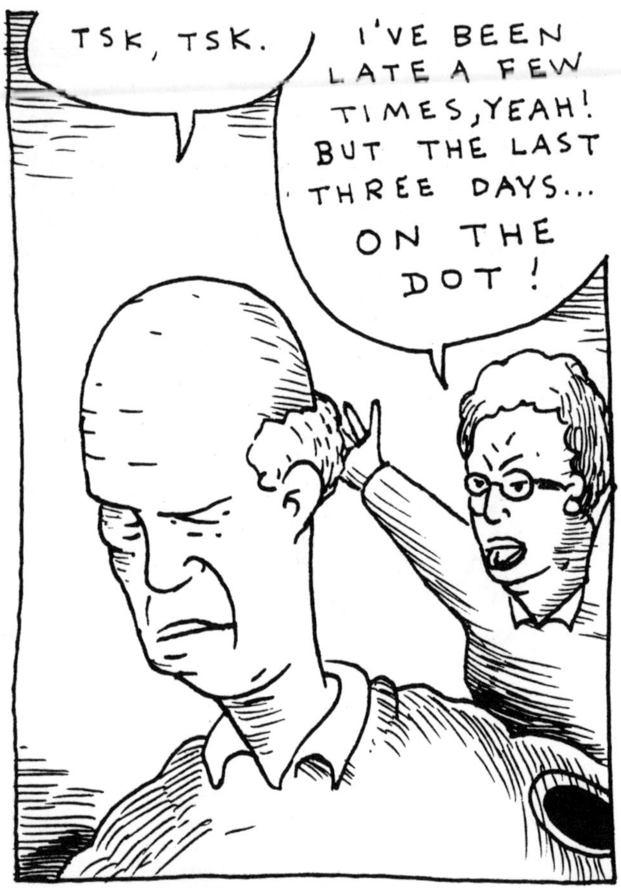
TSK, TSK.
I'VE BEEN LATE A FEW TIMES, YEAH! BUT THE LAST THREE DAYS... ON THE DOT!

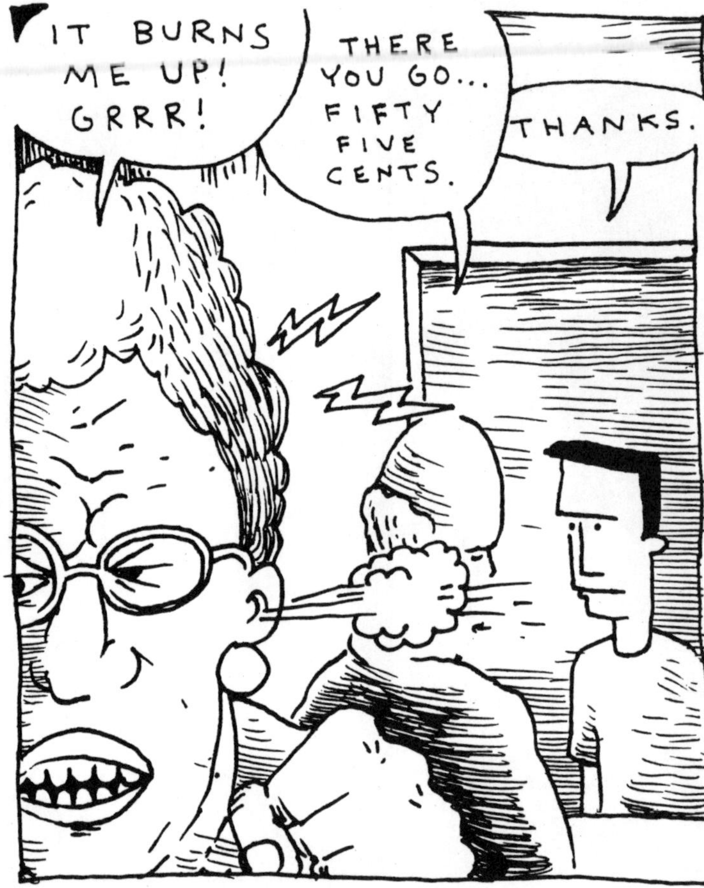
IT BURNS ME UP! GRRR!
THERE YOU GO... FIFTY FIVE CENTS.
THANKS.

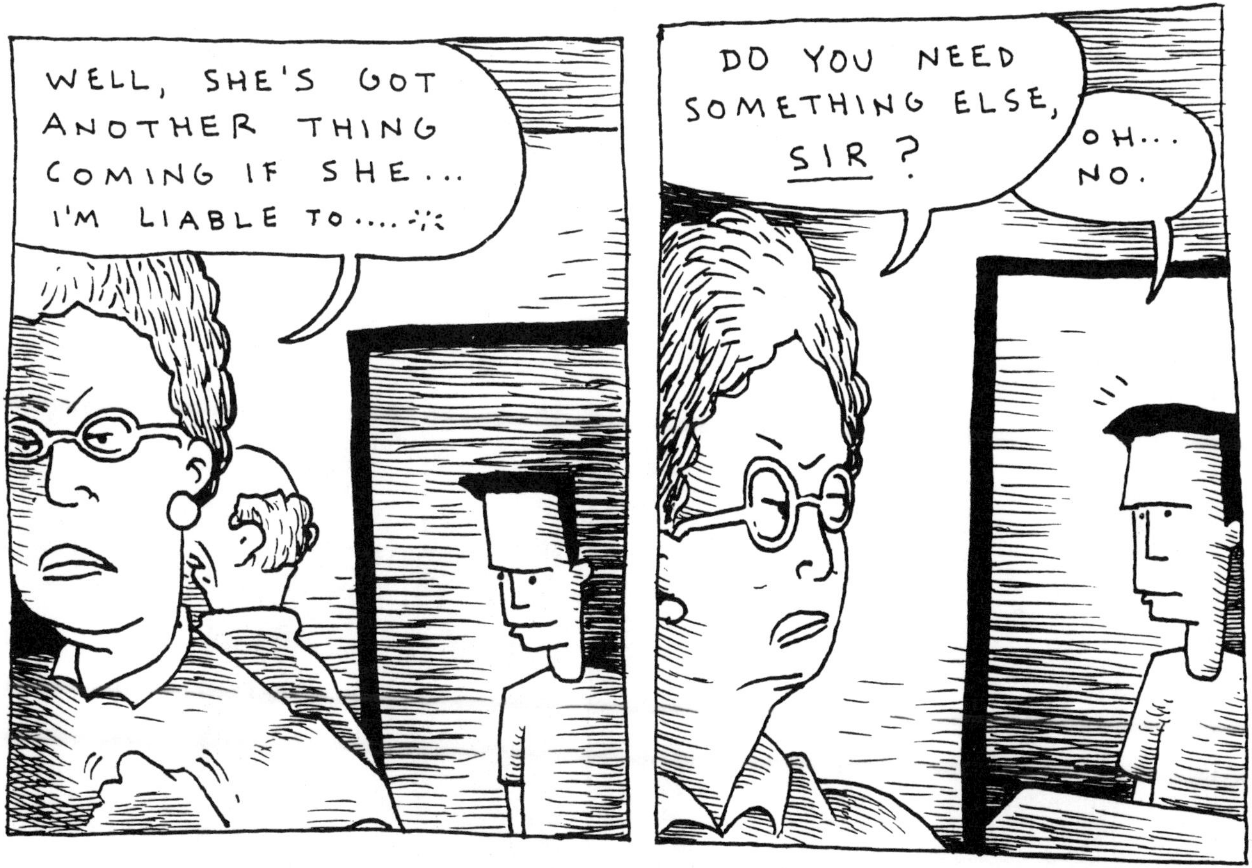
WELL, SHE'S GOT ANOTHER THING COMING IF SHE... I'M LIABLE TO....
DO YOU NEED SOMETHING ELSE, SIR?
OH... NO.

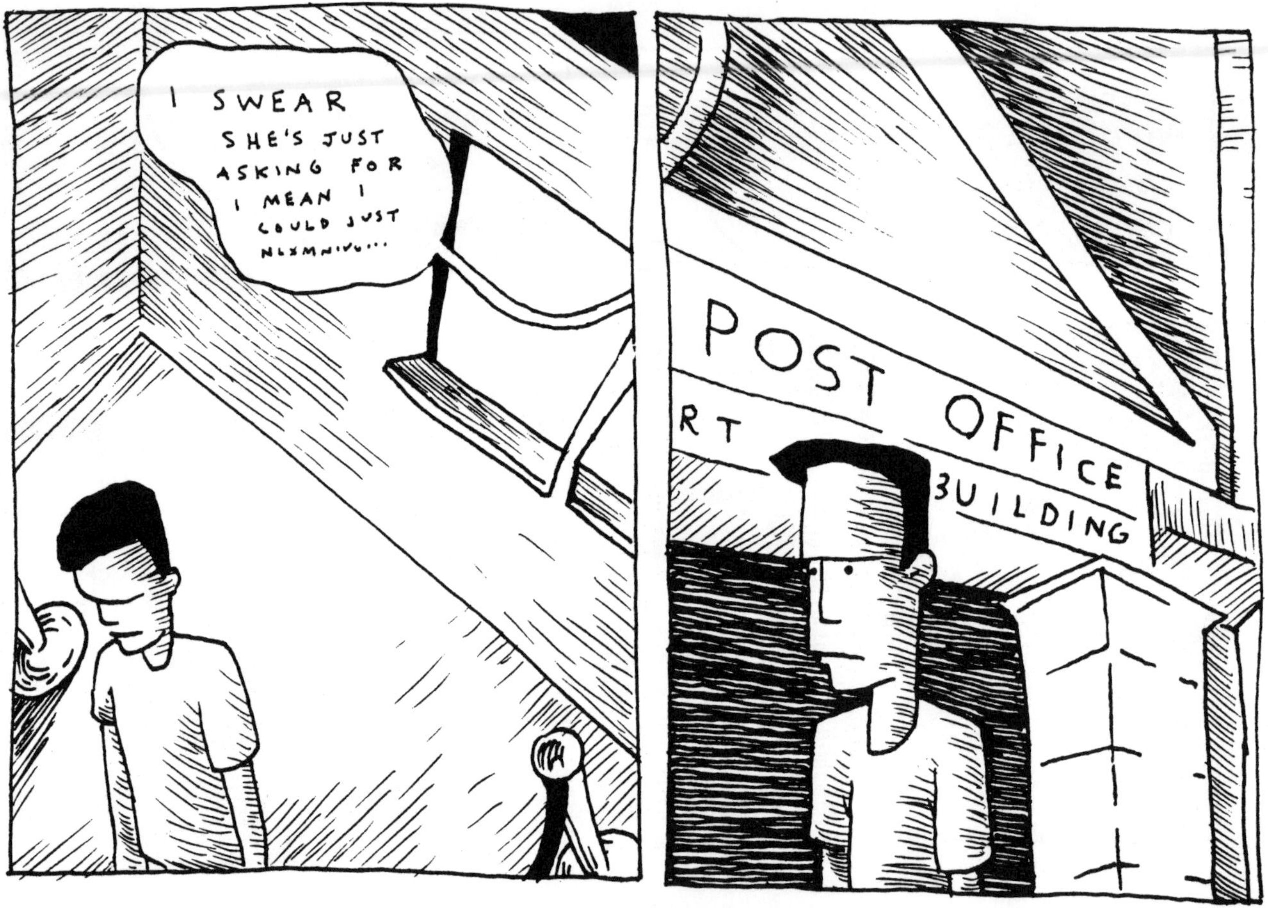
I SWEAR SHE'S JUST ASKING FOR I MEAN I COULD JUST
POST OFFICE
RT
BUILDING

9.

HALLOWEEN:
NO COSTUME. I FEEL LIKE
A DORK. IT'S INEVITABLE—
EITHER WAY I'LL FEEL LIKE
A DORK, COSTUME OR NO
COSTUME. IT'S A NO-WIN
SITUATION!

IT'S A STRANGE NIGHT. EVERYONE
LOOKS GOOD. GIRLS WALTZ AROUND
HAWTHORNE STREET IN STRANGE
GEAR AND FOR SOME REASON I
HAVE NOT SEEN A GIRL WHO
WASN'T THE MOST BEAUTIFUL
GIRL I'VE EVER SEEN FOR
SEVERAL HOURS NOW.

I LOOK STRAIGHT AHEAD AND TRY NOT TO STARE, THINKING OF SHAVING MY HEAD AND LISTENING TO GREGORIAN CHANTS; THINKING OF D.G. IN THE SOLITARY CONFINEMENT OF HIS BACHELOR APARTMENT AND THE QUIET DESPERATION IN HIS VOICE ("IT'S KIND OF LONELY") AND NOT WANTING TO HEAR THAT SAME DESPERATION IN MY OWN THROAT.

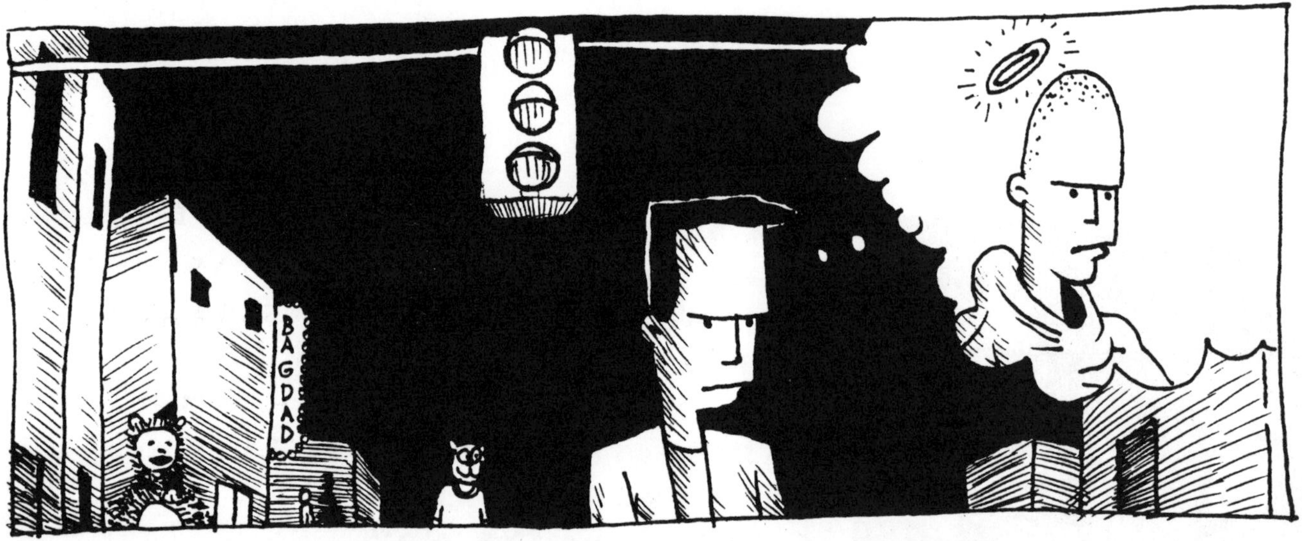
BAGDAD

THESE DAYS THINGS CHANGE IN SUCH DRASTIC AND MIND-BLOWING WAYS ALL THE TIME. EVERY NIGHT I GO TO SLEEP A CHANGED MAN. SOME EARTH-SHATTERER OF A DEVELOPMENT HAS POPPED UP BETWEEN SLEEP AND SLEEP TO READJUST MY CONCEPTUAL AXIS. IT'S NOT A BAD WAY TO LIVE, I GUESS. IT'S LIKE THE SEASON FINALE OF A TV SHOW EVERY DAY, EVERY DAY IS A CLIFF-HANGER. THE GUY IN THIS COFFEE SHOP WORKING THE COUNTER IS LISTENING TO PRETTY GOOD MUSIC. WE MAKE SMALL TALK; A LITTLE SPICE IN THE BLAND TOFU OF THE VEGAN ENTREÉ THAT IS THIS LIFE.

FOUR CUPS OF COFFEE.
I FEEL TOTALLY FUCKED
UP. THE AIR IS ABUZZ
WITH PEOPLE MAKING
PLANS, TALKING ABOUT
PARTIES, CRAP LIKE
THAT. I FEEL WEIRD.

A WOMAN ENTERS THE CAFÉ AND APPROACHES ME. "ARE YOU PETER?" SHE ASKS. I'M MOMENTARILLY CONFUSED, MY DAD'S NAME BEING PETER. "UM, NO..... I'M, UH ... UH, NO."

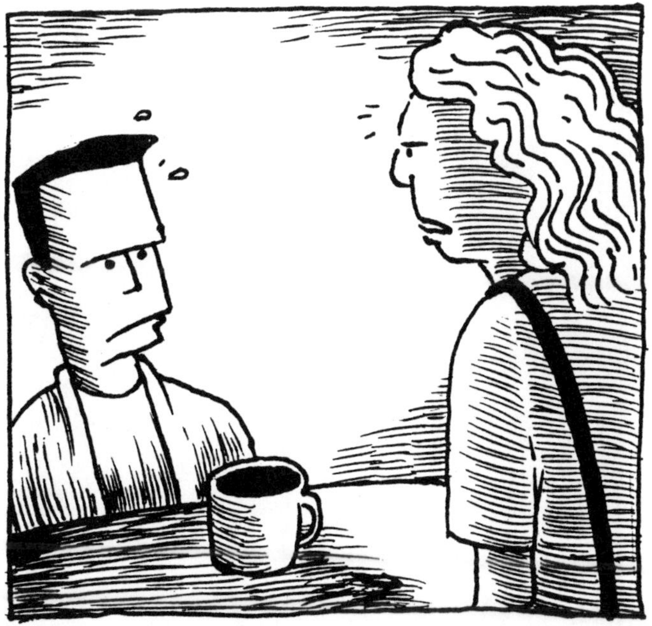

SHE SITS DOWN, BUT KEEPS GLANCING OVER AT ME. IT OCCURS TO ME THAT SHE'S SUPPOSED TO BE MEETING A <u>BLIND</u> <u>DATE</u> AND SHE THINKS I <u>AM</u> PETER BUT THAT I TOOK ONE LOOK AT HER AND DECIDED TO PRETEND THAT I WASN'T. HAPPY HALLOWEEN! I BECOME HYPER-AWARE OF EVERY GUY WHO WALKS IN, LOOKS AROUND, AND WALKS OUT. FINALLY, SHE LEAVES, GLARING AT ME. WHAT CAN I DO?

OUTSIDE ALL THE TRICK-OR-TREATERS ARE 20-SOMETHING SLACKERS WHO HAVE HALF-ASSED COSTUMES AND ARE JUST IN IT FOR THE CANDY. IT REALLY IRKS ME SOMEHOW..... I GO OVER TO T.D AND V.L'S HOUSE. T.D. CONVINCES ME TO WEAR HER HOSPITAL SCRUBS FOR A HALLOWEEN COSTUME. WHILE PUTTING THEM ON I KNOCK OVER A SHELF IN HER ROOM AND A PICTURE OFF THE WALL. TOO MUCH COFFEE.

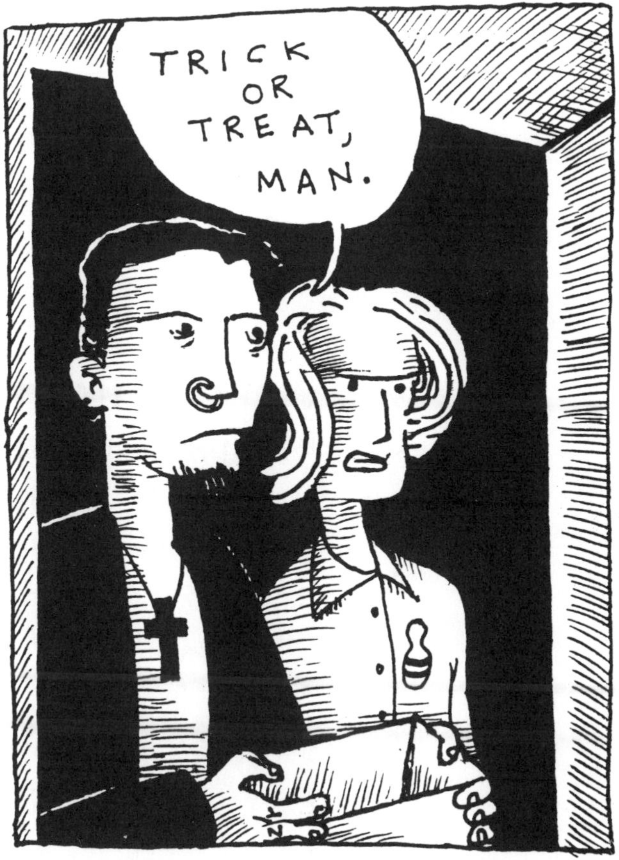
TRICK OR TREAT, MAN.

IN A FEW HOURS I
WILL BE DRUNK OFF MY
ASS AND KICKING OVER
A LIVING ROOM TABLE,
METICULOUSLY SCATTER-
ING THE COMPONENTS OF
T.D.'S MAKESHIFT SURGEON
COSTUME THROUGHOUT
EVERY ROOM OF THE
HOUSE.

I'LL WAKE UP THE NEXT
DAY WRACKED WITH GUILT
AND TRY TO GATHER
UP THE PIECES, TELLING
A.D. THAT T.D IS GOING
TO KILL ME. "MAN,
SHE WON'T CARE. YOU
WRECKED HALF HER ROOM
JUST TRYING THE COSTUME
ON." HE'LL CONSOLE ME.
"SHE HAD TO KNOW THIS
WOULD HAPPEN. THE
FACT THAT YOU DO THIS
KIND OF THING IS THE
WHOLE REASON SHE
LIKES YOU."

IT SEEMS LIKE A
WEIRD REASON TO LIKE
SOMEONE TO ME.

10.

SPRING LASTED ALL OF TWO DAYS THIS YEAR. THE FIRST DAY WAS PERFECT; CLEAR SKY AND NOTHING TO DO, I WANDERED AROUND TOWN AIMLESSLY AND EVERYONE I RAN INTO HAD THAT CURIOUS SMIRK WHICH MADE IT SEEM LIKE YOU COULD PROBABLY ASK THEM ON A DATE AND THEY'D SAY HELL YES. DAY TWO I CUT MY NICE PANTS, THE DRESS PANTS, WHAT MY FRIEND BILL MIGHT CALL "JOB INTERVIEW PANTS" (ALTHOUGH THE BRIGHT ORANGE PAINT WHICH A BAND IN PROVIDENCE THREW ON THE AUDIENCE WHILE THEY WERE PLAYING NEVER DID REALLY COME OUT IN THE WASH, BUT THEN AGAIN, WHAT WAS I DOING IN PROVIDENCE, WEARING MY JOB INTERVIEW PANTS TO A ROCK SHOW ANYWAY), INTO SHORTS. A BOLD DECLARATION OF SEASONAL COMMITMENT ON MY PART.

BUT NOW TODAY IT'S SUMMER. SITTING ON THE
FRONT PORCH OF MY HOUSE IT IS TOO HOT TO MOVE.
IN THE GLARING SEA OF BAKING PAVEMENT IN
FRONT OF THE HOUSE YOU CAN SEE SHADOWS, AMOR-
PHOUS WAVES OF HEAT WHICH SPIRAL AROUND SLUGGISHLY—
IT'S SO HOT YOU CAN SEE IT! THE HEAT IS A
PHYSICAL THING, IT CASTS A SHADOW, IT PRESSES
YOU DOWN AGAINST THE CHAIR. ON A DAY LIKE
THIS YOU SWEAT WHEN YOU'RE STANDING STILL, YOU
PERSPIRE JUST FOR EXISTING. THIS DAY MAKES
ME GLAD THAT I QUIT THAT JOB I GOT; AS I
BIKED THERE ON THE FIRST DAY OF NICE WEATHER
I REALIZED THAT YOU CAN'T MAKE COMMITMENTS
TO BEING INDOORS WHEN THE WEATHER IS LIKE
THIS.

I DO LOVE THE TRANSITIONAL
SEASONS, THE FIRST NICE DAY
WHEN YOU START MAKING
GRANDIOSE PLANS FOR HOW THE
REST OF YOUR LIFE IS GOING TO
GO FROM HERE ON OUT, BEFORE THE
REALITY OF HEAT AND STASIS KICKS
IN, AND YOU CAN'T DO ANYTHING.
I FEEL LIKE I GOT A LITTLE CHEAT-
ED ON SPRING THIS YEAR — BEING
MOST COVETED, IT ALWAYS GOES
BY FASTEST, BUT STILL, CAN YOU
HAVE A SEASON WHICH LASTS A
FRACTION OF A WEEK? IT SEEMS
RIDICULOUS. THIS WEATHER IS
LIKE A HAIRCUT — YOU GET IT A
LITTLE TOO SHORT IN ANTICIPATION
OF THINGS TO COME. TWO WEEKS
INTO IT IT'S PERFECT FOR ABOUT
TWO DAYS AND THEN ALREADY
TOO LONG AGAIN.

AS I'M SITTING IN MY ROOM WRITING THIS, MY HOUSEMATE
WALKS IN AND WE TALK A LITTLE ABOUT THE WEATHER,
AND THE TOWN'S RESULTANT SPRING FEVER.

"YOU DON'T SEEM TO HAVE ANY PROBLEMS IN THAT
DEPARTMENT," SHE SAYS, "LOOK, YOU'VE GOT A HICKEY
ON YOUR NECK."

"I DO?" I SAY, SURPRISED.

SHE TAKES A CLOSER LOOK. "OH, WAIT," SHE SAYS.
"THAT'S A SCAB."

"FIGURES," I SAY. IT DOES. IT PRETTY MUCH SUMS
UP ALL OF MY PROBLEMS: ALL OF MY HICKEYS
ARE ACTUALLY SCABS.

11.

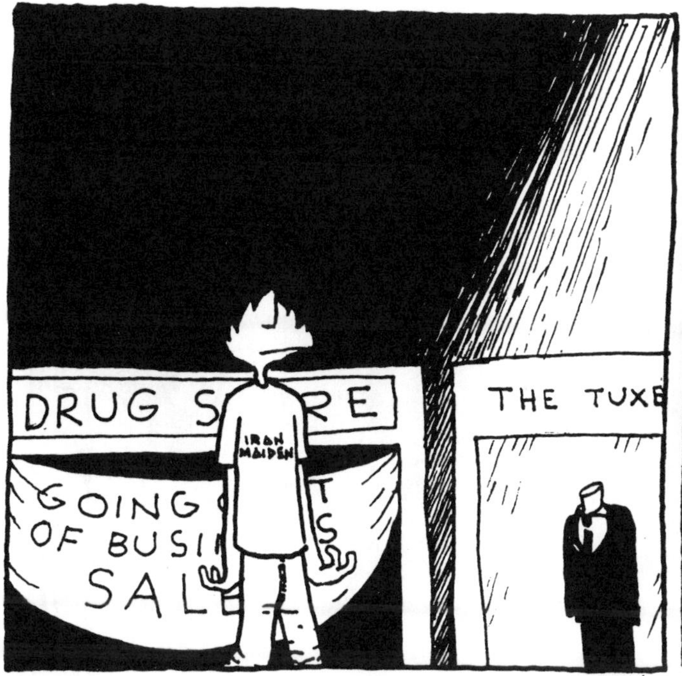
DRUG S RE
GOING T OF BUSI S SAL
IRON MAIDEN
THE TUXE

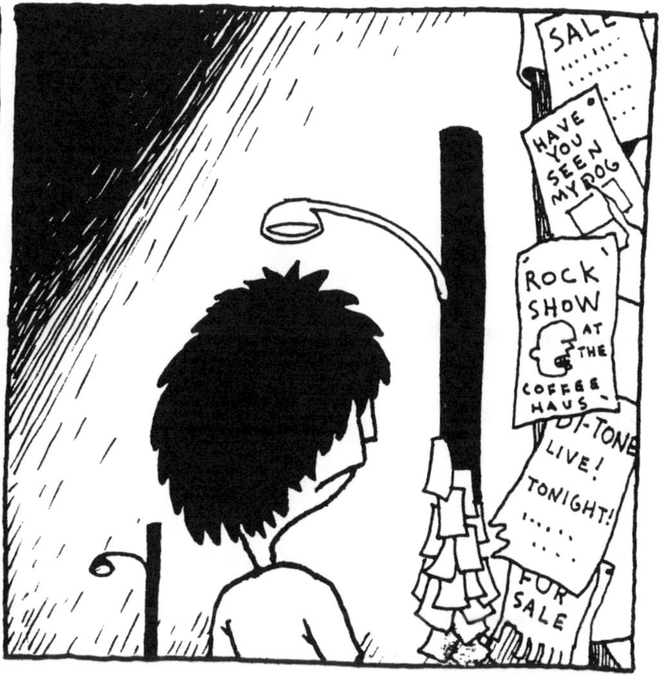
SAL
HAVE YOU SEEN MY DOG
ROCK SHOW AT THE COFFEE HAUS
LIVE! TONIGHT!
FOR SALE

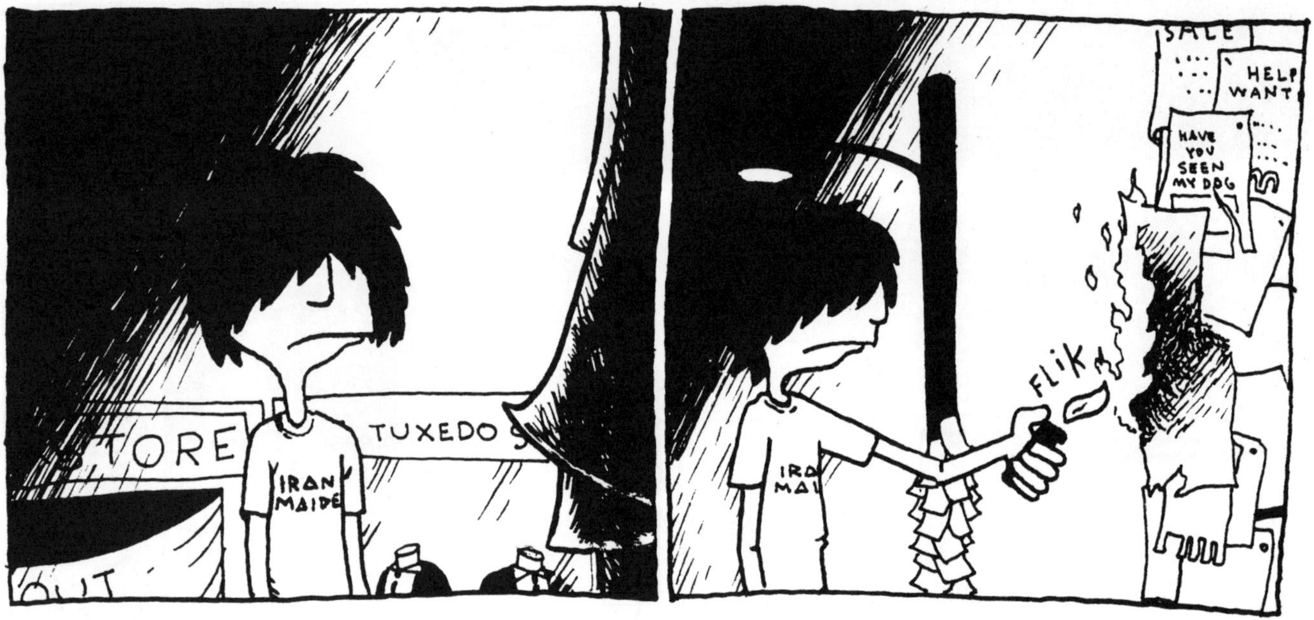

STORE
TUXEDO S
IRON MAIDE
OUT
SALE
HELP WANT
HAVE YOU SEEN MY DOG
IRO MAI
FLIK

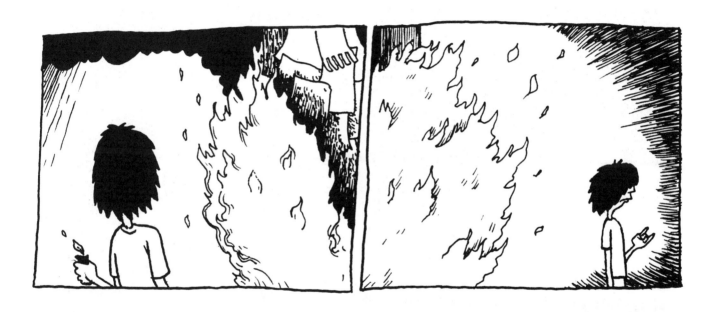

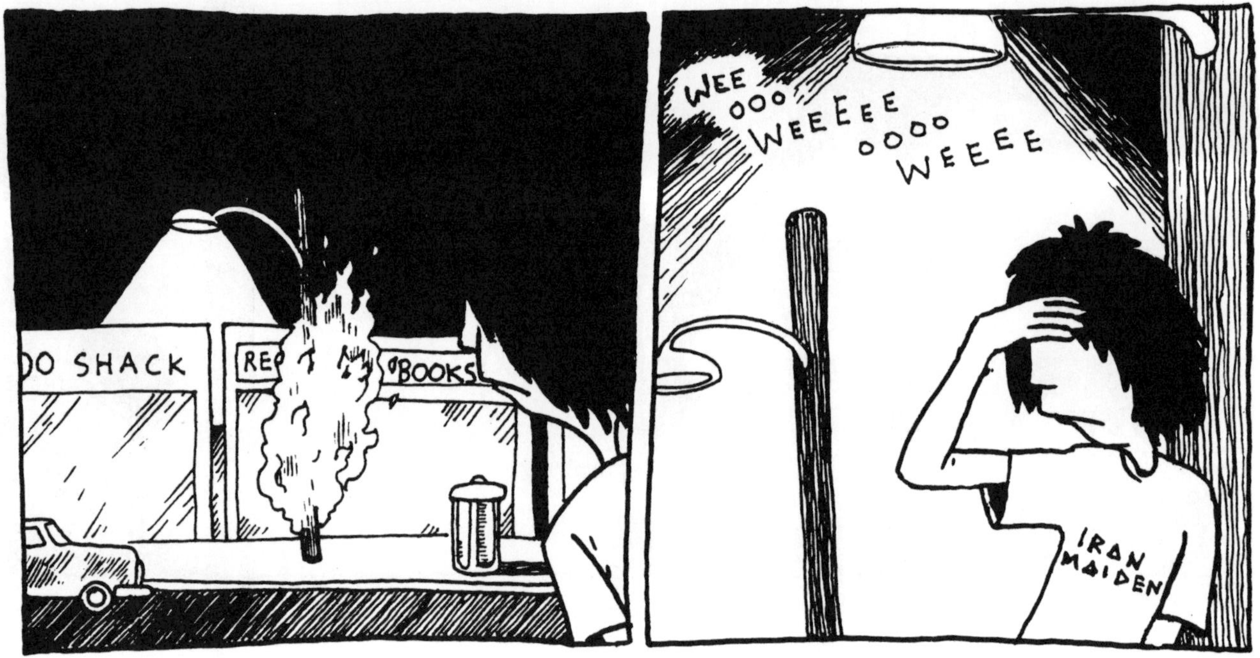

O SHACK
RE
BOOKS
WEE OOO WEEEEE OOOO WEEEE
IRAN MAIDEN

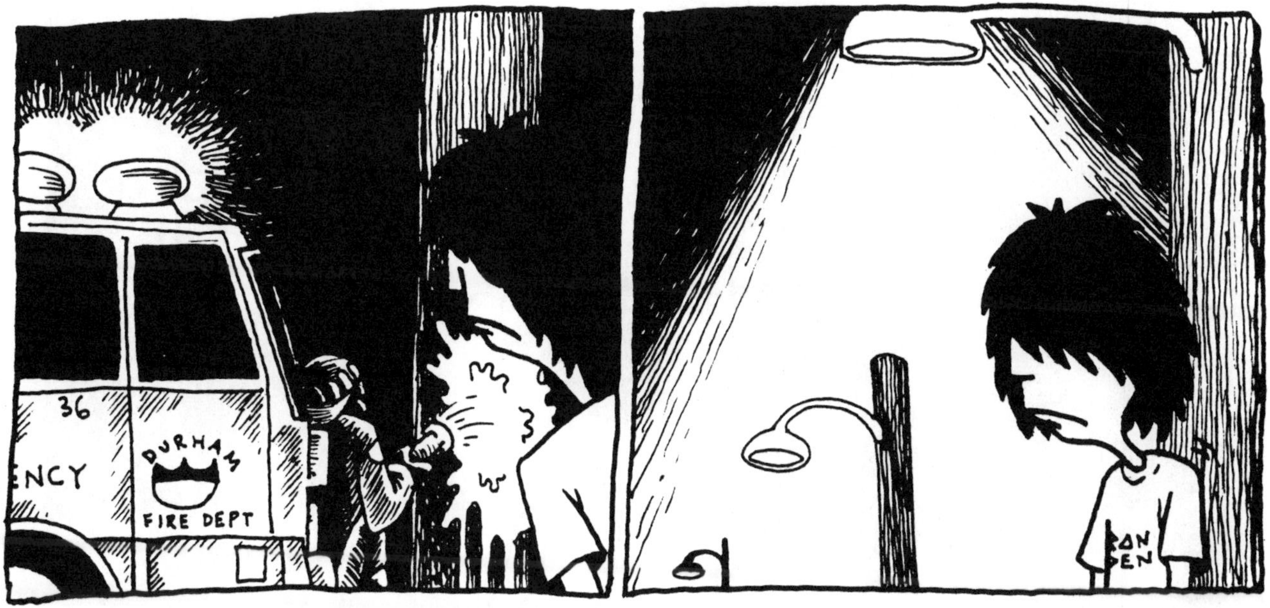
36
ENCY
DURHAM
FIRE DEPT

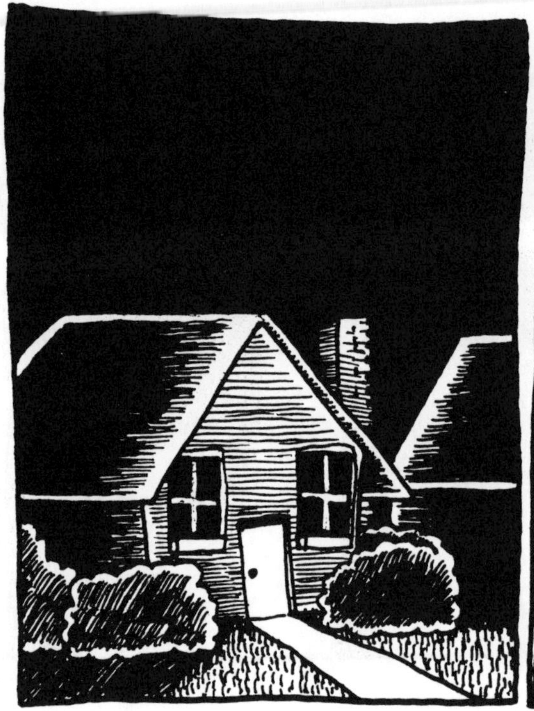

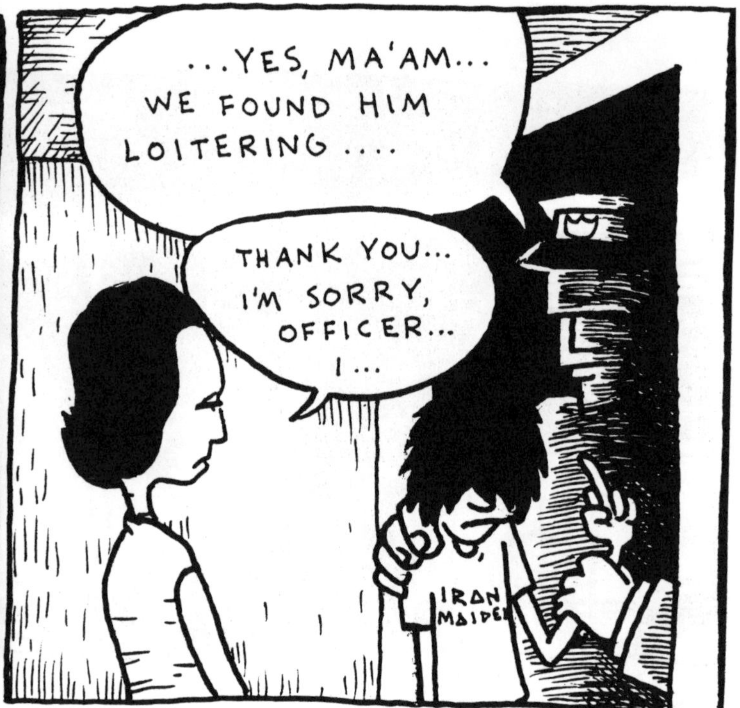
...YES, MA'AM...
WE FOUND HIM
LOITERING....
THANK YOU...
I'M SORRY,
OFFICER...
I...
IRON
MAIDEN

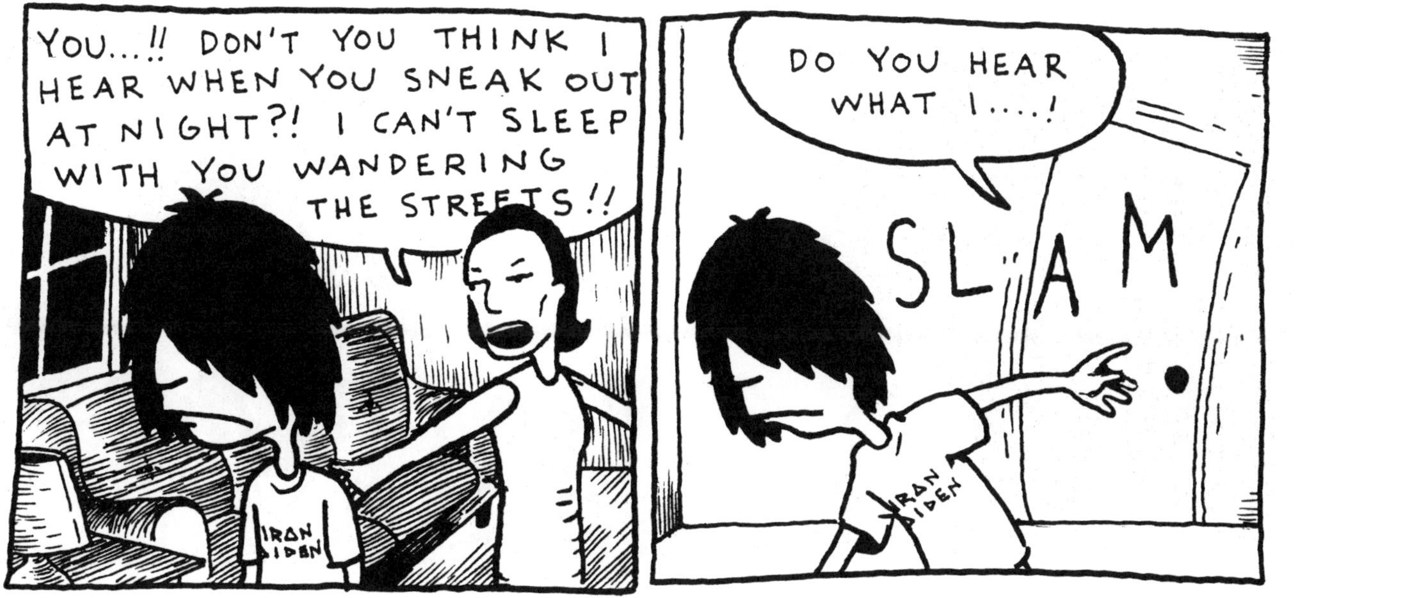
YOU...!! DON'T YOU THINK I HEAR WHEN YOU SNEAK OUT AT NIGHT?! I CAN'T SLEEP WITH YOU WANDERING THE STREETS!!
IRON AIDEN
DO YOU HEAR WHAT I....!
SLAM
IRON AIDEN

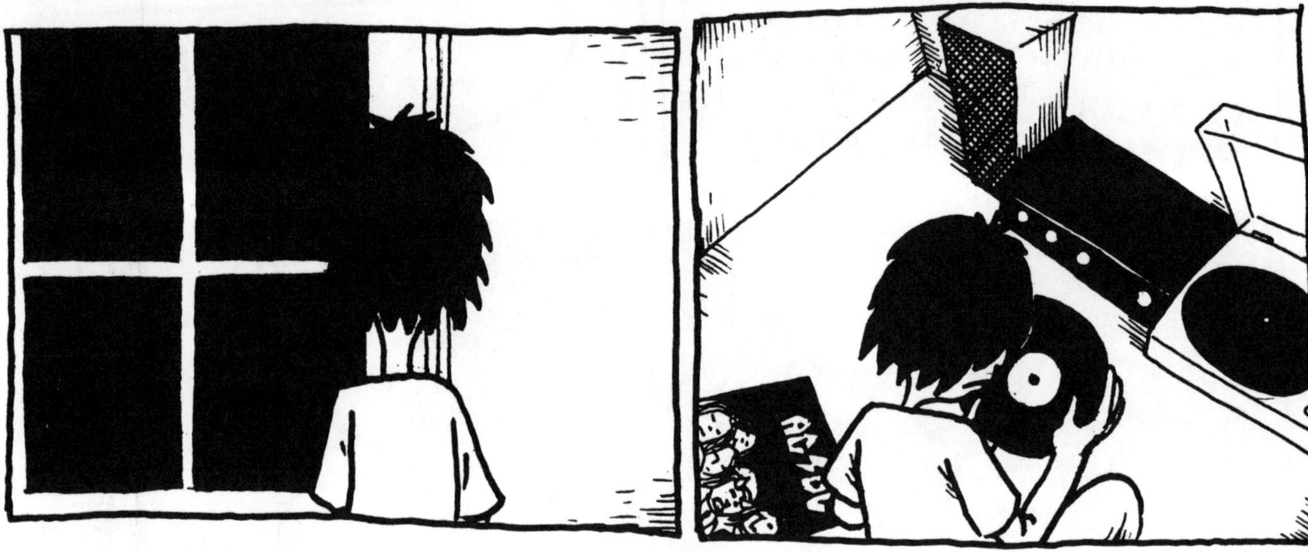
AC/DC

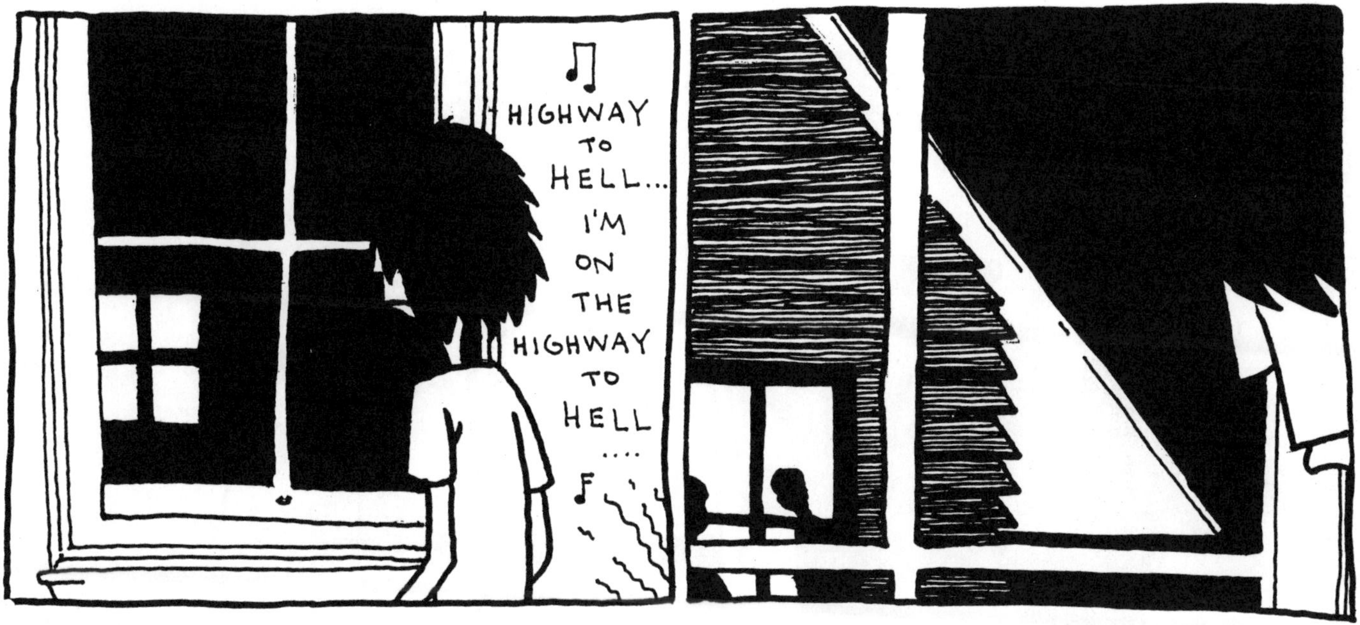
♫ HIGHWAY TO HELL... I'M ON THE HIGHWAY TO HELL ....

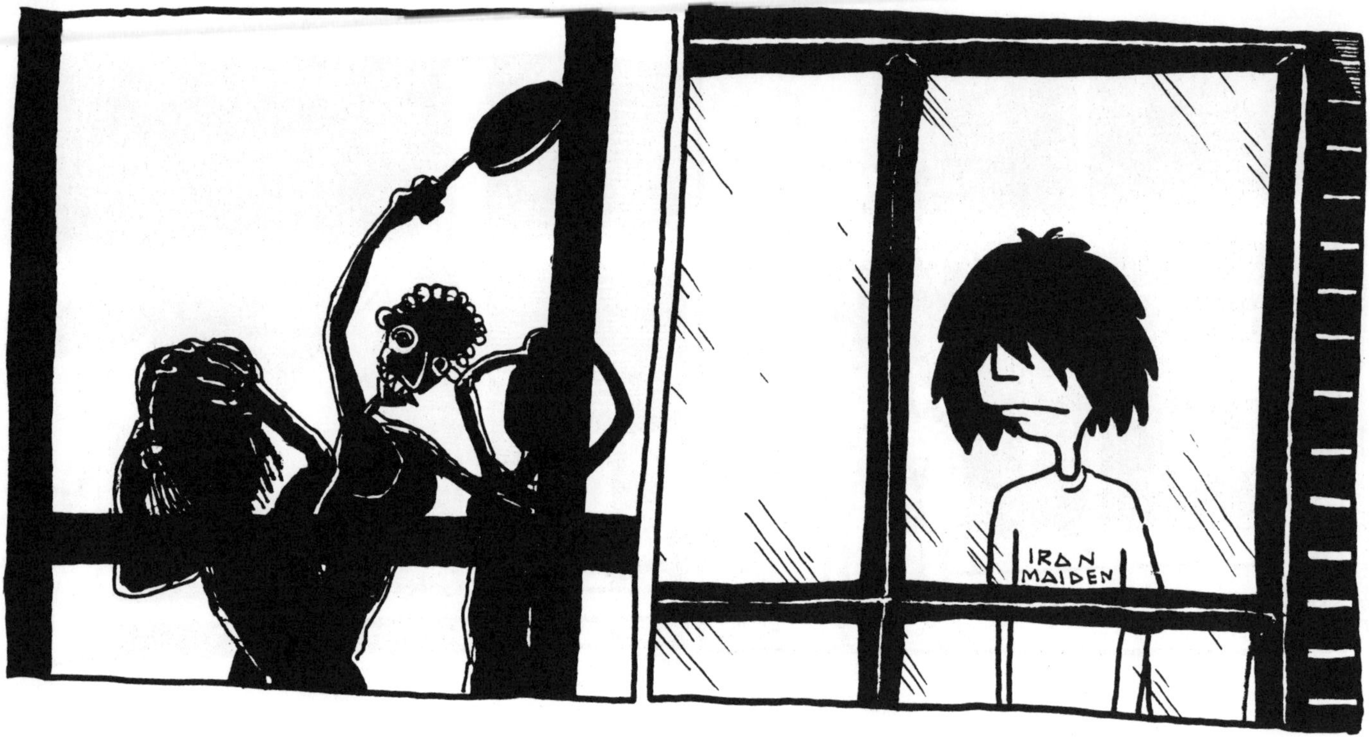
IRON
MAIDEN

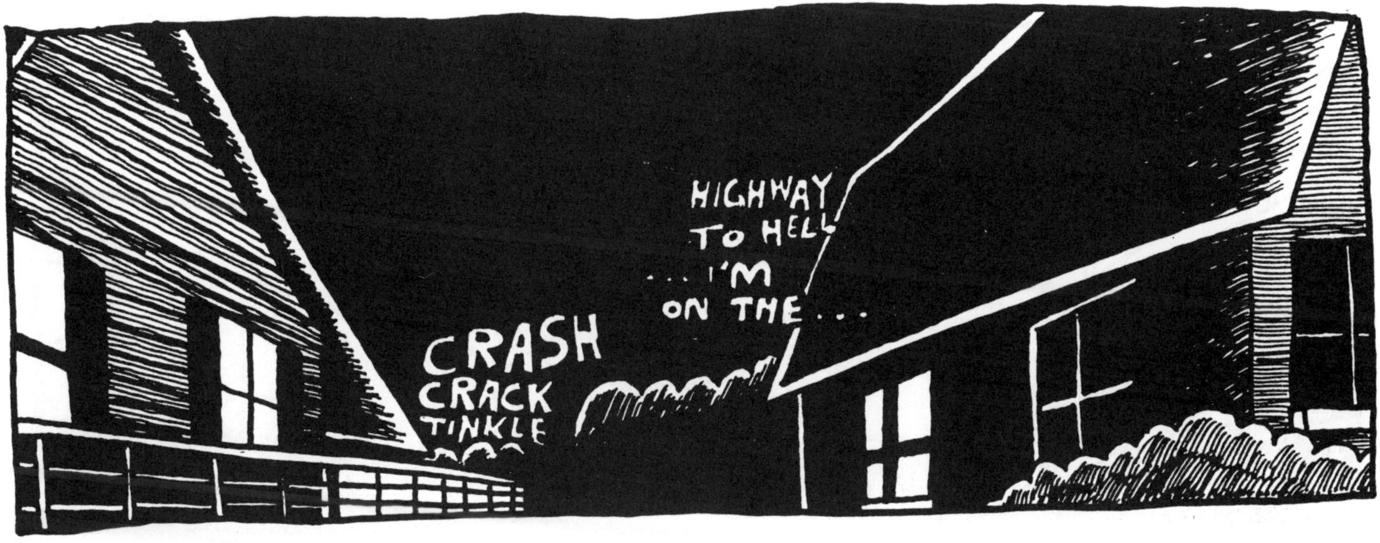
CRASH
CRACK
TINKLE
HIGHWAY
TO HELL
... I'M
ON THE...

———AS NEAR AS I CAN RECALL BEING
A TEENAGER IS ALL FIGHT OR FLIGHT. THERE WAS
THE PARENTS' DIVORCE, THE THREAT OF NUCLEAR
WAR, THE ALMOST PATHOLOGICAL FEAR OF HAVING
AN INTERACTION WITH ANYONE YOUR OWN AGE....
ACROSS THE STREET THE DAD, A COP (WHEN
I WAS A KID I'D GO OVER THERE TO PLAY WITH
THE NEIGHBOR KIDS AND I'D WATCH HIM CLEAN HIS
GUN) HAD JUST SPLIT AND THAT FAMILY UNIT
WAS UNRAVELING AS WELL. EVERY HOUSE SEEMED
LIKE ONE CELL IN AN ORGANISM, EACH CELL
BURSTING WITH CANCER, STRETCHING AT THE
SEAMS WITH PUS AND BILE. THE NEIGHBORHOOD,
THE CITY, THE WORLD, TRYING TO KEEP A
POKER FACE AS ITS GUTS ROTTED OUT————

BUT THAT'S HOW IT SEEMS IN
RETROSPECT. BACK THEN? WHO CAN SAY.

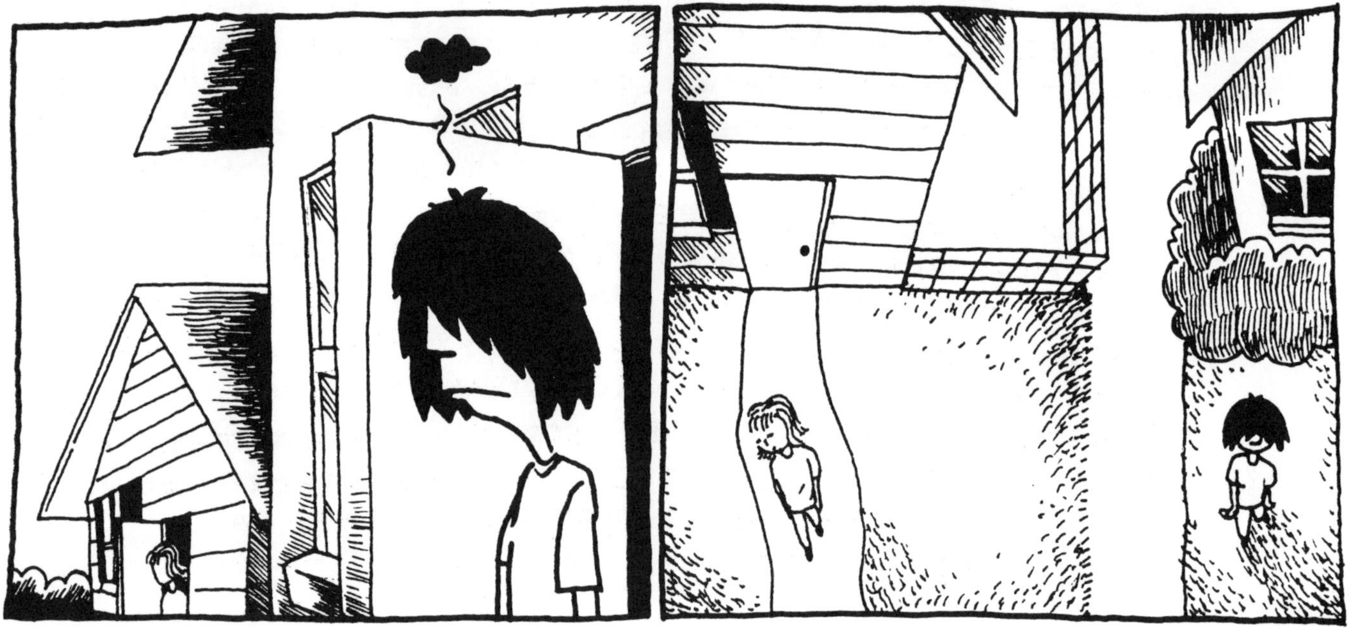

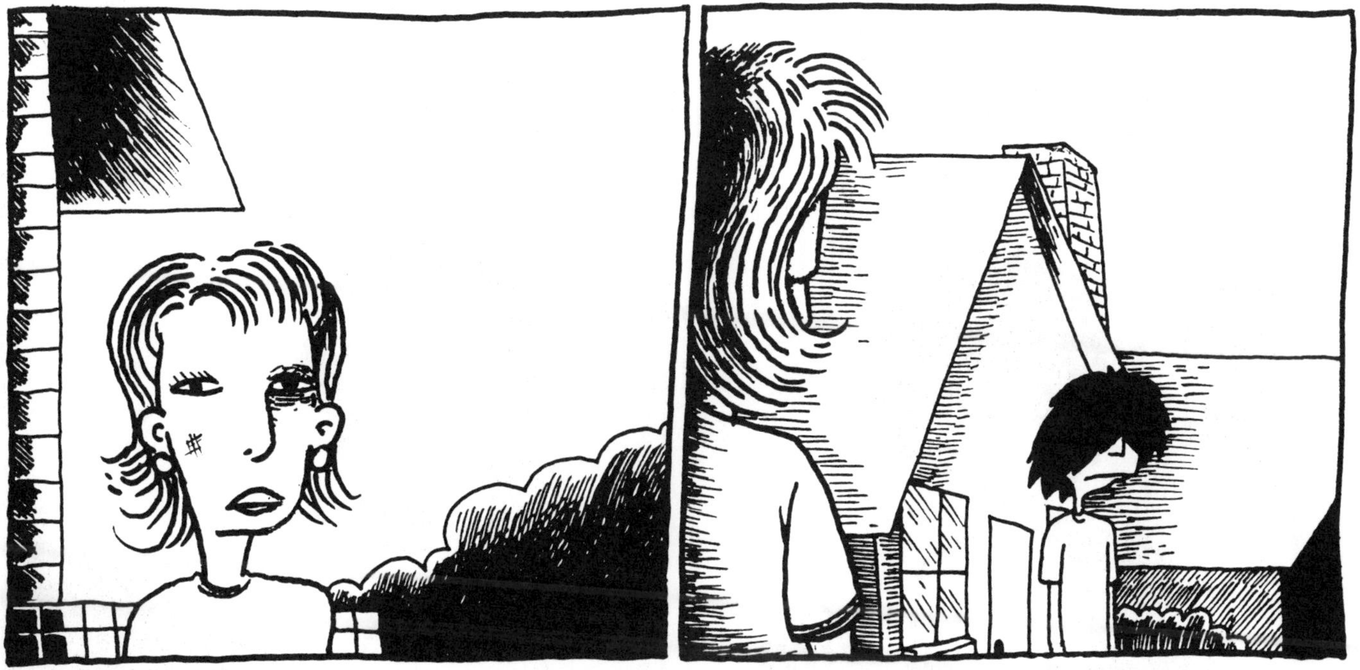

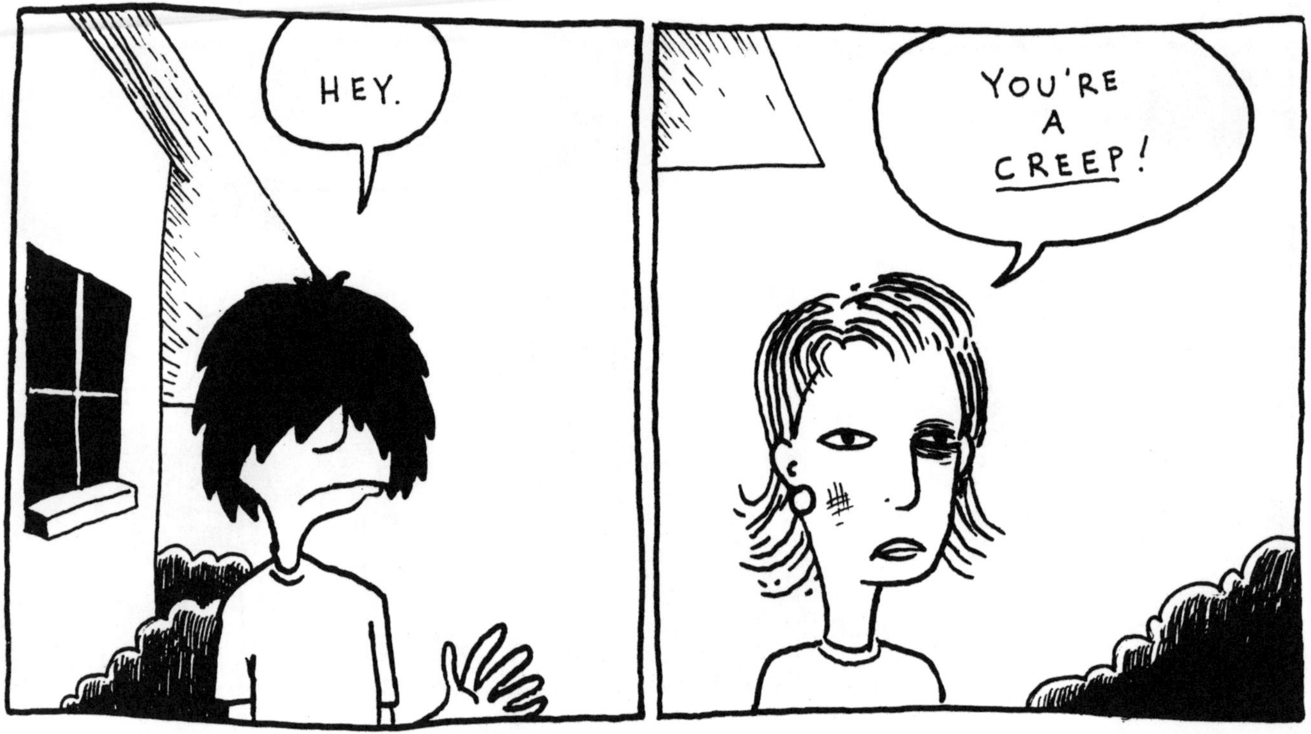
HEY.
YOU'RE A CREEP!

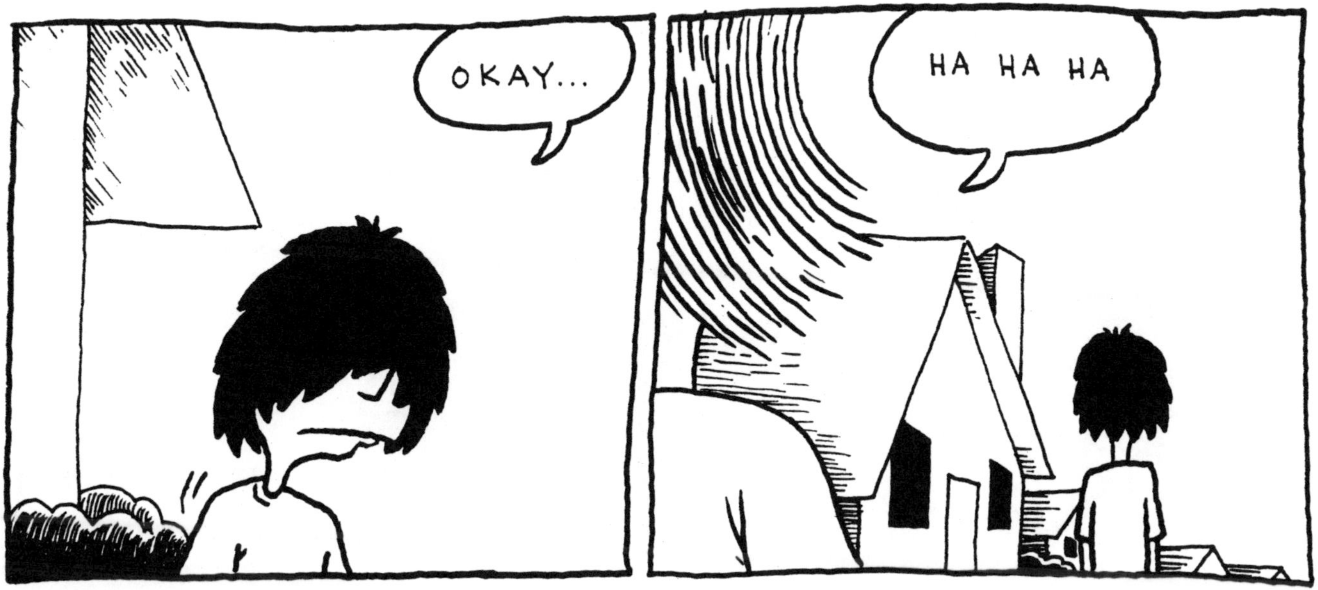
OKAY...
HA HA HA

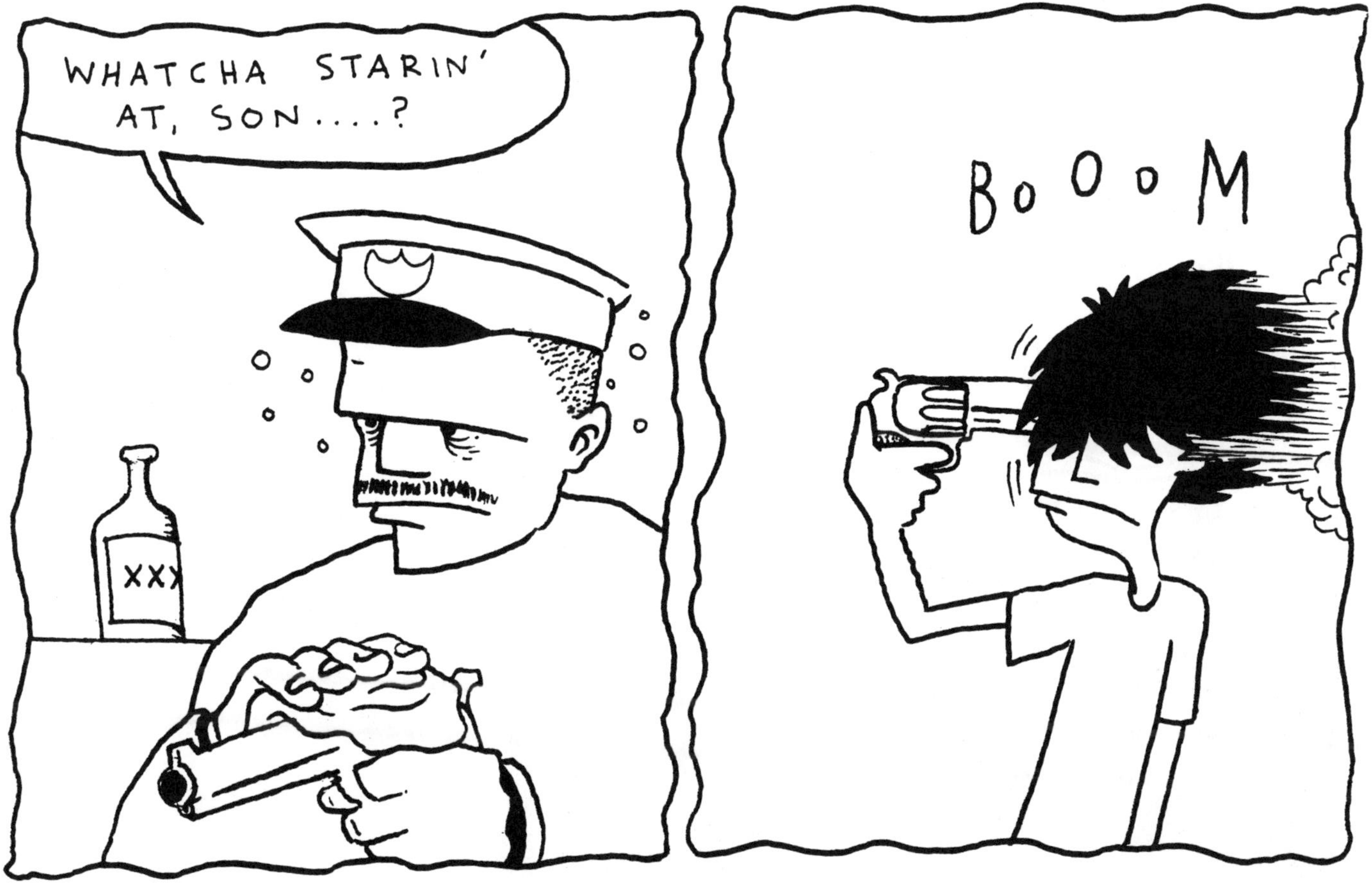
WHATCHA STARIN' AT, SON....?
XXX
BoOoM

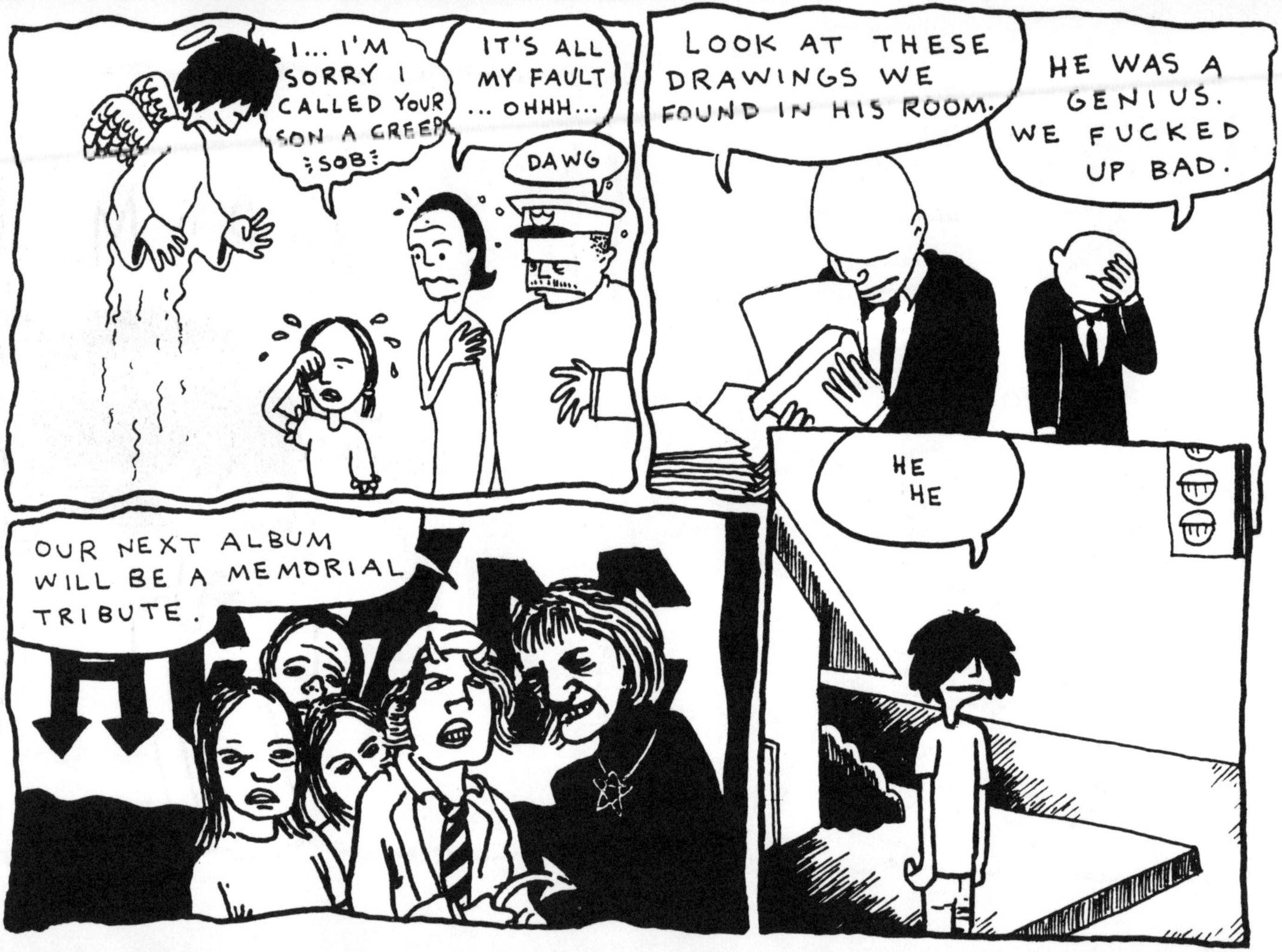
I... I'M SORRY I CALLED YOUR SON A CREEP
SOB
IT'S ALL MY FAULT ... OHHH...
DAWG
LOOK AT THESE DRAWINGS WE FOUND IN HIS ROOM.
HE WAS A GENIUS. WE FUCKED UP BAD.
HE HE
OUR NEXT ALBUM WILL BE A MEMORIAL TRIBUTE.

12.

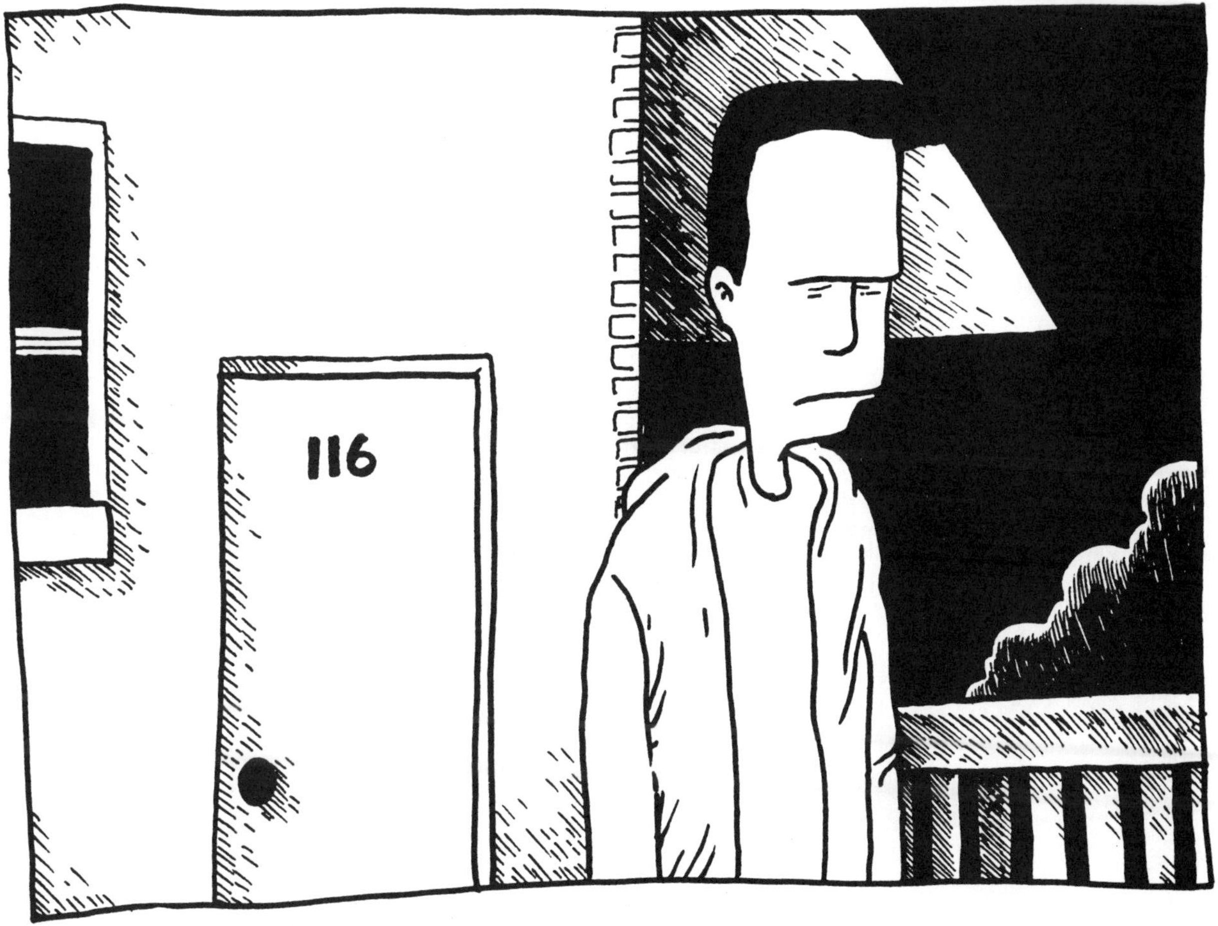
116

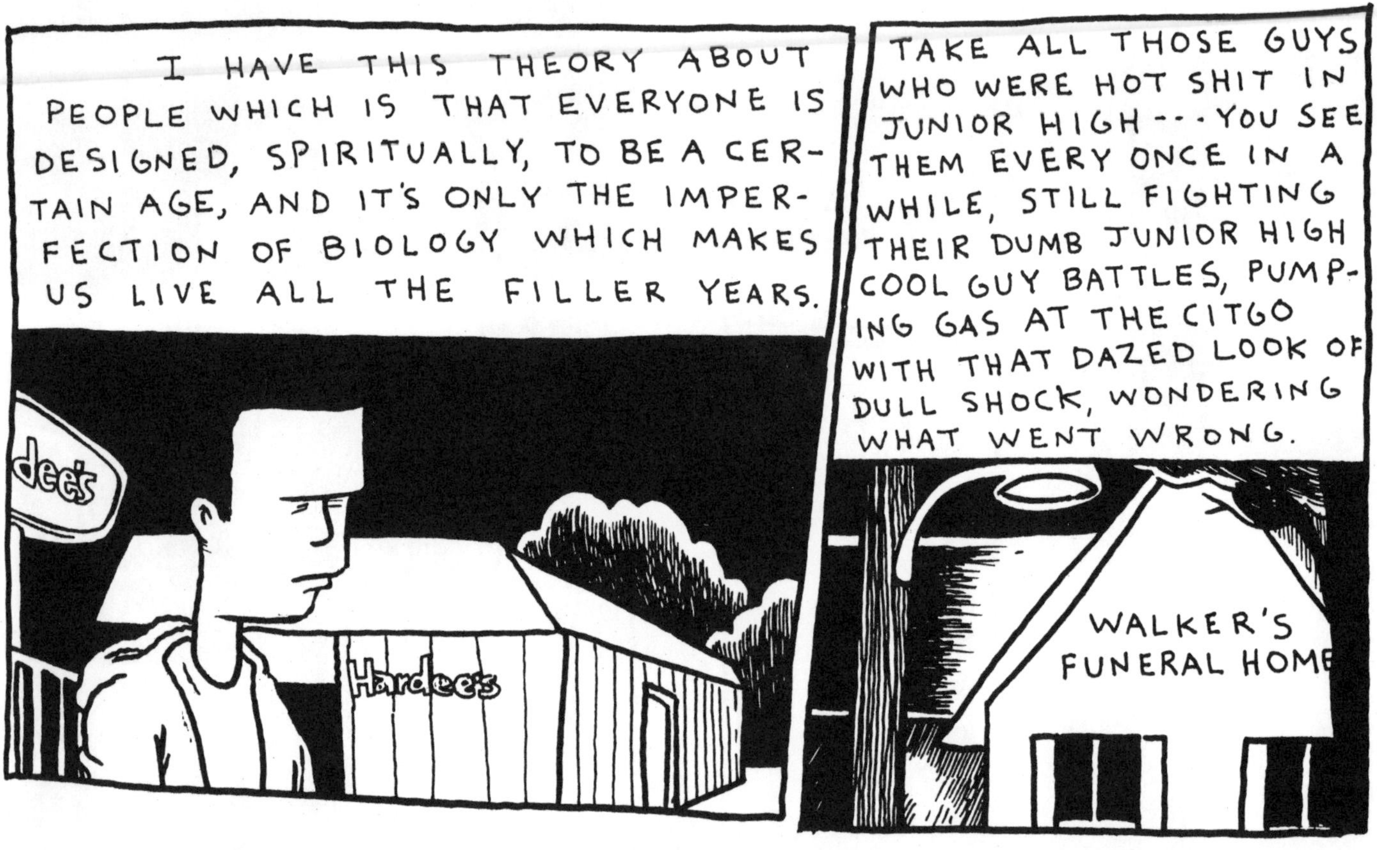
I HAVE THIS THEORY ABOUT PEOPLE WHICH IS THAT EVERYONE IS DESIGNED, SPIRITUALLY, TO BE A CERTAIN AGE, AND IT'S ONLY THE IMPERFECTION OF BIOLOGY WHICH MAKES US LIVE ALL THE FILLER YEARS.
dee's
Hardee's
TAKE ALL THOSE GUYS WHO WERE HOT SHIT IN JUNIOR HIGH --- YOU SEE THEM EVERY ONCE IN A WHILE, STILL FIGHTING THEIR DUMB JUNIOR HIGH COOL GUY BATTLES, PUMPING GAS AT THE CITGO WITH THAT DAZED LOOK OF DULL SHOCK, WONDERING WHAT WENT WRONG.
WALKER'S FUNERAL HOME

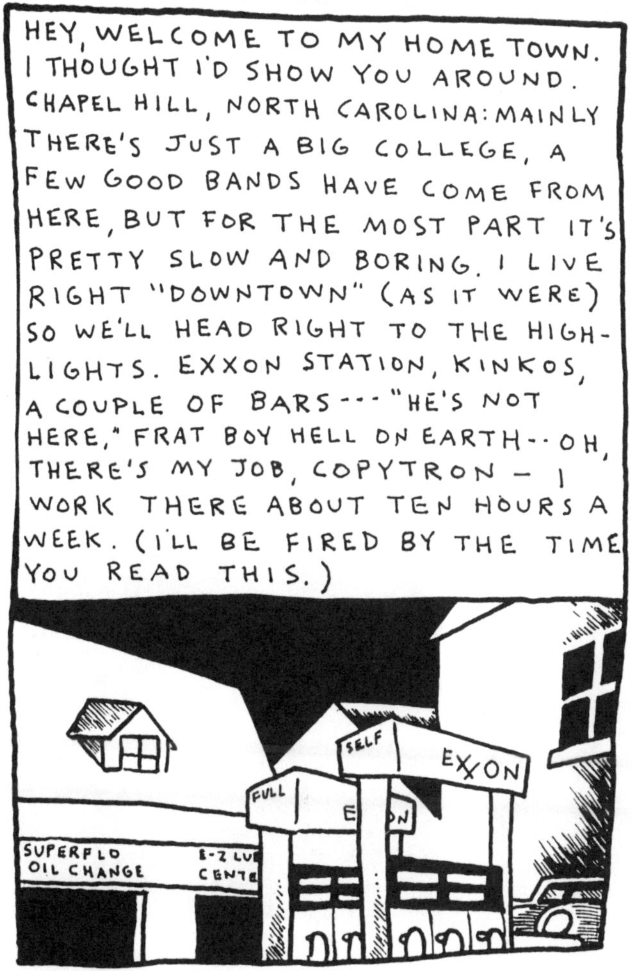
HEY, WELCOME TO MY HOME TOWN. I THOUGHT I'D SHOW YOU AROUND. CHAPEL HILL, NORTH CAROLINA: MAINLY THERE'S JUST A BIG COLLEGE, A FEW GOOD BANDS HAVE COME FROM HERE, BUT FOR THE MOST PART IT'S PRETTY SLOW AND BORING. I LIVE RIGHT "DOWNTOWN" (AS IT WERE) SO WE'LL HEAD RIGHT TO THE HIGHLIGHTS. EXXON STATION, KINKOS, A COUPLE OF BARS--- "HE'S NOT HERE," FRAT BOY HELL ON EARTH--OH, THERE'S MY JOB, COPYTRON — I WORK THERE ABOUT TEN HOURS A WEEK. (I'LL BE FIRED BY THE TIME YOU READ THIS.)
SELF
EXXON
FULL
SUPERFLO OIL CHANGE
E-Z LUB CENTE

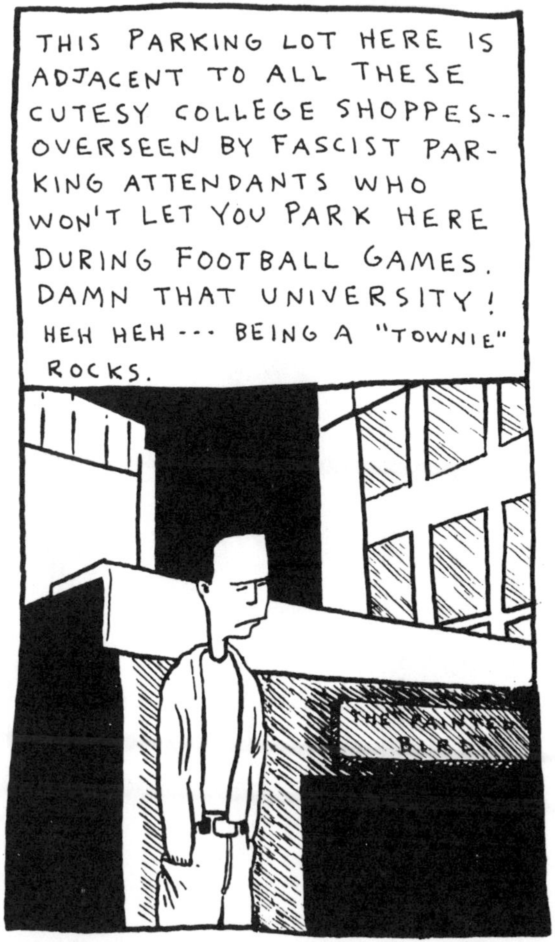
THIS PARKING LOT HERE IS ADJACENT TO ALL THESE CUTESY COLLEGE SHOPPES-- OVERSEEN BY FASCIST PARKING ATTENDANTS WHO WON'T LET YOU PARK HERE DURING FOOTBALL GAMES. DAMN THAT UNIVERSITY!
HEH HEH --- BEING A "TOWNIE" ROCKS.
THE PAINTED BIRD

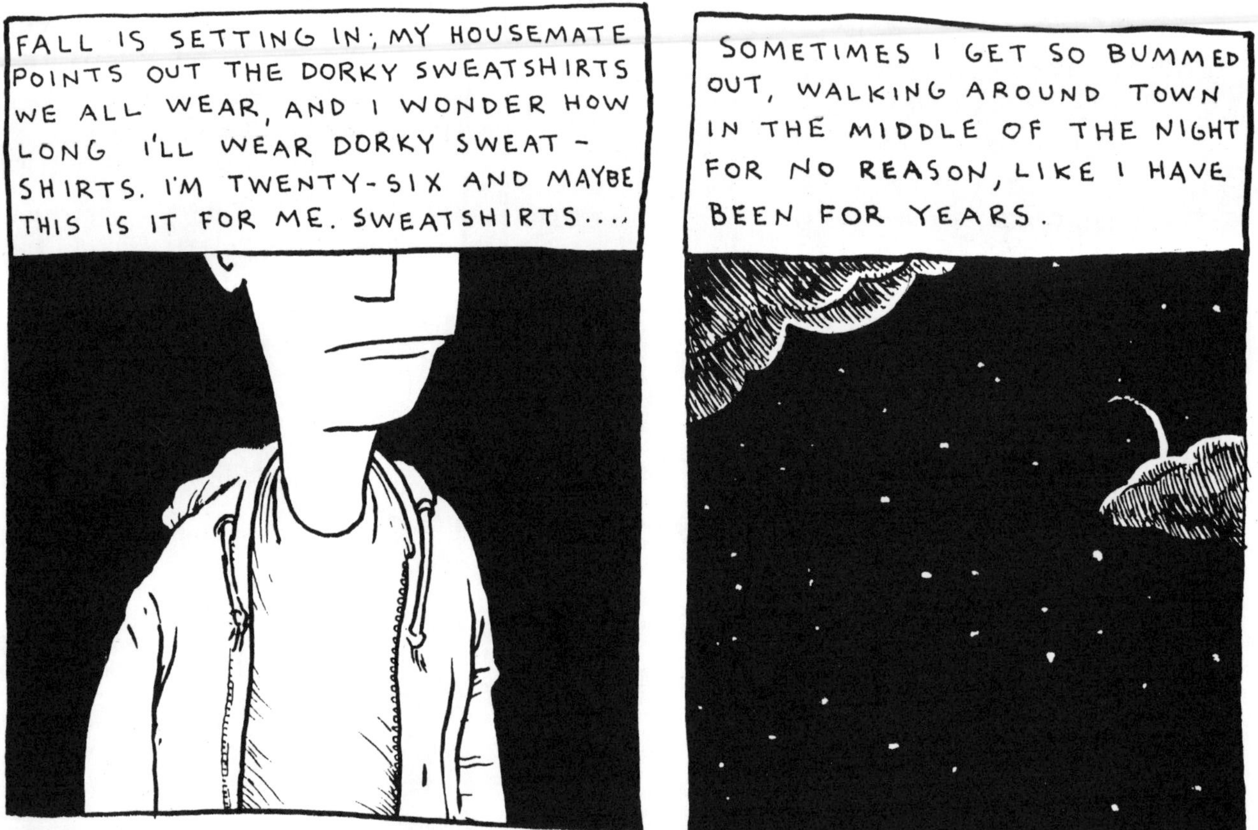
FALL IS SETTING IN; MY HOUSEMATE POINTS OUT THE DORKY SWEATSHIRTS WE ALL WEAR, AND I WONDER HOW LONG I'LL WEAR DORKY SWEAT-SHIRTS. I'M TWENTY-SIX AND MAYBE THIS IS IT FOR ME. SWEATSHIRTS....
SOMETIMES I GET SO BUMMED OUT, WALKING AROUND TOWN IN THE MIDDLE OF THE NIGHT FOR NO REASON, LIKE I HAVE BEEN FOR YEARS.

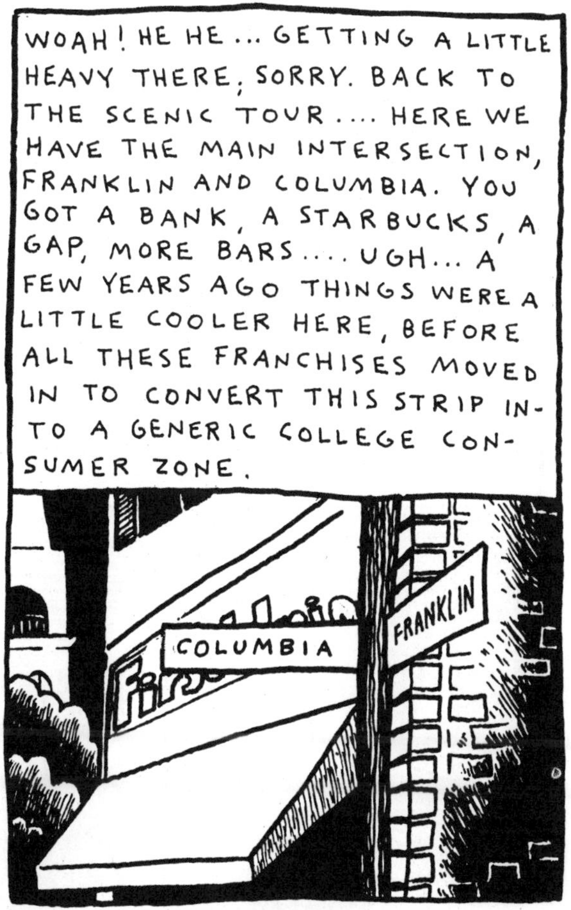
WOAH! HE HE... GETTING A LITTLE HEAVY THERE, SORRY. BACK TO THE SCENIC TOUR.... HERE WE HAVE THE MAIN INTERSECTION, FRANKLIN AND COLUMBIA. YOU GOT A BANK, A STARBUCKS, A GAP, MORE BARS.... UGH... A FEW YEARS AGO THINGS WERE A LITTLE COOLER HERE, BEFORE ALL THESE FRANCHISES MOVED IN TO CONVERT THIS STRIP INTO A GENERIC COLLEGE CONSUMER ZONE.
COLUMBIA
FRANKLIN

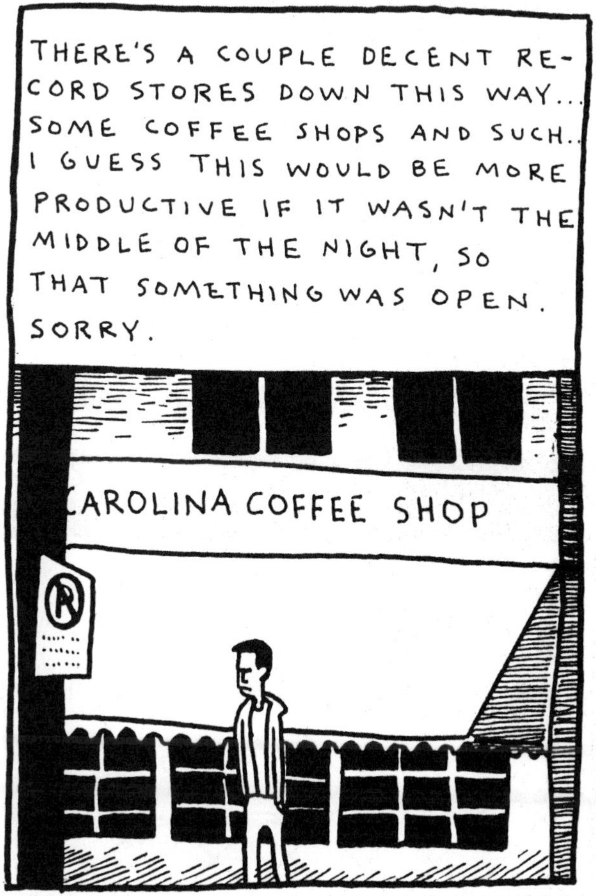
THERE'S A COUPLE DECENT RECORD STORES DOWN THIS WAY... SOME COFFEE SHOPS AND SUCH.. I GUESS THIS WOULD BE MORE PRODUCTIVE IF IT WASN'T THE MIDDLE OF THE NIGHT, SO THAT SOMETHING WAS OPEN. SORRY.
CAROLINA COFFEE SHOP

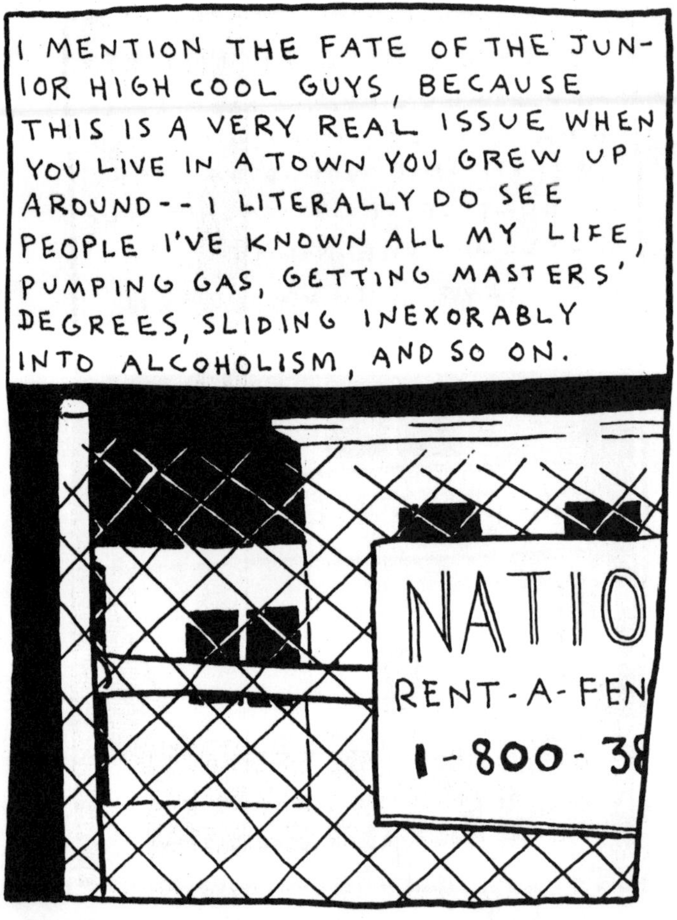
I MENTION THE FATE OF THE JUNIOR HIGH COOL GUYS, BECAUSE THIS IS A VERY REAL ISSUE WHEN YOU LIVE IN A TOWN YOU GREW UP AROUND -- I LITERALLY DO SEE PEOPLE I'VE KNOWN ALL MY LIFE, PUMPING GAS, GETTING MASTERS' DEGREES, SLIDING INEXORABLY INTO ALCOHOLISM, AND SO ON.
NATIO
RENT-A-FEN
1-800-38

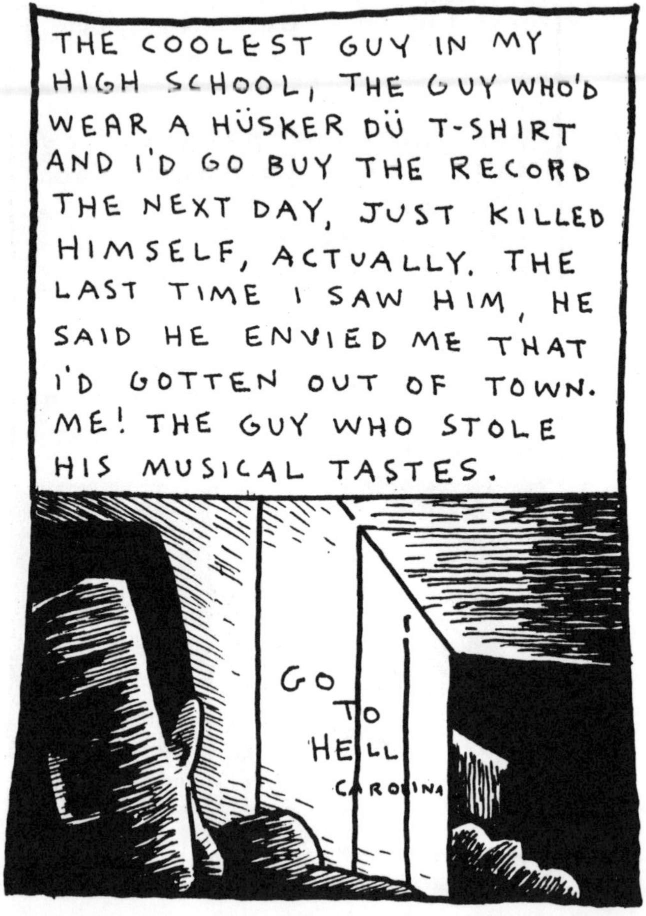
THE COOLEST GUY IN MY HIGH SCHOOL, THE GUY WHO'D WEAR A HÜSKER DÜ T-SHIRT AND I'D GO BUY THE RECORD THE NEXT DAY, JUST KILLED HIMSELF, ACTUALLY. THE LAST TIME I SAW HIM, HE SAID HE ENVIED ME THAT I'D GOTTEN OUT OF TOWN. ME! THE GUY WHO STOLE HIS MUSICAL TASTES.
GO TO HELL
CAROLINA

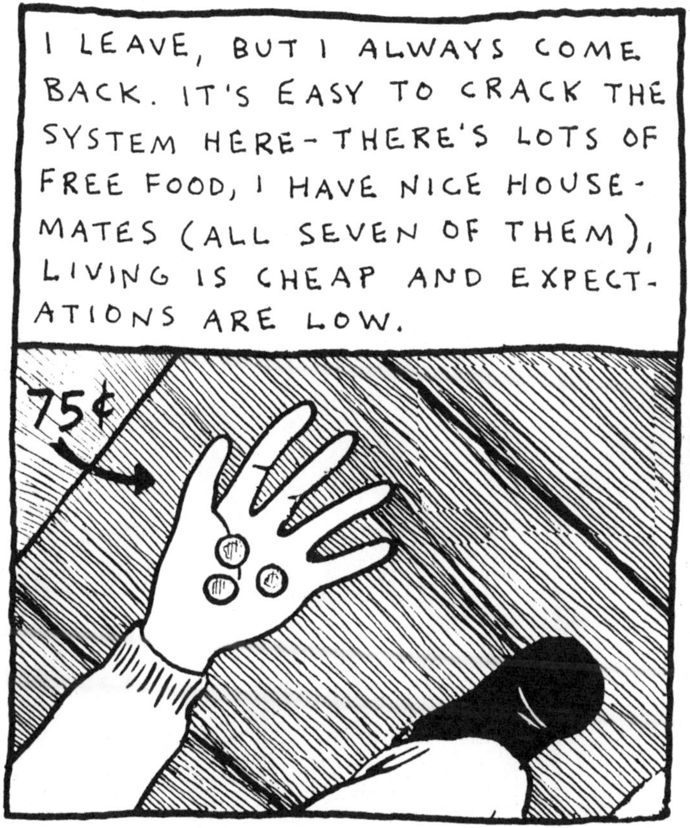
I LEAVE, BUT I ALWAYS COME BACK. IT'S EASY TO CRACK THE SYSTEM HERE- THERE'S LOTS OF FREE FOOD, I HAVE NICE HOUSE-MATES (ALL SEVEN OF THEM), LIVING IS CHEAP AND EXPECT-ATIONS ARE LOW.
75¢

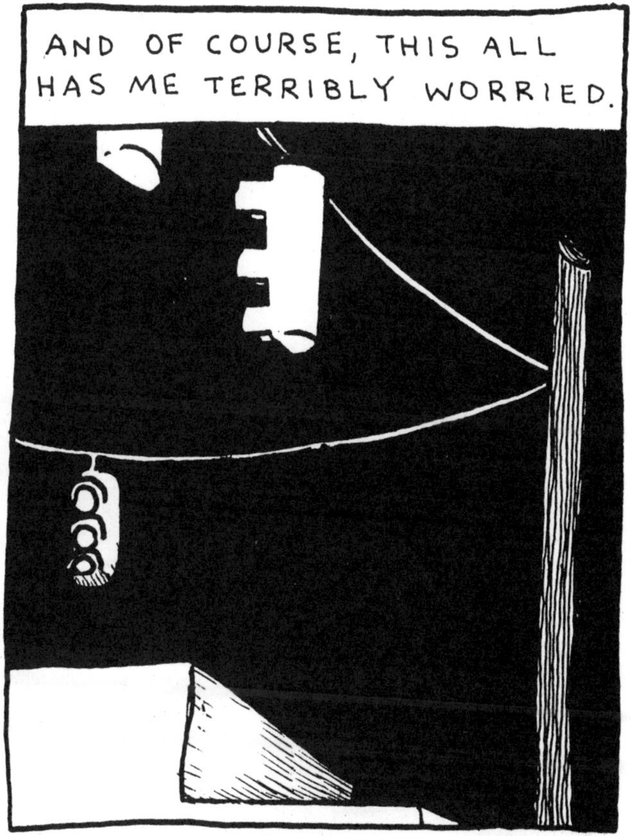
AND OF COURSE, THIS ALL HAS ME TERRIBLY WORRIED.

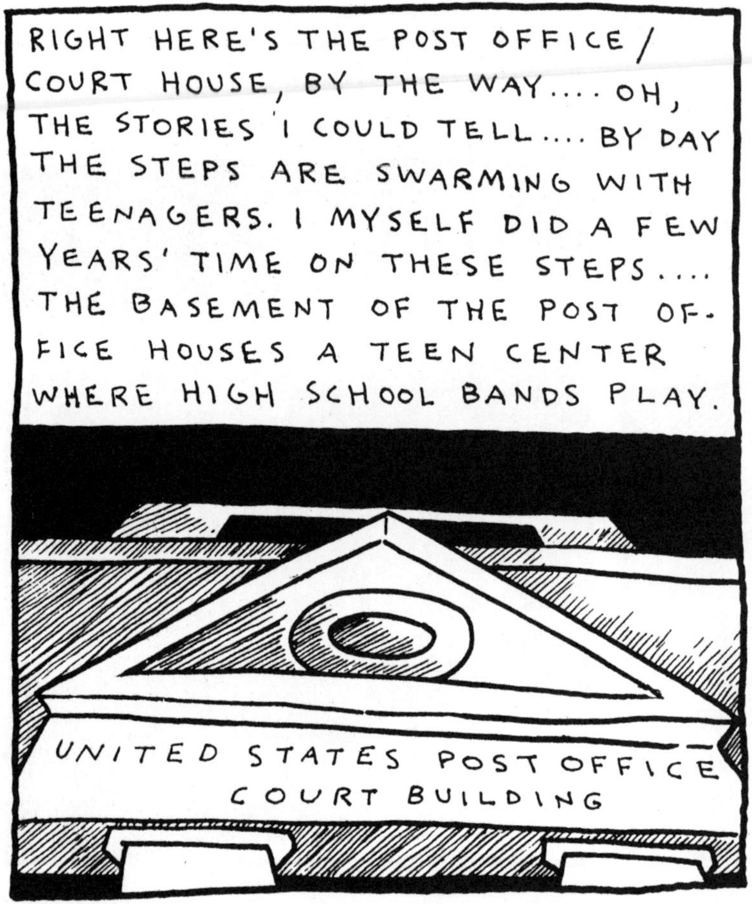
RIGHT HERE'S THE POST OFFICE / COURT HOUSE, BY THE WAY.... OH, THE STORIES I COULD TELL.... BY DAY THE STEPS ARE SWARMING WITH TEENAGERS. I MYSELF DID A FEW YEARS' TIME ON THESE STEPS.... THE BASEMENT OF THE POST OFFICE HOUSES A TEEN CENTER WHERE HIGH SCHOOL BANDS PLAY.
UNITED STATES POST OFFICE
COURT BUILDING

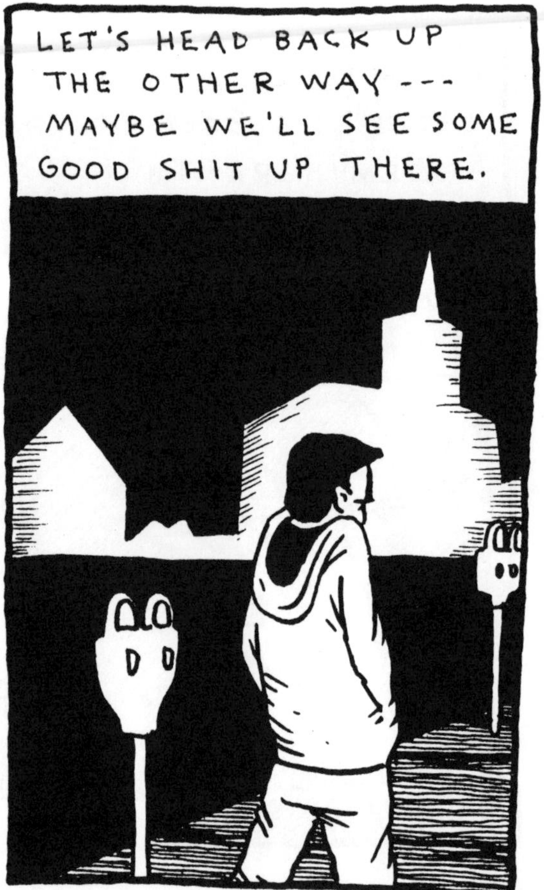
LET'S HEAD BACK UP THE OTHER WAY--- MAYBE WE'LL SEE SOME GOOD SHIT UP THERE.

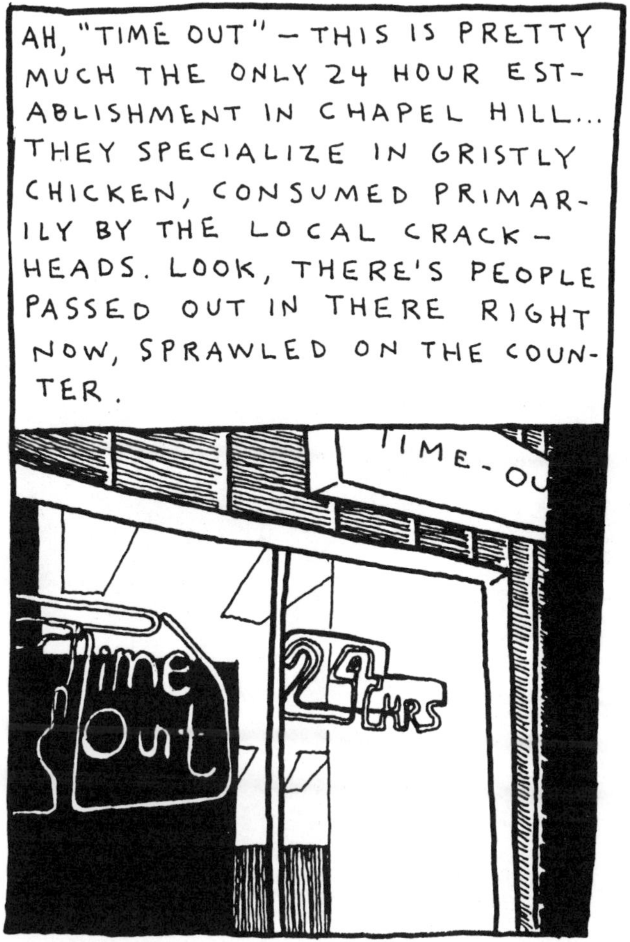
AH, "TIME OUT" — THIS IS PRETTY MUCH THE ONLY 24 HOUR EST-ABLISHMENT IN CHAPEL HILL... THEY SPECIALIZE IN GRISTLY CHICKEN, CONSUMED PRIMAR-ILY BY THE LOCAL CRACK-HEADS. LOOK, THERE'S PEOPLE PASSED OUT IN THERE RIGHT NOW, SPRAWLED ON THE COUN-TER.
TIME-OU
Time Out
24 HRS

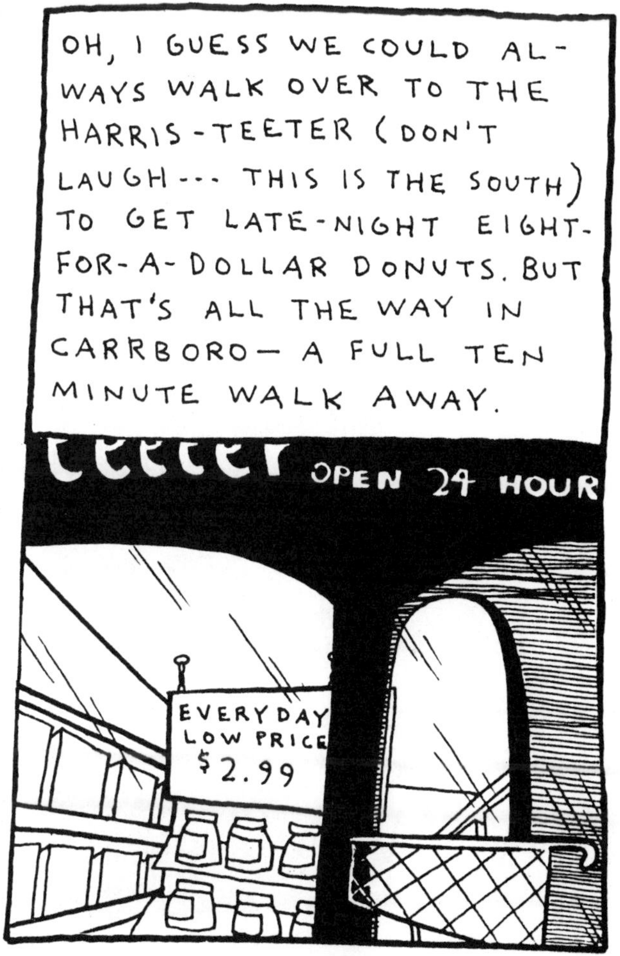
OH, I GUESS WE COULD AL-WAYS WALK OVER TO THE HARRIS-TEETER (DON'T LAUGH--- THIS IS THE SOUTH) TO GET LATE-NIGHT EIGHT-FOR-A-DOLLAR DONUTS. BUT THAT'S ALL THE WAY IN CARRBORO— A FULL TEN MINUTE WALK AWAY.
teeter OPEN 24 HOUR
EVERY DAY
LOW PRICE
$2.99

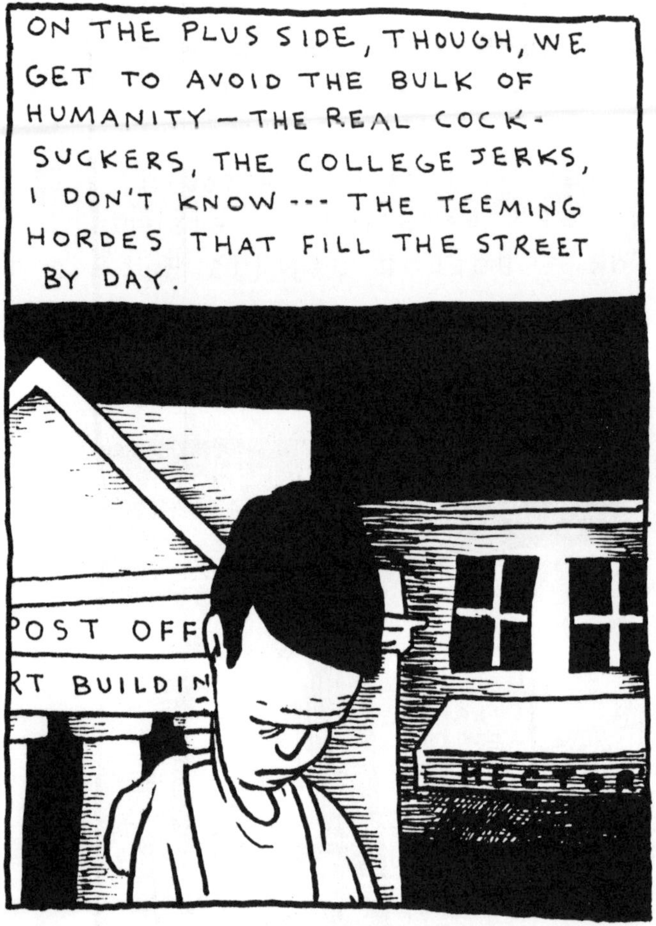
ON THE PLUS SIDE, THOUGH, WE GET TO AVOID THE BULK OF HUMANITY — THE REAL COCK-SUCKERS, THE COLLEGE JERKS, I DON'T KNOW --- THE TEEMING HORDES THAT FILL THE STREET BY DAY.
POST OFF
RT BUILDIN
HECTOR

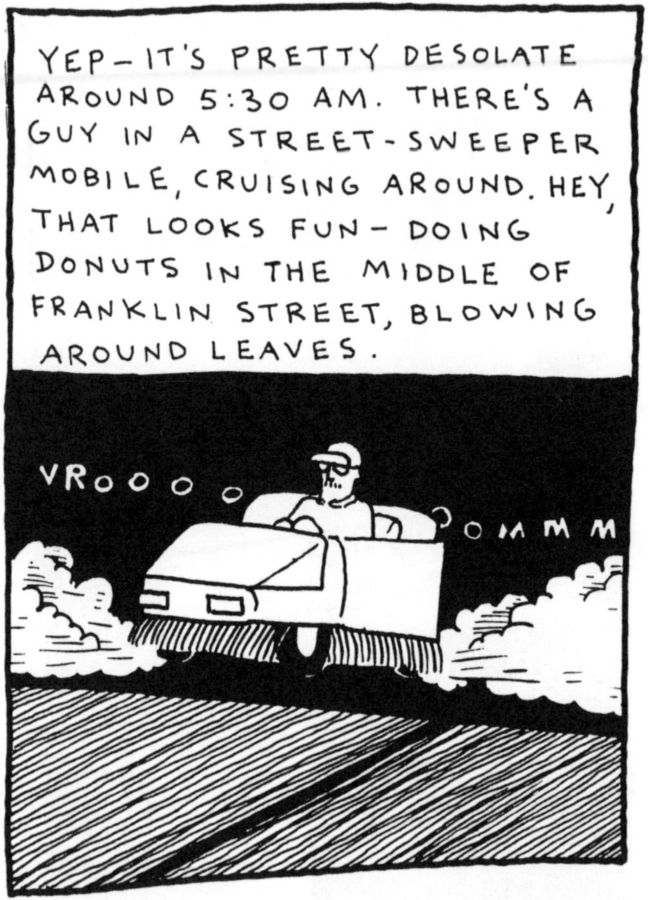
YEP — IT'S PRETTY DESOLATE AROUND 5:30 AM. THERE'S A GUY IN A STREET-SWEEPER MOBILE, CRUISING AROUND. HEY, THAT LOOKS FUN — DOING DONUTS IN THE MIDDLE OF FRANKLIN STREET, BLOWING AROUND LEAVES.
VROOOOOOOMMM

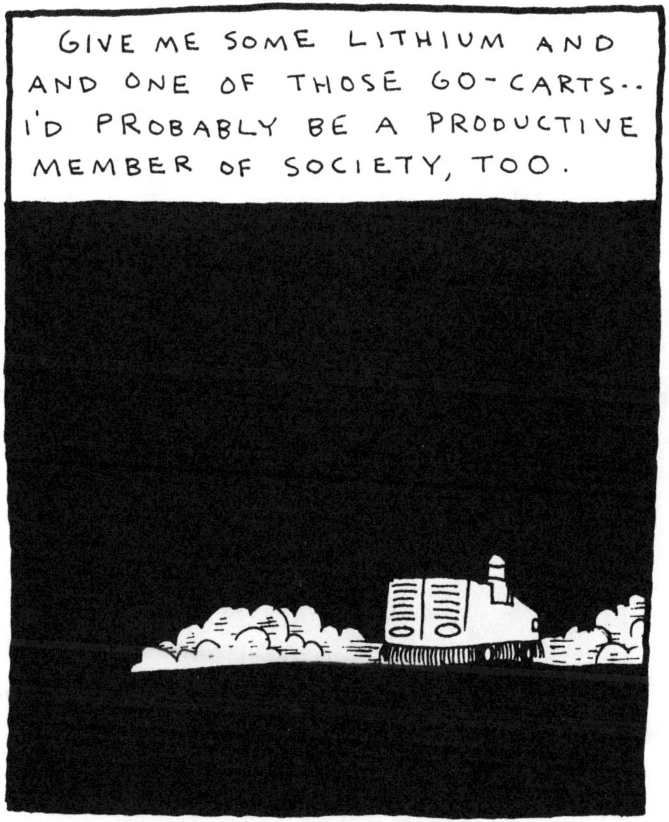
GIVE ME SOME LITHIUM AND
AND ONE OF THOSE GO-CARTS..
I'D PROBABLY BE A PRODUCTIVE
MEMBER OF SOCIETY, TOO.

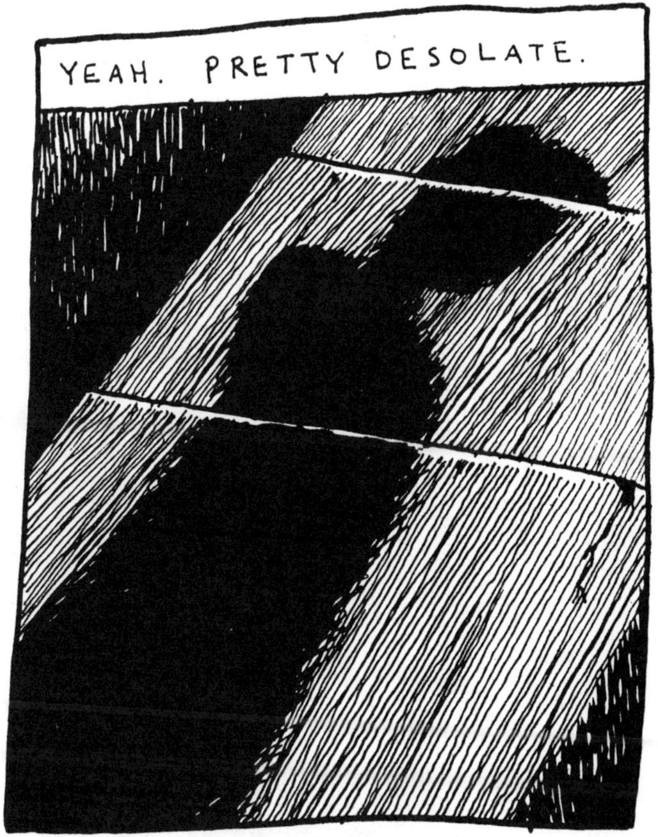
YEAH. PRETTY DESOLATE.

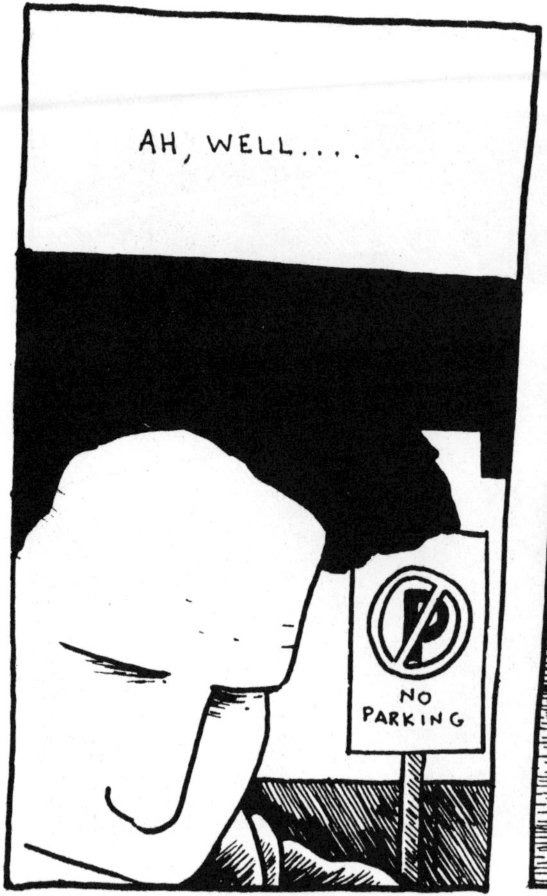
AH, WELL....
NO PARKING

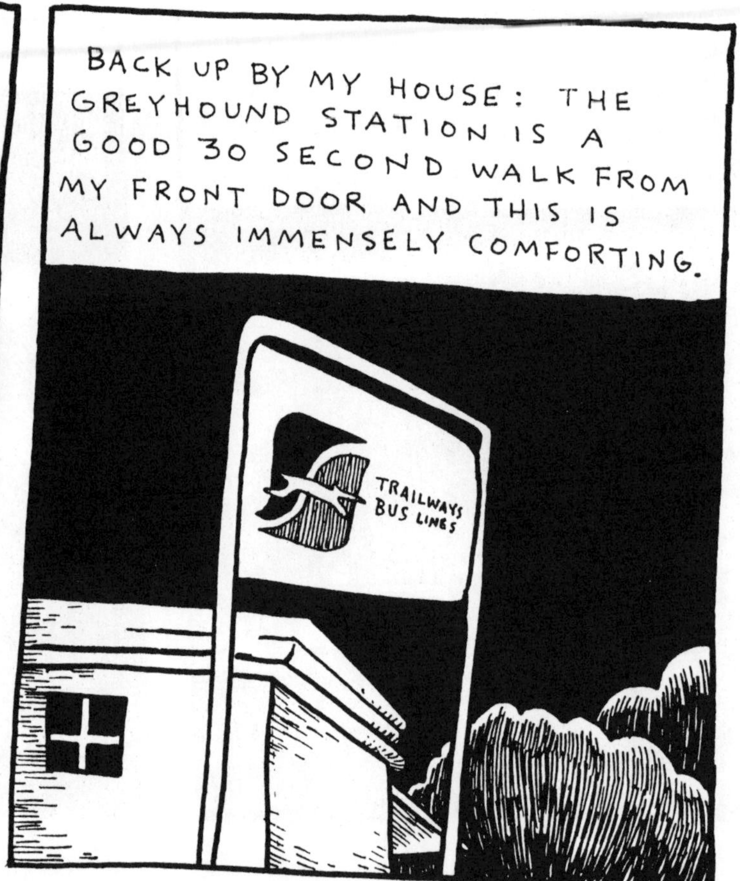
BACK UP BY MY HOUSE: THE GREYHOUND STATION IS A GOOD 30 SECOND WALK FROM MY FRONT DOOR AND THIS IS ALWAYS IMMENSELY COMFORTING.
TRAILWAYS BUS LINES

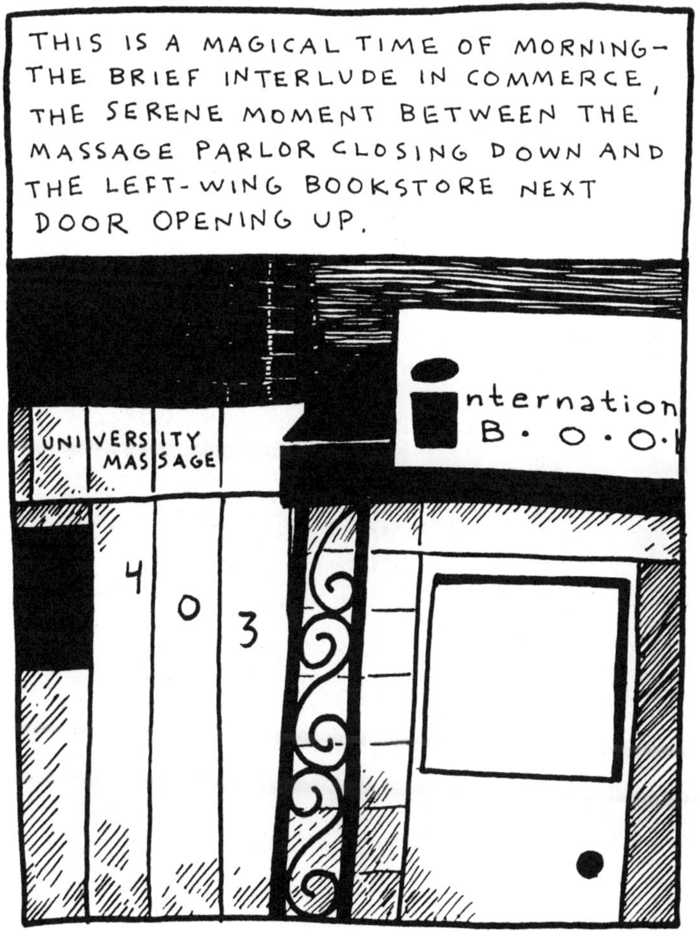
THIS IS A MAGICAL TIME OF MORNING— THE BRIEF INTERLUDE IN COMMERCE, THE SERENE MOMENT BETWEEN THE MASSAGE PARLOR CLOSING DOWN AND THE LEFT-WING BOOKSTORE NEXT DOOR OPENING UP.
UNIVERSITY MASSAGE
403

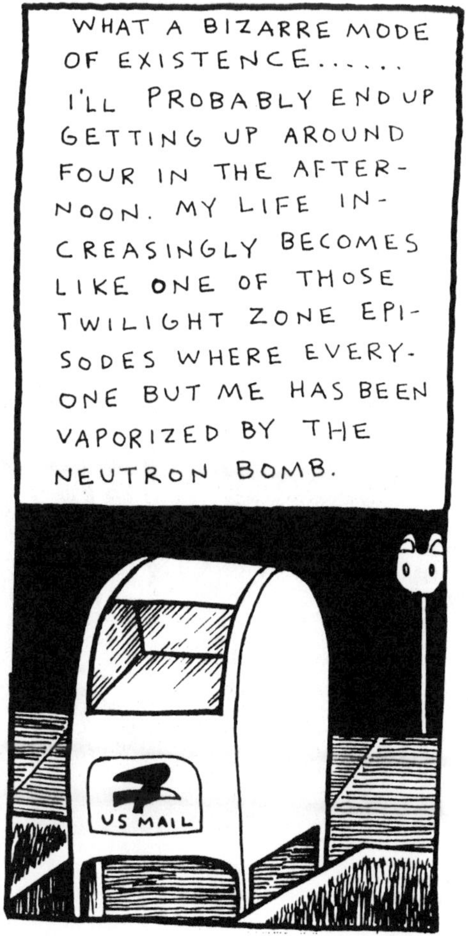
WHAT A BIZARRE MODE OF EXISTENCE...... I'LL PROBABLY END UP GETTING UP AROUND FOUR IN THE AFTERNOON. MY LIFE INCREASINGLY BECOMES LIKE ONE OF THOSE TWILIGHT ZONE EPISODES WHERE EVERYONE BUT ME HAS BEEN VAPORIZED BY THE NEUTRON BOMB.
US MAIL

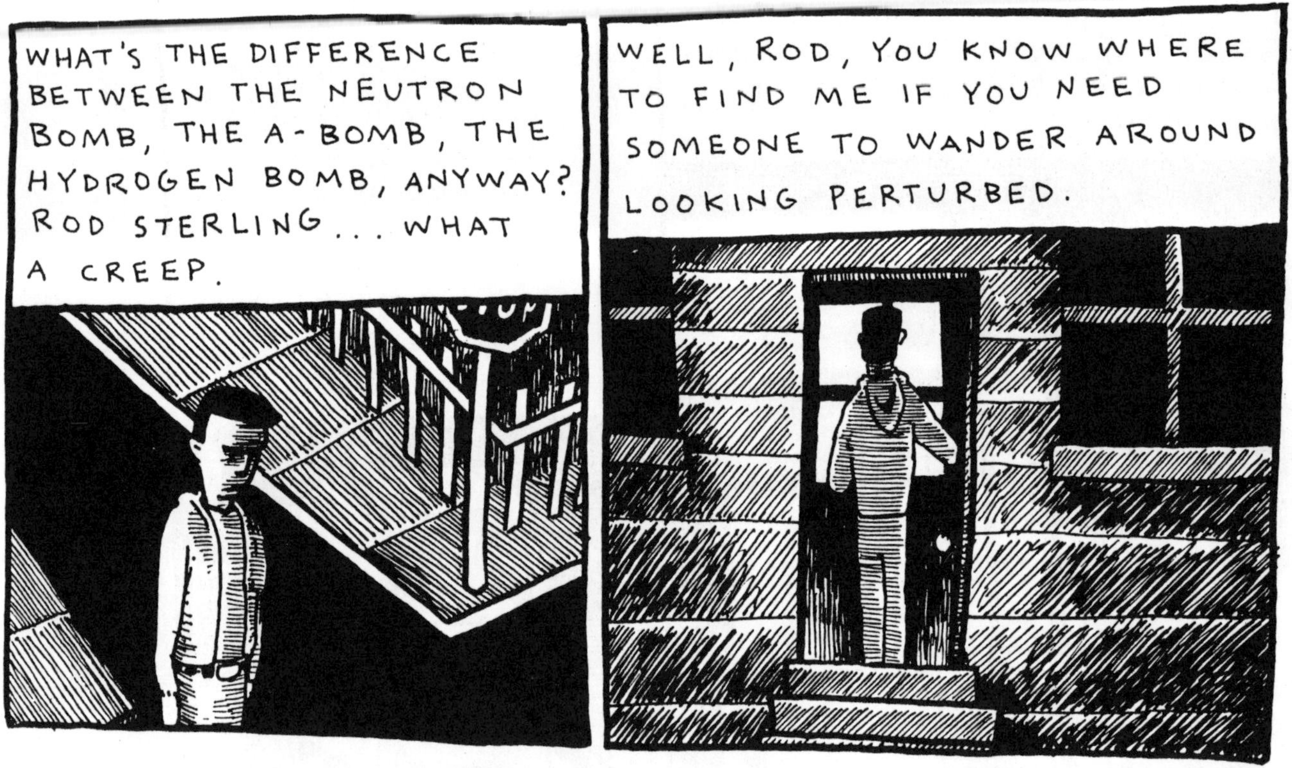
WHAT'S THE DIFFERENCE BETWEEN THE NEUTRON BOMB, THE A-BOMB, THE HYDROGEN BOMB, ANYWAY? ROD STERLING... WHAT A CREEP.
WELL, ROD, YOU KNOW WHERE TO FIND ME IF YOU NEED SOMEONE TO WANDER AROUND LOOKING PERTURBED.

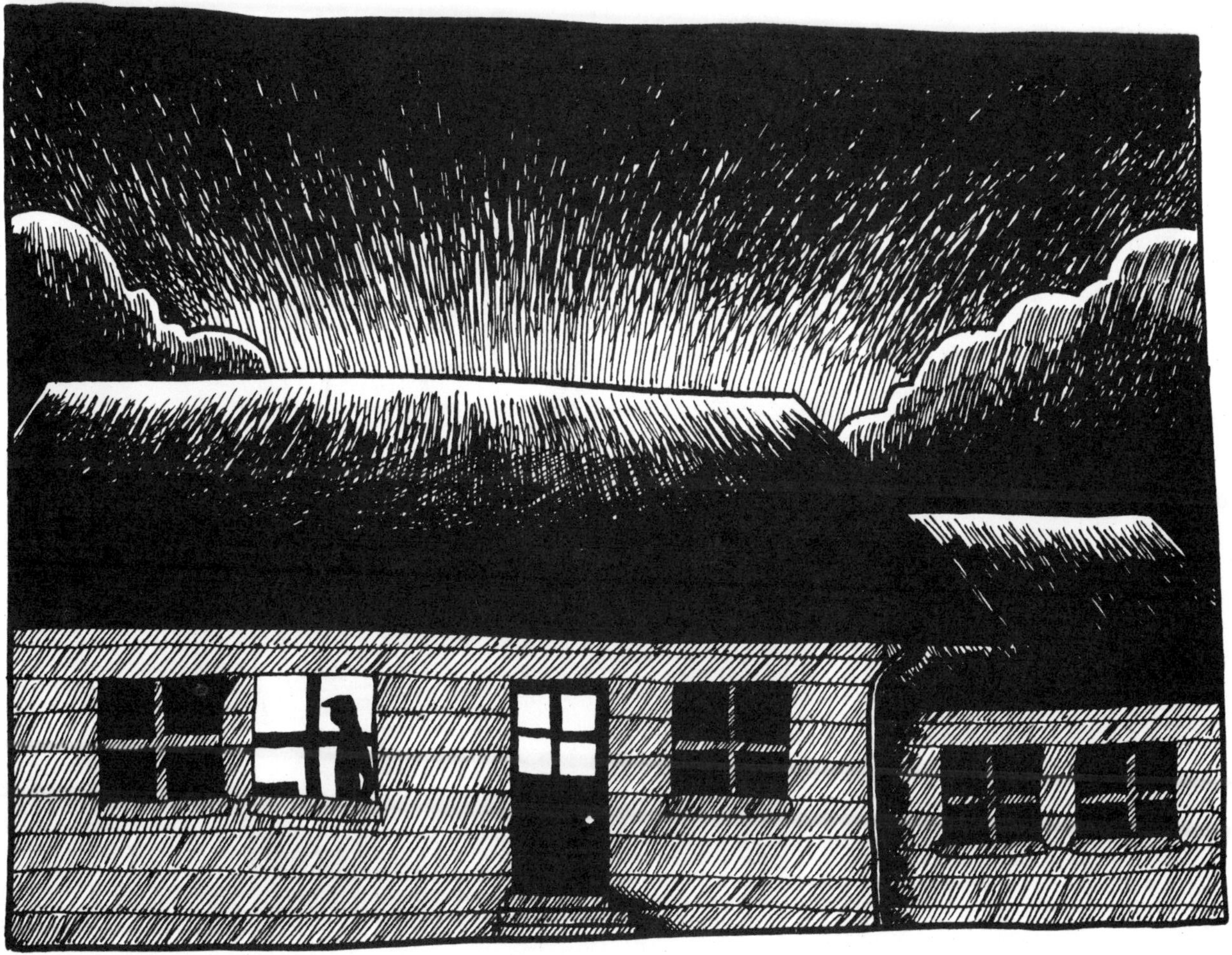

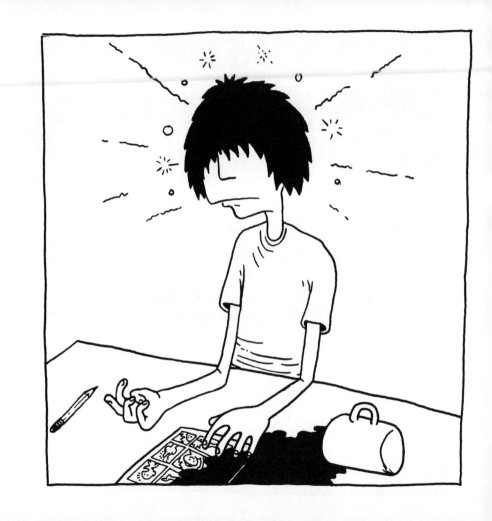

THESE COMICS OWE THEIR EXISTENCE TO A MAN NAMED IAN LYNAM, WHO WORKED FOR YEARS IN THE PRODUCTION WAREHOUSE OF A MAJOR PHOTOCOPYING FIRM AND OPERATED AN ILLICIT PUBLISHING CONCERN (A "ZINE LABEL," WE CALLED THEM IN THOSE MORE INNOCENT AND CAREFREE DAYS) OUT THE BACK DOOR. HE SEEMED LESS MOTIVATED BY A COMMITMENT TO THE ARTS THAN A DESIRE TO

STEAL REAMS AND REAMS OF PAPER. THUS, WHEN HE'D
RUN LOW ON ARTISTIC IMPULSE OF HIS OWN, HE'D
SOLICIT THE ARTISTIC IMPULSES OF OTHER
PEOPLE. I WAS ONE OF THOSE PEOPLE, AND WE WERE
A GOOD MATCH — I HAD SPENT QUITE A BIT
OF TIME TRYING TO RUN MY EMPLOYERS INTO
THE GROUND BY PHOTOCOPYING THEM OUT OF
EXISTENCE, TOO. SO, IN THE INTEREST OF
GUMMING UP GEARS AND REVENGING OURSELVES
FOR TOO FEW COFFEE BREAKS, I GRIT MY
TEETH AND DREW SOME THINGS, AND HE GRIT
HIS TEETH AND PRINTED THEM.

I LIVED IN PROVIDENCE, RI, PORTLAND, OR AND
CHAPEL HILL, NC DURING THIS TIME, AND DREW SOME

OF THESE IN EACH PLACE. IAN PUBLISHED IT
IN THREE INSTALLMENTS. COMPILING THEM
TOGETHER NOW, I AM SHOCKED AND
MORTIFIED AT HOW NAIVE AND EMOTIONALLY
ON-THE-SLEEVE IT ALL IS, AND HOW BADLY
DRAWN. BUT THERE IT IS, SUCH WAS THE
SPIRIT OF THE TIMES: THESE ARE THINGS
DRAWN ON NAPKINS IN AIRPORTS, XEROXED
ILLICITLY DURING WORK. THAT'S THE
SORT OF BEHAVIOR YOU ENGAGED IN, IF YOU
WANTED TO FEEL YOUNG AND FREE. SO
IAN: THANKS FOR THE COPIES. AND KEEPING
ME BUSY.

AL BURIAN
CHICAGO, IL
EARLY 2003